HELLFIRE

The Bugging Out Series: Book Seven

NOAH MANN

© 2017 Noah Mann

ISBN-10: 1545198225
ISBN-13: 978-1545198223

Nearly all men can stand adversity,
but if you want to test a man's character,
give him power.

Abraham Lincoln

Part One

Night

One

Not long ago, in the rage of a winter storm, bodies had spilled onto the shore from the churning Pacific. This morning, as a darkened dawn broke, two more forms emerged from the surf, very alive, wearing wetsuits and rebreathing SCUBA gear, the M4 rifles in their hands aimed at Corporal Enderson and me.

"SEALs," Enderson said, eying the approaching special operations troops.

We both had weapons in our possession, sidearms and long guns, but Enderson's M4, and my AR, both hung from slings across the front of our bodies. Neither of us wanted to present any threat to the warriors just coming ashore.

"Identify," one of the SEALs said, loud but not shouting.

"Corporal Morris Enderson," he said, the first time I'd ever heard 'Mo' willingly use his legal first name. "United States Army."

"Eric Fletcher," I said.

The pair of SEALS stopped a few yards from us and lowered their rifles. Beyond them, just off shore, a small rigid hull inflatable boat was riding the breaking waves, its helmsman steering it through tight circles to keep it on station. And, a greater distance out, closer to open water, the squat grey hull of the *Rushmore* was just becoming visible in the day's dim new light. To the east, ash had spread across the horizon, blotting the sunrise so that it was little more than a weak, jaundiced glow.

"Lieutenant Harker," the first SEAL said, identifying himself, then gesturing to the other member of his party. "This is Chief Nguyen."

"Welcome to Bandon," Enderson said.

"We need to speak with your senior officer on station," Harker said.

The natural response that Enderson could give was to tell the man that Sergeant Lorenzen was senior while Captain Angela Schiavo was absent. But the situation wasn't that clear, in technical terms.

"Our sergeant has operational control," the corporal replied, walking the finest line he could without actually avoiding the truth.

"I'm not here to talk to a sergeant," Harker said.

Enderson gave me a sideways glance, knowing where this was going.

"Commander Clay Genesee is the senior military officer in town," Enderson told the SEAL leader.

"Take us to him," Harker said.

* * *

I drove the Humvee which Enderson had used to bring us down to the beach after lookouts had reported a shadow on the horizon. A shadow the size of a ship. We'd suspected, correctly, that it might be the *Rushmore*, and were dispatched by Lorenzen to verify its presence off the coast as he completed the final preparations for our mission to locate and assist Schiavo, Martin, and Private Carters Laws, who'd begun their journey to Portland less than three days before. Twenty-four hours ago, Mt. Hood had erupted, spewing a constant gush of burning ash into the sky. So far, the cloud had not reached Bandon, but, as Enderson and I had earlier walked across the sand toward the water's edge, we both felt the change in the weather. The wind was cool, and light, but it was now coming from the north.

We could expect ash from the eruption to reach us within hours.

"Do you have supplies for us?" Enderson asked.

He sat next to me in the passenger seat, the SEALs behind, their gazes playing over the slumbering town as we cruised through. Each seemed almost shell shocked by the normalcy of what they saw. Houses. Dry land. Small trees alive and green in the sweep of the vehicle's headlights.

"We're not here for that," Harker said.

To this point, Nguyen had remained silent. I glanced over my shoulder at the junior warrior, a thirtyish man filled with experiences of one twice his age. He'd seen much. Too much, maybe.

"Chief," I said, alternating my view between him and the road ahead.

"Yes."

"Any information on what happened in San Diego?"

The chief looked to his lieutenant, their shared surprise just shy of obvious.

"How do you know about San Diego?" Harker asked.

I told him about the bodies. Bodies of people we'd known had once inhabited the San Diego survivor colony.

"San Diego is lost," Harker said.

Still silent, Chief Nguyen shifted his gaze out the side window, more an attempt at distraction than interest in the scenery.

"Lost how?" I pressed.

"We're not getting it back," Harker said, polite and bland, offering information without emotion.

"Was it the Unified Government?"

To my question, Harker nodded and looked away. The SEAL community had a deep connection to the area, with much of their rigorous training taking place on nearby Coronado Island. Losing such a place would be a harsh pill to swallow, and, from the reactions of both men, that was a reality they were having difficulty accepting.

"How much farther?" Harker asked.

"Almost there, sir," Enderson told him.

Neither Harker nor Nguyen had come to talk. At least not to me or the corporal. They were on their own mission, which, for some reason, Clay Genesee was the focal point of.

Two

Commander Clay Genesee lived in a small house less than a five-minute walk from the hospital, a mode of travel he preferred to using the Humvee that had been assigned to him. That vehicle sat at the curb, the one we'd arrived in double parked next to it, almost choking the narrow street as we walked up the stone path to the doctor's front door. Just as we reached the bottom steps to the porch a four-wheeled ATV came around the corner and sputtered to a stop facing the pair of military vehicles. Sergeant Lorenzen climbed quickly off and met us, shifting his weapon so it was slung across his back.

"This is Lieutenant Harker and Chief Nguyen," Enderson said, offering the introductions.

Lorenzen rendered a quick salute to the Navy officer. From the corner of my eye I saw a flash of subdued embarrassment on the corporal's face as he realized he hadn't saluted Harker when learning his rank on the beach. Even in the world as it was now, rank mattered.

But not enough for Harker to care, it seemed. He had more immediate concerns.

"Sergeant," Harker said. "Will you wake the commander?"

It wasn't given as an overt order, but that's precisely what it was. And Lorenzen obliged the stranger's directive, moving past us to mount the steps and cross the porch to thump his fist solidly on the front door. Before a second knock was needed the door opened and Genesee looked out, bleary eyed, wearing only a pair of blue sweats, his gaze swelling with confusion when he saw what had arrived upon his doorstep.

"What's... Who..."

"Doc, you have some visitors," Lorenzen said.

Harker gave the sergeant a sideways glance, reacting to the informality that Lorenzen was expressing toward his superior.

"What time is it?" Genesee asked, rubbing his eyes and glancing past us to the muted glow of the new day on the horizon, ash filtering the coming daylight to almost nothing as the pair of strangers on his doorstep each saluted him. "What's going on?"

"It's early, commander," Harker said, not waiting for the superior officer to return his salute. "May we come in? We have intelligence you're going to need."

Genesee puzzled openly at the SEAL's deference toward him, then let an actual chuckle slip past his lips.

"Lieutenant..."

"Harker," the senior SEAL prompted. "Michael Harker."

"Right," Genesee said. "Lieutenant Michael Harker, you don't want me. You want these folks right here."

Genesee gestured toward Lorenzen, Enderson, and me.

"I'm just a doctor."

"Pardon me, sir," Harker began, "but you're a commissioned officer in the United States Navy, and ranking officer here in Bandon. This is correct, yes?"

For a moment, Genesee was flustered, the early hour and unlikely interaction combining to dull his faculties.

"Lieutenant, I'm not your guy."

"Again, pardon me, sir, but according to what we've been told, you are our guy."

Harker's insistence finally broke the mental logjam which had stalled Genesee's acceptance of the inevitable, and the Navy commander, bare from the waist up, stepped aside and let his five early morning guests into his house.

* * *

Genesee excused himself to get a sweatshirt from his bedroom, leaving the five of us who'd awakened him to wait in his living room.

"Lieutenant, if this is going to take a while, Fletch here and I would like to get back to preparations for our mission," Lorenzen said. "We're leaving this morning."

It had been decided that Lorenzen and I would head out to locate and assist our expedition to Portland, which had to have been affected by the eruption of Mt. Hood. The sergeant had dispatched me and his second in command to investigate the reports of a ship offshore, with no expectation that we'd be returning to town with a pair of special operations troops. In fact, when reporting that very occurrence via radio to Lorenzen as we started back toward town, his reaction had bordered on disbelief. But there was no doubting the reality of the situation now, just as there was no question that we had to get back to readying our equipment and supplies for the arduous journey to begin in just a few hours.

"Is this a mission to find your people heading to Portland?" Harker asked.

It shouldn't have surprised us that the SEAL knew about the expedition which had set out to, presumably, reach Air Force One. The directions to expect a message had come from the *Rushmore*, which had obviously sent these men ashore in a small launch. But the manner in which Harker had made note of it hinted at some connection to his purpose here.

"It is," Lorenzen confirmed.

"You're going to want to put that on hold until we finish here," Harker said.

Lorenzen looked to me, both of us curious, and wary, that state of concern lasting until Genesee returned, dressed from neck to ankles now.

"So what is it you need to tell me?"

"Com aboard the *Rushmore* picked up a transmission from your people about six hours ago," Harker said, instantly seizing our full attention. "It was bounced off a satellite."

In the past, particularly during interference by the White Signal, we'd used a transmitter set up to relay messages using communications satellites passing overhead at specific times of day. That had been a fairly reliable method of defeating the signal which overwhelmed the airwaves. There was just one problem with what Harker was sharing.

"Lieutenant," I began, "they didn't have a satellite transmitter with them. Just line of sight radios."

"They found one," Nguyen said, speaking for the first time.

Harker nodded to his subordinate and the man retrieved a device from the gear vest strapped snugly across his chest. It was a waterproof GPS unit.

"GPS hasn't functioned for a while," I said.

"Yours hasn't," Harker said, making it clear that the military, or portions of it, were still able to access the constellation of Global Positioning System satellites.

"The contact was initiated from here," Nguyen said, pointing to a digital pin that had been dropped on the GPS's map screen. "North of Eugene around a town called Coburg."

"What was the communication from them?" Lorenzen asked.

Harker looked to Genesee to give his answer.

"They said they need a doctor."

Genesee absorbed that.

"What was the nature of the need?" he asked. "Who was hurt? What are the injuries?"

Nguyen shook his head.

"The *Rushmore* was only able to acknowledge their transmission before the contact was lost," the chief said.

"Could be atmospheric disturbance from the ash," Harker suggested. "Or something else."

Something else...

I didn't want to venture any guesses as to what those other possibilities could be, because none were as benign as too much volcanic dust in the air.

"You need to get there, Commander Genesee," Harker said. "That mission has to reach Portland, and if some injury is holding it up, that obstacle has to be removed."

The SEAL officer spoke of what might have befallen the expedition as though it were some benign growth that was easily removed. Except it wasn't. It was a mystery, and it existed far from where we stood, in possibly hellish conditions. To expect that Genesee, more civilian than military man, by his own choice and actions since being stationed in Bandon, could somehow fix an unknown was a hopeful thought at best.

"Lieutenant," I said, and Harker reluctantly shifted his attention to me. "Sergeant Lorenzen and I can get to them, and we can get whoever's hurt back here."

To that, Harker simply shook his head.

"The voice on the radio was male," he explained. "Captain Schiavo could be the one who is hurt."

Lorenzen processed that, clearly troubled by the possibility.

"She'd put herself in harm's way before she let someone else get hurt," the sergeant said.

"She can't be brought back to Bandon if she's hurt," Harker told us. "She's the one who has to make it to Portland."

"The only one," Nguyen added.

The statement was one of military fact, not some cold assessment of the expendability of those who'd accompanied Schiavo on the trek. Still, it made clear the reason for the SEAL's almost laser focus on speaking to Genesee. To them, and to whoever had concocted this new mission, he was a savior.

The reluctant Navy commander, though, did not see it that way.

"I'm not some field guy. I'm not you. Okay? I suture cuts and set bones."

"Noted, Commander Genesee," Harker said. "But this isn't an option. I'm relaying a direct order to you from Admiral Adamson. You are to go meet up with the mission already underway and ensure that Captain Schiavo is fit and able to reach Portland."

Genesee, still, wasn't buying into the premise of his necessity.

"Are you telling me I'm the only doctor available?" he challenged the SEAL officer. "When I came in on the *Rushmore* there were two other doctors. You must have one on board who can do this. You could put him ashore further north, which is a lot closer than we are to this Coburg place. And what about a helicopter? You had two Seahawks on board when I was there. You could drop that doc right to them and pull out anybody who's hurt. Hell, you could fly them to Portland in...that..."

Genesee suddenly realized how his protest was coming across. As though it was being delivered by a man afraid of the duty he'd signed up for long ago. Long before the blight turned the world into a daily battle for survival. And long before Mother Nature had decided to interject a reminder that she controlled all things beneath our feet, including the long dormant volcano which had left that state of quiet behind to add its own devastation to our corner of the world.

"Look, I don't know that I can do this," Genesee said.

Harker exchanged a look with Chief Nguyen, then fixed on Genesee again.

"Are you refusing the admiral's order, sir?"

The man who'd come to Bandon a cold and distant practitioner of medicine, but who'd slowly grown to be more a part of our town, and the community of people that inhabited it, looked to Lorenzen, Enderson, and me, his gaze steeling with each passing second. Finally he faced Harker again and shook his head.

"I am not, lieutenant," Genesee said. "I will do what I'm ordered to do."

"Good," Harker said, then nodded to Nguyen, who handed the GPS to the Navy doctor. "This will guide you to their last known position."

Genesee eyed the device, the digital pin marking the location flashing on the screen. A light circle surrounded it, indicating any probability of error, and showing that our friends could be anywhere within a half mile radius. Not quite a needle in a haystack, but not marked by some flashing neon sign, either.

"One question," I said, drawing Harker's attention to me once again. "Why not do what the doctor suggested? Have the *Rushmore* put someone closer? I know the helicopter idea is out because of the ash cloud, but you could put people a lot closer, and a lot faster. You could even transport us up the coast, put us ashore near Florence and we head inland. That could cut a day, maybe two off our trip."

Harker looked at me for a moment. Just looked. But there was no hint that he was even slightly entertaining the possibility of what I'd suggested.

"The *Rushmore* has its own mission," the SEAL officer said. "Once we're back aboard, she's heading out to sea."

"Lieutenant," Lorenzen said. "Pardon, but if Captain Schiavo getting to Portland is so vital, why are you all running for open water?"

"I'm not at liberty to discuss why the *Rushmore* and its crew is doing whatever it is it's doing," Harker answered, providing no answer at all. "Now if you're clear on what Commander Genesee is tasked with doing, can you transport us back to the beach so we can return to the ship?"

And that was it. Genesee stood there, seeming in a state of mild shock.

"Good luck, commander," Harker said, then led off toward the door.

Outside, Lorenzen told Enderson to take the ATV back to the garrison headquarters at the Town Hall as the SEALs climbed back into the Humvee.

"Looks like it's gonna be a party of three," Lorenzen said to me before we joined our guests in the vehicle.

That was not an unreasonable assumption to make, particularly after the briefing we'd just been privy to. But I didn't hold with that belief, and, after we'd seen the SEALs off back at the shore, I suspected that the sergeant would agree with me, though I was dead certain he would be furious at that forced reality.

Three

Lorenzen stopped the Humvee on the sand and left the headlights on. What should have been a beach basking in the glow of the new day was, instead, a strip of shore under false night, the first gritty bits of ash beginning to fall near the water.

The sergeant and I got out of the Humvee along with Harker and Nguyen, walking the two SEALs down to the waterline. Two hundred yards out, their boat still circled, waiting to return them to the *Rushmore*, which was anchored a good two miles off shore.

"Lieutenant," Lorenzen said as Harker took his swim fins from where he'd stowed them on the side of his compact rebreather.

"Yes?"

"What team are you? What unit?"

"Unit?" Harker repeated, regarding the sergeant with a bit of surprise for even needing to pose such a question. "You're looking at the unit."

Lorenzen nodded and gave the SEAL a salute. Harker returned it, then began wading into the surf with Nguyen. Only after they were chest deep would they put their fins on and begin the cold swim back to their launch.

"They're decimated," Lorenzen said.

"By what?" I asked rhetorically.

A strobe began to flash on the launch, guiding the SEALs as they swam through the surf toward the nimble boat. A few minutes later they climbed aboard and the small craft went dark as it turned away from shore and raced over the rolling surf toward the *Rushmore*, its mothership.

"Paul..."

The sergeant looked to me, the drizzle of grit from the sky increasing. Soon we would need dust masks, or bandanas over our mouths, to filter what we could of the damaging particles. But whatever the ash fall was like here, it would be ten times worse closer to the eruption. Precisely where our friends were.

And where Lorenzen would not be traveling.

"What is it, Fletch?"

"You have to stay here," I told the man.

"What?"

He was surprised by my statement, but more curious, I thought.

"Clay and I will go find them in Coburg," I said.

Lorenzen almost chuckled.

"Where is this coming from, Fletch?"

"Look out there," I said, tipping my head toward the *Rushmore*. "That ship has damage to the bow. I saw it when she made her brief appearance last week. And the SEALs aboard are down to two men. In ten minutes the ship will be running. *Running*. From what, Paul?"

What I was saying was hitting a nerve, but could not elicit a truth neither of us yet knew.

"I don't know," Lorenzen answered.

"Exactly. What if that trouble is coming here, and you're off chasing down our people in the middle of a volcanic eruption? You know what the captain would say about that."

"I do," he said, nodding, and angry that there was no way he could dispute the logic.

"You, Enderson, Westin, and Hart may be needed here."

"May," Lorenzen said, shaking his head. "That's what rubs me wrong about this. It's all a hypothetical."

"What isn't?"

The sergeant looked to the dark sky and held his hand out, ash dusting the palm of his glove.

"This," he said.

I don't believe he could have been more right about anything right then. We were facing a possible threat, and a definite one. If the first became a reality, the town might, once again, need to defend itself. The garrison's second in command would be an integral part of that.

"Genesee is gonna be a terrific traveling partner," Lorenzen joked, dumping the ash from his glove. "He's a civilian who ended up in khakis."

"You'd better talk to the mayor and let him know he's going to be Doc Allen again until we get back."

The elderly leader of our town, who'd been its sole doctor through most of the blight's aftermath, had soldiered on after the death of his wife almost a year ago. He'd slowed, both physically and in spirit, but his mind was sharp.

"Hart will help," Lorenzen assured me. "And we have Grace."

My late friend's wife served as the head nurse at our small hospital, with two other nurses assisting her. Truly, though, the realities of the blighted world had forced her to perform procedures that, normally, would have been handled by doctors. At my refuge in Montana, shortly after she and Neil and her daughter, Krista, had arrived, Grace had patched up the gunshot wound in my jaw, almost certainly preventing infection from settling in.

In short, she'd saved my life.

Now, another life needed to be saved. Schiavo's? Martin's? Carter's? The only way to know would be to reach them and render what assistance we could. The preparations we'd begun, including loading the Humvee with supplies, were almost complete when this new wrinkle arrived through the pounding surf. Now, with the SEALs almost back to the *Rushmore*, those preparations had to be completed—and altered.

"Can you get Genesee ready?" I asked. "Maybe Grace can help with any medical supplies that might be necessary."

Lorenzen nodded, understanding.

"Go home, Fletch. Spend a while with your family. I'll swing by and pick you up when it's time."

When it's time...

Two hours from now. That's when we'd planned to set out. There was no reason to delay that timetable, but two reasons I wanted to.

"I'll be ready," I said.

Four

My little girl smiled at me as I held her on my lap, facing me, hands supporting her back, her neck. Hands that, in a few short hours, would be out there again, in unknown lands, ready to do what needed to be done.

Even kill.

"You're going to need to see that the ash gets raked off the roof," I said to Elaine.

She sat a few feet away, in the comfortable rocker, watching the moment I was sharing with our daughter. With our Hope.

"Don't try to do it yourself," I reminded her. "Dave Arndt said he'll come by and keep you from breaking your neck."

"I can climb a ladder," my wife assured me, but offered no real protest toward my admonition. "But I'll let him handle it."

The ash fall, if it kept up, would add tons of weight for the roof structure to support. If it could. Across Bandon, some houses would fail. The trick was keeping that number low, and, more importantly, making sure no people were inside buildings that were at risk of collapse.

"I won't make a fuss about this," she told me.

"Thank you."

In another time, at another place, she would have challenged my desire to keep her out of harm's way. Now, with the world which had been recovering shrouded in darkness, she knew that her focus had to be on our child.

"As soon as you're back, you're on dish duty."

"Gladly," I said.

How many more minutes did I have with my daughter and my wife? Ten? Five? Lorenzen would soon be here to take me to the town hall, where Genesee, I assumed, would be waiting. We would leave from there and return...

"I don't know when I'll be back," I told Elaine. "I just have no idea what's out there."

"I know."

She'd been with me on our trek across the wasteland to Cheyenne and back. The feelings we'd had for each other had come out into the open on that journey. What we'd survived had strengthened us, and softened our hearts. What I was about to face, out there, in the hellfire of a most unexpected disaster, could only be imagined. And, though each of us knew that there was no certainty to my return, we would not entertain that possibility aloud.

I was coming home. I was.

"But I will come back to you," I said, looking to our Hope on my lap. "And to you, too."

Headlights swept across the curtains, cutting through the daytime darkness outside. That would be Lorenzen. In a moment he would park and come up the walkway and knock on our door. And I would leave with him.

But I had that minute, still. That brief bit of time with my family.

I stood, as Elaine did, and we stepped close, our daughter in the embrace between us. I kissed Hope, then my wife.

"I'm gonna say it," Elaine said. "Be careful. Really, be careful. This isn't like anything we've seen. Okay? You promise me."

It was a command she was giving me, not a request.

"I promise," I said, looking at her for a moment as the heavy steps of boots came up the front walkway. "I love you, Elaine."

"I love you, Eric."

The knock sounded at our door. Elaine's arms slipped around our daughter, taking her from me. She stepped back and managed a smile. For a moment I couldn't look away. Couldn't turn and go to the door.

Another soft flurry of taps forced the issue, and I turned away from my wife, and my daughter, and I took my AR and backpack from where they waited near the door. I didn't look back as I stepped out to the porch and pulled a bandana up to cover my mouth. Didn't look as I followed Lorenzen down the walkway to the waiting Humvee near our pickup, breathing through the thin material to filter out the still light ashfall.

But when I took my place in the passenger seat next to the sergeant, I did cast my gaze toward my house, and in the window next to the closed front door I saw my girls. Elaine lifted our daughter's tiny hand and moved it in a small wave. I smiled, my heart both warmed and pained by what I saw, because I wanted to see it again. Wanted to see them again.

That, though, was not a certainty, however confident I wanted to be toward the evolving mission I was about to set out on. That *we* were about to set out on.

"Is Genesee ready?"

"As ready as he's ever going to be," Lorenzen answered, a hint of doubt in his answer.

"Let's go," I said, and looked away from my wife and daughter as the sergeant drove us away into the black morning.

* * *

One of the garrison's Humvees had been loaded with supplies, including every medical device that could reasonably be taken with us. Grace was arranging the last of those items as Lorenzen and I pulled up outside the Town Hall. I stepped from the vehicle and approached, the sergeant disappearing into the building to find the man who would be joining me.

"Fletch," Grace said, lowering her white dust mask to flash me a smile that was bright beneath a worried gaze.

"Grace..."

I could think of no more to say than just to utter her name. To speak what my friend, her late husband, could no more. And it was a fitting name she bore. Much as my daughter personified the hope we all felt, Grace exemplified a manner of living, a way of surviving, that was, at its core, quiet intensity. Few would know what a fighter she could be, one who'd shot a helicopter out of the air to save her future husband and me. More would know the healer that she was. The mother. The wife and friend. Those parts of her were never in conflict. She was strength and steadiness in all that she did, and all that she'd suffered through.

"Everything the commander needs is already packed," she told me.

I nodded and studied her for a moment. That strength was there. That poise. That confidence. But another indicator of some thought or feeling shone through, from within. From someplace close to the surface. A place where things once hidden were slipping through cracks in the walls built to contain them.

Without much thought, I knew what it was that was revealing itself despite her best efforts to conceal it.

"You can call him Clay, you know," I said.

She looked me with eyes that registered both relief and terror. I'd sensed something in the way she related to the man who ran our town's hospital. The Navy man who was as ill at ease in the uniform as he was at the very idea that he was posted to a place like Bandon. Or had been, I reminded myself. Commander Clay Genesee had grown on the residents, slowly, inasmuch as he'd begun to feel part of the community himself. Part of that growing comfort and acceptance I attributed to the woman standing before me in the world so dark that it seemed impossible some light of promise could shine through.

But it was. From her, and through her, because of him. A flicker, at least, of something good. Something possible.

"I'm sorry, Fletch..."

I shook my head at her apology. Neil, my friend, her husband, had been dead just shy of a year. Were she to continue to grieve indefinitely, to shut herself off, there might never be another chance for happiness in the world that had been hollowed out of those sorts of joys.

"Grace, there's no reason to be sorry."

She managed a timid smile at my expression of acceptance.

"Neil hasn't even been..."

"You're not on some clock," I told her, searching for the right words to express what I wanted to say. "The Neil that I knew, that I really knew, wouldn't want you to let grief overshadow happiness. He wouldn't want you to mourn forever. He'd want you to live, and to laugh."

Without more prompting, she let out a soft giggle.

"He makes me laugh," she said. "Clay."

"I find that hard to believe," I teased her.

That smile that had been mostly suppressed blossomed a bit more, and she fixed a thankful gaze on me.

"When you two get back, we'll all get together for dinner. Elaine, the children, Clay."

"I'd like that. I know Elaine would, too."

The door behind Grace opened, Genesee and Lorenzen coming out. The Navy man held an M4, one clearly issued to him from the garrison's small armory. The sergeant had also outfitted him with a set of Army BDUs, and a load bearing vest stuffed with magazines and every item that a fighting man would bring into battle. On his belt a holster hung low, strapped to his thigh, a Beretta M9 secured within.

"Paul insists I be ready to face some zombie attack," Genesee said.

"Going blue to green?" I asked the man playfully, referencing a term used when someone serving in the Navy transferred to the Army.

"If the benefits are better, who knows?"

Genesee opened the back door of the Humvee and put his vest on the back seat, and was about to stow his rifle when I stopped him.

"You're riding shotgun first," I said. "There aren't zombies out there, but there are other things."

The Navy commander looked to his rifle. He was uncomfortable wielding the weapon of war. Scalpels and sutures and stethoscopes were the instruments of his calling, but he had raised his hand and taken the oath to support and defend the constitution. That document might be nothing more than ashes now, but its ideals endured.

"You'd better hit the road," Lorenzen said.

"Before it gets dark?" I asked him, glancing to the false night raining down around us.

"Get there, and get back," the sergeant said.

I nodded. Genesee looked to Grace, and she to him. Whatever existed between them, it was too new to allow an overt expression of affection. But it did not preclude everything.

"Be careful," Grace said, directly to him. "Please."

Lorenzen, who clearly hadn't noted the hints of some budding emotional connection between them, flashed a mildly surprised look my way.

"We will," I told Grace, then looked to Genesee. "Ready?"

He gave Grace a last look, then walked around the Humvee with his rifle and climbed in. I took my place behind the wheel and closed the door, listening to the gritty ash fall upon the vehicle, its sound akin to some sort of sizzling rain.

"This isn't going to be easy," Genesee said, staring out into the swirling blackness cut by the headlights.

"No, it isn't," I agreed, then started the Humvee and pulled slowly away.

We drove out of town, passing masked residents raking ash from rooftops, and the ranch crew leading livestock to a group of empty buildings downtown that had been hastily repurposed as sheltered pens. An additional supply of food for the animals had been hastily processed and stored, as had water, taken from the Coquille River and stored in a pair of tanker trucks before it could be contaminated by ash and debris.

"If this keeps up, Fletch," Genesee said, shaking his head at the disaster raining from the black sky above.

"The wind will shift," I said, and he looked to me with little hope, but brimming doubt.

"You a weatherman?"

I shook my head.

"People can't breathe this indefinitely," Genesee said, lifting up one of the many flimsy dust masks we'd brought with us. "These will only do so much. And the water is going to be undrinkable."

"The town has a supply," I reminded him. "Four weeks."

"If everybody conserves," he said.

"And they will. They'll do what's necessary."

"You sound awful certain," Genesee said, no agreement at all in his words.

"I am."

"Why?"

"Because we've come too far to be beaten by this," I said, gesturing with a nod to Mother Nature's fury outside the vehicle. "No way. Not by this."

Genesee regarded my statement with silent skepticism, but there was no hyperbole in what I'd professed. We would reach our friends. We would return. The winds would shift. The mountain would quiet. I knew this.

Because we'd earned a future.

Five

Paper maps ruled the day.

"Right here there was an avalanche," Mike DeSantis told us as we stood in the abandoned outpost across the highway from the town's houses. "It cut the road to Camas Valley."

Behind him, Nick Withers was leading a crew readying the old general store for immediate habitation. An endeavor of necessity.

"Ash has already taken down one roof," Mike said. "Another is on the verge."

"Anyone hurt?" Genesee asked.

Mike shook his head, thankful to be able to offer that bit of good news.

"Let's keep it that way," I told the man.

He was one of the settlers who had split from Bandon to form their own community forty miles inland. Up the road fifteen miles was the survivor colony at Camas Valley, parties to a formal alliance which Schiavo had envisioned and brought to fruition over doubts and difficulties.

"We have roof crews clearing any ash accumulation," Mike said. "Rebecca's supervising that."

Rebecca Vance, a woman who hid a soft humanity within a hard shell of grief, would see that any such task was completed. Or she'd do it herself.

"How bad is the highway blocked?" I asked Mike. "We have to get through to Camas Valley and over to the Five."

Interstate 5 cut through the western part of Oregon, heading north from California and continuing on through Washington to the Canadian border. It was our best shot to reach our friends north of Eugene in the least amount of time. Or so we'd thought.

Just getting to Remote had taken six hours of maneuvering around drifts of ash and fallen trees. The clogged flow of one creek had backed up over the roadway near a bridge whose concrete supports were in danger of being undermined should the dammed water let loose. But we'd made it, with some light left in the day, though that was a misnomer at best. There was no light. At three in the afternoon it was as dark as midnight. And we still had far to go.

"We can't get through with the vehicles we have here," Mike said, pointing to the slide's location on the old topographic map spread out on the counter. "I tried to head up there in my four-by, to see how they were holding up, but I couldn't get through it. In the Humvee...maybe."

"Maybe is all we've got," I said.

Genesee, though, wasn't so sure about that.

"Unless we backtrack and head up the coast," he suggested. "Follow the route they took."

We'd already considered that before departing. At least Lorenzen and I had.

"Too many bridges," I told the Navy man. "Just like that creek we passed, a backed up flow that breaks through a blockage could wipe out any crossing. We just have to get inland to the Five."

My explanation didn't fully clear any doubt that Genesee held, but he wasn't going to protest. This wasn't his arena, out here, dealing with situations of daunting odds against survival. He knew that. I was glad about that, because I didn't have time on this trek we were undertaking to educate the man about the ways of this world we'd been plunged into. As much as I, myself, could, that was. What we were facing, the violence of Mother Nature on full display, was unlike anything I'd been faced with. I had to trust that my instincts, honed by hours and days and weeks fighting to stay alive in other hellish places, would be enough to get us to our friends, and then back home again.

"Fletch..."

"Yeah, Mike?"

"Does anybody have any idea how long this will last? I mean, is it gonna clear soon?"

I shook my head. We were at the mercy of geology and weather. Wind could push the ash cloud east, and the mountain could go quiet, ending its release of choking gas and pulverized pumice.

"It'll pass," I said. "This will all pass."

Mike nodded, but I could see it in his eyes. The same thing I was wondering.

When?

* * *

We reached the avalanche site an hour after leaving Remote. We weren't the first to do so.

"We've got company," Genesee said from the passenger seat.

I could see what he'd noticed through the falling ash. A light, sweeping back and forth. Just barely, beyond the beam, silhouettes of people stood out, as did the hulking shape of a large vehicle. A vehicle I recognized.

"It's their tow truck," I said, recalling the wrecker that had been dispatched to haul our damaged Humvee into Camas Valley after the ambush we'd survived.

I pulled as close to the avalanche as I could, the mound of ash and earth and rock four feet high, a snapped tree protruding from the pile. Genesee and I climbed out, the engine off but headlights burning. We scrambled slowly up the blockage and over to the far side, the dark shapes in the darkened landscape that I'd seen now quantifiable as two people, one of whom I recognized.

"Lo."

The man who'd led the mission to save us from the ambush on this very road offered me a gloved hand, and I shook it. He lowered the bandana wrapped around his face.

"Fletch."

I looked to his companion, a face I recognized from our brief time in Camas Valley, and from supply runs between there and Remote during my stay in the settlement, but whose name I could not recall.

"This is Paula," Lo said, introducing the woman.

"Good to meet you," I said, taking the opportunity to make sure both knew the man I was travelling with.

Then, the reality of our reason for being on the road took over the conversation, and I quickly explained what we had set out to do.

"The road to Winston is passable," Lo told us.

"How recent is that report?" I asked.

"I rode it myself this morning," Paula said.

Rode...

The inhabitants of Camas Valley, in addition to manufacturing batteries and supplying them to Bandon as part of our alliance agreement, had constructed a number of all electric motorcycles which would have wowed even in the old world. That the nimble vehicles required no air pulled through a filter which could clog was a major plus in this environment, but riding one through the ash fall, on roads coated with the fine, hot grit, could not have been easy.

"That must have been a sporty trip," I told the woman.

"It'll be easier for you with four wheels under you," she said.

"You all are holding up okay?" I asked.

"For now," Lo said. "I can't say we thought a volcanic eruption was in our initial events to prepare for, but there's overlap, I suppose."

The Camas Valley survivor colony had begun before the blight had even been the twinkle in some mad scientist's eye, a collection of individuals who'd expected some event to trigger the collapse of society. They planned accordingly, training and supplying themselves to survive a grid-crippling EMP attack, or economic meltdown, a surprise nuclear attack, or coordinated terrorist operations which would bring down water, power, and communications. In essence, they'd hardened themselves against a myriad of ways society could crumble, not knowing that they would face the literal end of the world.

And, now, a violent earth making its supremacy known.

"We were about to clear this when you pulled up," Lo said.

I glanced past him to the tow truck, its headlights burning and engine idling.

"Does that have a dozer blade I can't see?" I asked, unsure of how the beefy vehicle could clear the road without one.

Paula pointed past us to the thick tree trunk sticking upward from the avalanche.

"That could act like an anchor if it slid with soil," she explained. "We're going to attach the tow cable to it and pull."

I was understanding now, and the idea was simple, as well as inspired.

"You could clear a path through the debris just by yanking it out," I said, seeing how the trunk and root system of the dead tree could act like a rake, sweeping enough away to allow passage through.

"Let's see if it works," Lo said.

It took him and Paula just a few minutes to turn the tow truck around and extend a cable from its rear winch, which was then secured low around the tree. Genesee and I stood aside, clear of any danger should the cable snap. With Paula at the wheel and Lo guiding her with shouts and flashlight signals, the engine revved and the cable went taut. The tip of the tree leaned toward the wrecker, and debris at its base began to shift, small avalanches to either side opening a crack in the blockage, then a gully, and finally a valley as the remains of the old, dead pine slid free, dragging soil and ash up the road as Paula pulled the tow truck to the shoulder and stopped.

"That should get you through," Lo said.

I nodded, looking to the man as Genesee jogged back to the Humvee to drive it through the opening. Something had suddenly struck me. A wondering and a realization all in one.

"Lo, why were you two here?" I asked. "With the truck?"

That both of us would have shown up at the avalanche almost simultaneously was not something any odds would point to. Unless one looked deeper, I was about to learn.

"Dalton sent a patrol out early on to check on Remote," he explained. "They reported the slide and we came out to clear it."

The alliance, it appeared, was solid. More solid than even the formalities had suggested. What I'd just witnessed was one group of people looking out for another. That spoke to a connection beyond agreements. That spoke to growth, and to a belief that we were all in this together.

"I'm glad you were here," I told the man.

Genesee pulled the Humvee through the breach and stopped alongside me. Just ahead, vaguely visible in the filtered glow of the headlights, Paula had unhooked the cable from the tree and was winching it back to the truck.

"You want to follow us back to Camas Valley?" Lo asked.

"Lead the way," I said, and climbed in next to Genesee.

"You okay with me driving?" the Navy commander asked.

"Just stay on their tail," I said.

That was precisely what he did as we made our way along the highway, his attention focused forward. Most of the time.

"Fletch..."

"What is it?"

Genesee looked to the mirror on his side of the Humvee, then pointed past me to the one on my side.

"I see daylight behind us," he said.

I looked, and just as he'd said, there it was. A real sliver of sunlight cutting through the seemingly constant fall of ash behind us. It was thin and faint, a line of muted brightness just above the top of the dead woods, but it *was* there. It was real.

"That's due west," I said.

Genesee nodded and glanced to me as we neared Camas Valley.

"It might be clearing at the coast," he said.

A few minutes later, as we stopped in front of the old school building that was the center of the survivor colony led by Dalton, I stepped from the Humvee and felt the most wonderful thing I could imagine. Wind. Coming from the west.

"Do you feel that?" I asked Genesee as he climbed from the vehicle.

"It's blowing east," he said, looking to me, the smile upon his face plain even beneath the dust mask he'd just donned.

"Someone up there likes us..."

I looked toward the voice and saw Dalton approaching from the building. Beyond him, the tow truck was pulling into its shed up the street. Already the air seemed clearer, if only by a bit.

"I'll take any help from anyone," I said.

The man reached out and shook my hand.

"Commander Genesee," Dalton said, offering his hand.

"Have we met?" Genesee asked, lowering his mask as he shook the man's hand.

I laughed lightly, and saw a hint of smile on Dalton's face. The extent to which Camas Valley had scouted our town and surveilled its residents had been troubling at first, but had quickly evolved into moments of amusement, triggered by what Genesee was experiencing now.

"I'll explain later," I told my companion, then turned my attention to Dalton. "We heard that the road to Winston is doable."

"What's in Winston that would bring you out in this?"

I explained the situation to Dalton, including the impetus for our sending a delegation to Portland.

"The president," he said, any lightness in his mood gone as if never there.

"It looks that way," I said.

"He snaps his finger and you all are ready to jump?"

Our communities had grown closer due to the alliance, but there was still a deep mistrust of the government that had, as the blight spread, let its people down. I was one of those people who'd held such feelings. Dalton was me times fifty.

"We don't know what they want," I said. "But Schiavo follows orders."

"So do I," Genesee said, quite unexpectedly, backing up the reasoning I was giving Dalton.

The man shook his head and looked upward, into the thinning ash, more of the day's waning light bleeding through.

"That plane won't be in Portland," he said. "Not with this falling."

"That's not my concern right now," I said. "Getting to our people is."

Dalton seemed to accept at least that part of our effort.

"I wish our repeater tower hadn't gone down in the initial quake," he said. "You might be able to reach them. Get some more information."

"I wish we could, too," I said.

Once more he looked upward, and to the west, the slight clearing seeming to hold. For now.

"This won't be the same the closer you get to the mountain," Dalton cautioned us.

"I know," I said.

There might be clearing here, if only slightly, but as we made our way north that was certain to lessen. In fact, we could expect the ash fall to intensify, even if the eruption had subsided, which we had no indication of. More tremors had shaken the earth since the large earthquake which signaled that Mt. Hood had exploded back to life after a lengthy slumber.

"Do you want to stay the night?" Dalton asked.

"Thanks, but no," I answered. "We need to put some more miles behind us. At least just past Winston to Roseburg. That will put us on the interstate tomorrow."

"Roseburg to Coburg," Dalton said, mulling the challenge of that journey. "It's been a while since we scouted up that way. Never made it past Eugene. But if nothing has damaged the roads and bridges, I'd say you can make that by tomorrow night."

"That's only, what, eighty miles?" Genesee asked, mildly doubting the estimation. "You think that will take us all day?"

Dalton eyed my companion, masking the hint of pity that I detected. He could tell that, even in the world as it had become since the blight, the Navy man was sheltered. This was his first true foray into an unknown beyond his comfort zone. In essence, he was facing a new reality for the very first time.

"You're heading into the beast's maw, Commander," Dalton said, truth in his words despite the injection of drama. "Tomorrow's not Sunday, so don't expect a Sunday drive."

Genesee chose not to respond, wisely. Dalton let that silent response linger for a moment before looking to me.

"Do you need anything?" the leader of Camas Valley asked.

"We're supplied well."

Dalton nodded at my assurance.

"If it clears more, I'll have Lo put a crew together to finish clearing the road to Remote."

"I know they'll feel better with that route open," I told him, then looked to Genesee. "We should get moving again."

"Yeah," he said, his agreement subdued. "We should."

"Dalton, thank you," I said, offering my hand once more. "We'll see you on the way back."

He shook my hand and watched as I got behind the wheel, Genesee already in the passenger seat. I pulled slowly away, not wanting to kick a larger cloud of ash up as we left.

"He's not the warm and fuzzy type," Genesee said once we were back on the highway.

"Warm and fuzzy can get you killed," I told him.

The man didn't challenge my statement, or its truthfulness. He simply stared out the windshield as we cruised slowly along the two lane road, heading toward our friends.

And into another thing that could get us killed—the unknown.

Six

We woke to skies still hued black, the only hint of clearing now far to the west and south. Where we'd stopped for the night, in the front showroom of a looted used car dealership half a mile east of the interstate in Roseburg, darkness reigned. Any sunrise that might have warmed and buoyed us was solidly blocked by a rain of ash which, I had to admit, seemed to be increasing.

"Do you need a hand with that?" Genesee asked.

I stood at the front of the Humvee, just forward of the passenger door, my hands beneath the opened hood as I worked to replace the vehicle's air filter. We'd brought an extra six of the parts, knowing that the choking atmosphere would wreak havoc on any engine. We couldn't afford to not reach our friends, and had to ensure that every mechanical part functioned well enough to get us there, and then back.

"Isn't there something about doctors needing to protect their hands?"

Genesee put the cup of orange drink he'd just mixed up down on the left fender and showed me his palms.

"These would rather be working on the sixty-eight Camaro in my garage," he said, chuckling to himself after a moment. "I'd like to think someone stole it and mounted quad fifties on it for some duel in the desert, but it's probably rusting in some roadside ditch."

"I'd pay money to see that," I said, finishing with the filter. "The duel in the desert—not the rusting in a ditch."

He took his cup of orange drink and sipped, spitting the mouthful out before swallowing.

"The damn ash is everywhere," he said.

I closed the Humvee's hood and watched Genesee toss what remained in his cup aside.

"Canteen water for the duration," he said.

It was a quiet moment. But it couldn't last. A few minutes later we were back in the vehicle, our gear stowed. I pulled out of the empty showroom, through the space where large windows had once let shoppers view the newest models of Fords from the street. A short drive up a four-lane road brought us to Interstate 5, and a quick turn onto the onramp put us on that thoroughfare.

Ten minutes later, as we maneuvered around an overturned delivery truck, Genesee shook his head at the view out the windshield.

"It's getting worse," he said.

He wasn't wrong. The ash fall was increasing. Already there were a good six inches on the roadway, with drifts up to a foot and a half. Our top speed was a painfully slow fifteen miles an hour, making Dalton's estimation of our trip's duration more accurate than Genesee had thought at the time.

"It's not going to get any better," I told him.

Past the truck, we had clear road for an hour, then a partially collapsed bridge forced us to detour off the highway and creep along the flat edge of a shallow creek before we found a spot to cross. The Humvee's wheels spun on the far bank, the slope slick with a mix of wet ash and mud. After a tense few minutes I drove us back up onto level ground and turned toward the highway.

Genesee took the map and spread it on his lap. He studied it as I steered us back onto the interstate.

"We still have rivers to cross," he said, pointing to several on the map. "Bigger than that creek we just got past."

"I know."

"This rig can't swim across a river," he said.

"Hopefully it won't have to."

That didn't do much to reassure him, but he held his worry and folded the map and stuck it back in its space atop the boxy dash. For the next ten minutes the road was clear and Genesee was silent. The wipers swatted ash from the windshield, the constant sweep of grit across the glass slowly working on its clarity. By the time we returned to Bandon I thought it might be nearly opaque.

"We should have brought spare wiper—"

"I think I'm in love with Grace," Genesee blurted out, interrupting the mundane with the momentous.

I glanced right and saw the man looking straight at me, worry and determination both plain on his face.

"You *think*?"

He quickly reconsidered his wording.

"I'm in love with Grace," he said.

I stayed focused on the road ahead, unsure of what I should say, particularly since my exchange with Grace just prior to leaving. To know that the feeling was mutual, to a degree, at least, was not a surprise. Grace was more than a good woman—she was a beautiful person. She exuded kindness and joy, even in times which had tested her.

"I feel like I need to tell you this, Fletch. Because..."

"Because of Neil," I prompted when he hesitated.

Genesee nodded. He was reaching out to me, as one might to the father of an intended bride. In this instance, I was the surrogate of that role. The friend of the man who had been Grace's husband. Who had fathered a child with her. I didn't suspect that he was looking for my approval, or some blessing on my part. Instead I sensed that he was concerned, about reactions, possibly.

I was wrong.

"Fletch, am I..."

"Are you what?"

Once more he hesitated, that concern I'd noticed a moment before more apparent now. More tangible.

"Am I good enough for her?"

I wanted to look to the man, but forced myself to keep my eyes on the road. What he was asking was an impossibility to define. It was an intangible measure. Still, I understood why he had sought my counsel on the matter, though what assurance, or dissuasion, I could offer him was uncertain. The best I could do, without trying to weigh this man's life against that of the friend I'd known almost my entire life, was to provide some perspective. Of a more personal nature.

"Elaine and I would have never been together before the blight," I said. "Never. But then things changed."

I heard Genesee laugh lightly at my choice of words.

"Have they ever," he said.

"Old considerations went out the window," I told him. "I looked at the world and everyone left in it with new eyes. That allowed me to see Elaine for who she was, and I loved what I saw. And I didn't care what anyone thought about it, because the time we have now is too important to waste on worries. Even worries about yourself."

Genesee thought on that for a moment.

"Neil was your friend," he said. "Even with all that's happened, I know he still means a great deal to you."

"He does," I confirmed. "But he's gone, Clay. I've come to terms with that, and the reasons behind his death. I think Grace has, too."

I sensed that his concerns weren't completely assuaged by what I'd said so far. So I decided to hold nothing back.

"You've been kind of an ass," I said.

There was no immediate response from the man to the judgement I'd just handed him as to his character. No quick defense or justification. In fact, from the corner of my eye, I saw him nod lightly to himself.

"That doesn't mean that you are now," I told him. "Or that you have to be going forward."

"This is going to sound selfish," Genesee warned me. "Before everything went to hell because of the blight, I was looking to get out of the Navy. I'd done my time and then some. I had plans. Private practice. Make some actual money. Travel. Hell, I didn't even want to find anyone and settle down. I wanted to live, on my own terms. But..."

He quieted for a moment.

"All that seems so trivial now," he continued. "I was bitter about it, though. About losing a chance at that life."

"And now?"

"I still want out of the Navy," he said, adding a chuckle which I joined. "But I don't want to spend the time after that alone. Not anymore."

The man wasn't seeking some grand understanding of whatever change had come over him. I thought right then as we drove through the dark rain of ash that he'd already come to the conclusion that the future he wanted included Grace.

"Clay, I know you're not looking for my approval, but let me just say that everyone deserves a chance at happiness. Grace does, and so do you."

"Thank you, Fletch LOOK OUT!"

The abrupt shift of his words from appreciation to warning coincided with my own eyes seeing the old van appear in our path. I slammed on the brakes and steered left, but the layer of ash upon the surface of the road had, at times, made the vehicle react as if we were driving on ice. This was one of those times.

"Hold on!"

I shouted the warning as the nose of the Humvee swung left, then right, its beefy bumper slamming hard into the stationary old van, long ago abandoned on the highway. The impact shoved the boxy Ford hard to the right and into the guardrail. We slid past it and skidded to a stop near the same barrier which had prevented the van from going over the highway's edge.

"You all right?" I asked.

"Fine," Genesee said, just slightly shaken by the incident.

I reached for my AR and the door at the same time.

"Let's check our front end," I told my companion. "Grab your weapon."

The reminder made Genesee hesitate as he was about to climb out empty handed. He retrieved his M4 and followed me out, each of us securing dust masks over our faces as we stepped into the swirl of blowing ash. A wind with no constant direction was spinning the warm grit at us from every direction. I wondered it the volcanic event could create its own weather pattern, one that would intensify and become more erratic the closer we came to its origin.

"Nothing major," I said, shining my flashlight on the front end of the Humvee.

"Fletch..."

I looked to Genesee, his form almost erased by the rain of ash between us. He was maybe twenty feet away, standing at the driver's door of the van we'd hit, but at that scant distance he was already difficult to see.

"What is it?"

"Come here," he said, shining his light through the broken driver's window.

I went to where he stood and looked to the interior of the van, my heart hurting as soon as I saw what he had.

Two adults and one child, father at the wheel, mother and daughter holding each other in the passenger seat. There was little ash inside, indicating the broken window had been intact before our collision. Just a smattering of black granules had been deposited on the desiccated bodies, the remains partially mummified, skin pulled taut over the bones beneath, mouths gaping in some grotesque silent scream.

"They died on the highway," Genesee said, slightly shaken by the discovery. "They ran out of gas, or broke down, and that was it. There was no one to help them. No one to call. They just gave up."

"Clay, we've gotta get moving," I told him.

He shifted his light, focusing on the mother and child.

"They died first," Genesee said. "At least a year ago. Probably closer to two."

"Clay..."

The beam moved again, to the father, his slack corpse leaning back in the driver's seat.

"If they'd all died together, he'd be huddled with them. But he kept driving until something gave out. Then he gave up. He sat in that seat and waited for it to come. Death."

"We've gotta go," I prodded him.

Genesee switched his flashlight off and looked to me, nodding. There'd been shock in his eyes just seconds before. Now, though, something else had replaced it. Some fire. Some determination.

"No more dying," he said. "No more."

He turned and headed back to the Humvee, returning to the passenger seat. I joined him, taking my place at the wheel. The man, the officer, the doctor, was staring straight ahead into the blizzard of black lit by our headlights.

"You all right, Clay?"

He shook his head slowly, as honest a reply as I'd ever seen from the man.

"I've seen death, Fletch. Doc Allen's wife from the virus. The child from the same. Your friend shot down by Olin. All those bodies that washed ashore. But this...it has to stop."

"You can't lay a marker like that, Clay. Not in our world."

"I can today," he said, looking to me. "I can for the people I know. They're not going to end up dead in a

Humvee on some highway somewhere. Not like this family did. So let's go get them."

I nodded, understanding his fervor, wanting desperately to believe that his desire would find its ultimate satisfaction.

"All right," I said, turning the Humvee back onto a straight course along the interstate.

Seven

Five hours after waking and setting out, we reached Eugene.

Or what had been Eugene. The only indicators that we'd arrived in the once pretty city on the Willamette River were intermittent signals on the GPS we'd been given and reflective lettering on green road signs blazing briefly in the dimmed glare of our headlights. Otherwise the place might have been just a hellish moonscape, black grit falling from the unseen sky, dusting everything with smoking, choking ash.

"What's our best route?" Genesee asked. "The interstate skirts the east side of the city."

The answer to his question came in the form of a skid, the Humvee sliding on the layer of grit coating the roadway as I slammed on the brakes. I'd caught just a glimpse of what had necessitated our sudden stop, an absence of the familiar directly ahead. Had I been going fifteen miles per hour instead of ten, Commander Clay Genesee and I might have ended up riding the Humvee as it tumbled over the severed edge of the bridge that crossed the Willamette.

"Jesus!"

Genesee shouted the exclamation as the vehicle lurched to a stop, its bumper just feet from the end of pavement, a dark abyss filled with swirling ash before us.

"Find us another way across, Clay."

"Right," he said, coming down from the rush of fear which had just filled him. "Just a minute."

I backed the Humvee away from the broken edge of the span and turned around as Genesee checked the paper map on his lap.

"There's a bridge to the west of here," he said. "Just get off the interstate and follow a road that parallels the river.

I followed his directions, as well as one could driving through the volcanic soup falling from the sky. At times we barely crawled forward, slowing to gently push wrecks to the side so that we could pass. Ten minutes after swinging around and leaving the fallen bridge we reached our other chance to cross the Willamette River.

"Coburg Road," Genesee said, comparing the name on the map to the bent-over street sign just outside his window. "Maybe this will take us right to them."

"It's got to get us across the river first," I said.

I turned onto the road and felt it begin to slope up, rising toward the span that, hopefully, would bring us to the other side. Five miles per hour was the top speed I was willing to chance as glimpses of the bridge's steel structure appeared overhead.

"Keep your eyes on the road," I told Genesee.

"It looks good so—"

KTHUNK

The left front of the Humvee dropped, metal frame and suspension smashing into the road surface as we drove into a hole. It was nothing as dramatic as the complete failure of the interstate bridge, but, for the moment, it stopped us dead in our tracks.

"I've gotta back us out of it," I said.

Doing so was not as easy as saying so. The vehicle had sufficient power, but something had hung up on whatever solid support members lay beneath the road surface.

"Come on..."

Urging the Humvee didn't work, nor did rocking back and forth, through forward and reverse gears, as one might when stuck in soft earth.

"You want me to get out and check it?" Genesee asked.

"No, just give me a minute here."

I stopped trying to force our way out of the hole with brute force and, instead, shifted to a plan of finesse, however much that was possible in the beefy military transport. With light pressure on the accelerator I shifted into reverse, nursing the wheel backward. Metal scraped on the road as we crept to the rear, then I felt the tire's rubber find purchase on the edge of the hole.

"It's working," Genesee said. "Keep it up."

A little more pressure on the gas and the nose of the Humvee came back up, the tire climbing fully out of the hole. Genesee reached over from the passenger seat and gave me a congratulatory slap on the shoulder.

His glee, though, was short lived, as the entire bridge began to shake, swaying back and forth.

"Earthquake," Genesee said.

"Hold on!"

I shouted the warning and jammed my foot down on the accelerator, steering right to miss the hole that had almost ended our journey. The tires spun for a second, then grabbed pavement beneath the ash that the treads cut through. We lurched forward as the bridge shuddered, the steel framework that supported it actually screaming. A series of loud, metallic bangs cut through the shaking as pieces of the arch above began to break away, the tremor a final nail in the span's structural integrity.

"Fletch!"

Genesee saw what I did, a twisted length of something resembling a sculpted I-beam fall right in front of us. I had no time to react to avoid the obstacle and simply kept my foot on the gas, slamming into the metal support. It bounced off the Humvee's already tested front end and was launched clear, disappearing into the ash.

"We're gonna make it," I said.

I didn't know if my companion believed me. The truth be told, I wasn't sure. Everything around us was whipsawing left and right, the bridge swinging severely east and west. What worried me, though, was not what I could see, but what I couldn't. Beyond the veil of ash the entire span might be coming apart—or might have already just ahead of us, much like the interstate bridge had. We'd been able to turn back, there, but here...here there was no turning back.

"I see the end," Genesee said.

Through the gritty smoke, as the shaking slowed, I, too, saw road that lay upon solid earth, not suspended over churning waters. A few seconds more on the gas and we were clear of the bridge. I slowed and stopped, taking a look in the side view mirror. What I could see behind us no longer resembled a piece of exact engineering.

"It's leaning," I said.

Genesee looked, shaking his head at what he was seeing.

"We're not getting home that way."

"We'll find a way," I said, and got us moving again.

* * *

"Coburg," I said, reading the signage on a post near the curb.

It had taken just twenty minutes to reach the town after our close call on the bridge. But this place was no more a recognizable town than any we'd passed through. It was little more than vague glimpses of buildings seen through the gauzy black rain of ash.

"How far are we?"

Genesee looked to the GPS. Its signal was still dubious, at best, but the pin that marked the location where our friends were, or had been, glowed bright on the small screen, as did the circle around it. He laid the device atop the paper map on his lap and compared the two.

"We're inside the circle," he said.

"They're close," I said, about to tap on the vehicle's horn when Genesee jabbed a finger toward the left, pointing at something.

"There!"

I slowed and stopped, looking to what he'd spotted, my heart sinking as the image became clearer through the steady fall of ash. The Humvee in which Schiavo, Martin, and Carter had left Bandon was nosed into the corner of a building just off an intersection, the upper part of a wooden telephone pole embedded in its left rear door, penetrating into the back seat area.

"Good God," Genesee said.

He climbed out, forgetting his weapon. I didn't as I left the driver's seat and approached the wrecked vehicle, my AR slung, eyes scanning the immediate area that I could see for any signs of an ambush, past or present.

"It's empty," Genesee said after checking the interior. "I don't see any blood."

And I didn't see any indication of a firefight. There were no impacts on the vehicle, nor any char marks which would point to some explosive round disabling the Humvee.

"Their trailer's gone," I said, eyeing the empty space behind the vehicle. "The hitch is snapped off."

Before whatever had happened here, something violent had ripped what they were towing free.

"Where the hell are they?" Genesee wondered, looking in all directions.

That was the question of the moment, and one we had to answer.

"Cover your ears," I said, drawing my Springfield from its holster on my hip.

Genesee followed my instructions. I raised my pistol, flipped the safety off with my thumb, and fired three fast shots into the air. Then, we waited, listening.

"I don't hear anything," Genesee said.

"Give it a minute," I told him. "They probably aren't standing outside with a weapon waiting for this kind of—"

Bang. Bang. Bang.

The reply was obvious. And close.

"Down the street," Genesee said, pointing in the direction we'd been driving.

We were back in the Humvee in a few seconds and cruising down the street, looted and rubbled storefronts barely visible to either side.

"I don't see anything," Genesee said.

I honked the Humvee's horn, its anemic blast barely registering. But, it was enough.

"Lights," Genesee said, pointing ahead and to the left.

I saw them, too, the beams of two flashlights crisscrossing each other as they swept back and forth, the person wielding them resolving through the ash as I steered the Humvee toward the curb and stopped in front of a bank building. Carter Laws lowered the lights when he saw us.

"Carter!" I shouted as both Genesee and I climbed from the vehicle.

"Fletch!"

The young, newly minted private ran up and threw a bear hug on me. A second later, Schiavo raced out of the bank building, her presence and Carter's appearance leaving no doubt as to who was hurt.

"Where's Martin?" Genesee asked.

"He's inside," the captain answered.

"Help me with the medical supplies," Genesee said.

I left Schiavo and Carter to do just that and hurried into the building.

Eight

Martin lay on his right side on a makeshift bed in the teller area of the bank. Two desks that had been righted and pushed together had formed the base of where he rested, with a collection of scavenged blankets and old bedding folded beneath his body to offer some cushion against the hard surface.

"Martin," I said, approaching and putting my AR aside. "Fletch..."

The man who'd mastered the art of firm graciousness, a quality I'd experienced soon after arriving in Bandon, reached a hand slowly toward me. I slipped my gloves off and took hold of it, holding tight, with an arm wrestler's grip.

"You don't look half bad," I told him.

"I'd hate to see the other half," he quipped.

Genesee came in a moment later, Schiavo and Carter with him, each carrying bags and boxes of medical supplies and equipment.

"Martin," Genesee said. "Grace tells me you had a pretty hard hit from a telephone pole."

"It won," Martin joked, coughing suddenly, his face grimacing in pain.

Genesee put a hand on the man's shoulder and looked to me.

"Fletch, the oxygen bottle and mask."

I retrieved the items for him. A moment later a slow flow of oxygen eased Martin's discomfort slightly as

Genesee checked him over, focusing on the large bruise and swelling beneath his left armpit.

"What happened?" I asked. "We saw your Humvee down the street."

"When the big quake hit we were just starting through that intersection," Schiavo said, shaking her head as she recalled the moment. "It was violent, Fletch. So violent."

"I was driving," Carter said, some guilt seeming to inhabit his tone.

"It's wasn't your fault, private," Schiavo said. "You just happened to be at the wheel when it hit."

"What was that piece of telephone pole in the back?" I pressed.

"It snapped off, Fletch," Schiavo said. "The whole top of the pole was whipping back and forth so hard in the quake that it broke away and flew into the vehicle. Right where Martin was sitting in the back seat."

"I think you've got a couple fractured ribs," Genesee said. "And a minor pneumothorax."

"Air in the chest cavity," I said.

I'd picked up enough from medical television shows in the old world, and from interactions with people like Grace and Doc Allen, to recall that which Genesee was describing.

"Classic impact injury," Genesee said, giving Martin a quick shot to numb some of his pain. "I'm going to have to put in a chest tube. I'm getting breathing sounds on the left side, but they're reduced. My guess is it's only a minor puncture in the lung. The ribs appear to have reset themselves, so we're not going to have jagged ends in there causing more damage, as long as he takes it easy."

The doctor went about performing the procedure that was necessary to remove air from the cavity around the left lung. We assisted as best we could, sterilizing our hands before wielding lights and passing bandages. It was all done in twenty minutes, a large bandage covering Martin's left side and a snug wrap circling his torso to help secure his injured ribs.

"You're going to be sore for a while," Genesee said.

Martin nodded, smiling groggily through the transparent oxygen mask.

"Thank God you were monitoring the satellite frequencies," Schiavo said to me. "It was blind luck that we found a SATCOM unit a few blocks over."

"There must have been a unit stationed here as the blight hit," Carter said. "Probably a roadblock on the interstate."

Checkpoints. That's what they'd been. My first encounter with the violence and breakdown of order brought on by the blight had occurred on a road in Montana, near Arlee. It made perfect sense that such a restriction on movement, hopeless as it was, would have been put in place where Carter suggested.

What Schiavo had thought, though, was not as accurate.

"We weren't the ones who heard you," I said.

It took a few minutes to explain what had transpired, from the arrival of the SEALs to our setting off on a mission to save a mission.

"You're apparently pretty important to someone," Genesee told Schiavo.

"We need to get moving," I said, ending the moment of sharing. "We're going to have to head west instead of south to find a passable bridge. If we're lucky, it will be clearer at the coast. We can be back in Bandon day after tomorrow."

Schiavo thought on that for a moment, then shook her head.

"I can't go back," she said. "I have to get to Portland."

Martin coughed and reached up to ease the oxygen mask away from his face, but said nothing, just regarded his wife with a mix of worry and wonder.

"Angela," I said, taking the moment to a more personal level, "there's duty, and then there's futility. Going on is futile. The situation is untenable."

"There's no way Air Force One will be in Portland," Genesee said. "They would have evacuated at the first sign of the eruption."

"The message you received from the SEALs came after the eruption," Schiavo pointed out. "Long after. And according to you they stated that I have to get to Portland."

"That's moot now," I said. "There's one vehicle between us and we have to get Martin back to Bandon."

The man tried to sit, but only managed to prop himself on one elbow. Genesee reached to steady his patient.

"I'm not going back," Martin told us, though his gaze was fixed fully on his wife. "Not if she's not, and, in case you haven't figured it out yet, she's pressing on."

Schiavo didn't want to smile, but a hint of that very expression spread slowly upon her face as she regarded the man she loved, and his undeniable devotion to her.

"You can't be serious," Genesee said, reading what the silence between them was telling him. "This man needs rest, and you can't walk to Portland. Not from here."

She looked away from Martin, to Genesee, and shook her head.

"We're not walking," she said. "The other Humvee is just banged up. We can get that running. Wouldn't you think so, Private Laws?"

Carter seemed taken aback by the proposition. Not of continuing the mission, but of getting their wrecked transport on the road again.

"I can give it a look, ma'am," Carter said.

He shouldered his weapon and turned toward the door, but never made it a single step as I reached out and put a hand to his shoulder to stop him.

"Let's just stop," I said.

"Fletch," Schiavo said, the tone that wrapped my name plainly admonishing me for resisting her decision.

But I wasn't doing that. Not at all.

"No," I said, shaking my head at her, then looking to each of those gathered around our wounded friend. "Let's just not play this back and forth like some of us are going to head for home and some of us are going to keep going. We're not splitting up. At the end of any discussion or argument we're going to have, we'll come to the same conclusion."

"We're sticking together," Martin said, adding a quick nod toward me.

"We are," I said.

Genesee, though, wasn't fully grasping what I'd just said. And what we'd all just agreed to. Even him, by default.

"Wait," the Navy doctor said, an inkling of what I'd just stated beginning to sink in. "You're not serious."

"You saw their Humvee," I reminded Genesee. "The left front suspension is shot."

When the vehicle had been pushed off the street and over the curb, multiple supports that allowed proper ride and steering had been bent, the wheel at that corner of the Humvee canted at more than a 45 degree angle. There was no chance that the vehicle would get them to Portland, or even out of Coburg.

"Martin needs to stay immobile," Genesee said.

"Like he would be riding in our Humvee back to Bandon?" I challenged him. "How is that different from him riding in our Humvee heading north?"

Genesee chuckled with disbelief and shook his head.

"She's going north, Clay," I said.

"So am I," Martin added.

"Me, too," Carter said, adding a half-raised hand to emphasize his commitment to go on.

"Every minute we debate this the ash gets thicker out there," I said.

Genesee stepped close to me, hardly a foot separating us.

"And do you have any idea what it will be like in Portland?" he pressed me. "What kind of hell we'll find there?"

I didn't. But that didn't matter. If our friends were going, I was going. I'd tried to convince myself after Olin's death that I could separate myself from what needed to be done to keep Bandon on a prosperous path. That I could, without malice, turn my back on tasks and necessities which I was suited to perform. I wanted to be home with my family. With Elaine. And Hope.

But Bandon had survived, and begun to thrive, because of me. And because of others just like me. None of us were heroes, but to a man, and a woman, we were all integral to what had been accomplished. If each of us who'd contributed to the town's resilience in the face of the blight simply decided to no longer walk that path, all that we'd sacrificed for would settle into a state of stagnation. That, almost certainly, would mean failure. And death.

We had to move forward, and part of making that a reality was what I could bring to the table in this very endeavor. I had no true idea what we would find in Portland, nor why Schiavo had been summoned there by, presumably, the highest authority in our battered and fractured nation, but it was her duty to complete the mission she'd been given. And it was my place to see that she had every chance to succeed, because at the end of this journey she, and we, might find something vital to our town's survival.

"Get Martin ready to move," I told Genesee.

Martin, though, didn't wait for any assistance. He levered himself to a sitting position and then slid off the makeshift bed, standing next to it, unsteadily at first.

"I just need help with my shirt," Martin said.

"This is crazy," Genesee said.

Schiavo didn't take the man's bait. She simply stepped past him and helped Martin get his shirt on and his gear ready. I didn't engage with Genesee either, having learned over our short time alone together that, despite his protestations, the man knew he had something, and someone, worth fighting for. His reluctance to go beyond this point was fueled largely by a desire to return to Grace. Once he considered the gravity of the mission Schiavo had been given, though, I knew he'd come to understand that by helping her, he was helping Bandon. And without Bandon...

"Just plain nuts," Genesee mumbled, then began to repack the medical supplies that had been brought in from the Humvee, readying himself to move out.

He'd committed himself to reaching our friends and bringing them home. Only half of that desire had been achieved. In his reaction I saw the hint of fear that those we'd found, along with the two of us, might end up dead along the highway somewhere to the north, much like the family we'd stumbled upon in their van.

He might be right, I knew. We'd all cheated death in some way since the blight, some more than once, in places near and far, and in situations that were clearly dire.

But not as dire as this. I had to admit that. This, what we were about to attempt, bore the greatest threat that I had faced. We were going up against Mother Nature, in all her glorious fury. A few people, I supposed, had done so before and lived to tell the tale.

A few...

I hoped that we would soon join that very exclusive club of survivors.

Part Two

Portland

Nine

There was no day. Only night. And though we might have rested in Coburg for the remainder of the day until the unseen dawn arrived the next morning, we did not. We began the journey to Portland as soon as we'd loaded the Humvee and not two minutes after Carter had swapped out the air filter. A hair over a hundred miles separated us from our destination, a distance that, on a normal day in the old world, we would have covered in less than two hours.

In the blighted world, with the rage of Mt. Hood's eruption choking the air and fouling the land, it took almost twelve. We used our remaining air filters just reaching the city's outskirts, delineated only by faded and broken road signs like the ones that had marked our arrival in Eugene.

We also had a guide.

"Bear left if you can," Carter said.

He was riding shotgun as I drove. A paper map lay open on his lap, though he hadn't looked at it once. His attention was fixed out the windows as we crept deeper into the city. His city. His hometown.

"If it's clear ahead, we can have a pretty straight shot toward the airport down Columbia Boulevard."

I followed his directions, driving slow, weaving around rotting vehicles and debris from rubbled buildings which had collapsed into the street. We'd left the interstate a while back, taking city streets east toward the airport. Carter peered through the falling ash, navigating almost by feel.

Through memories that had been sullied by too many realities since the blight, this new nightmare included.

"Everything used to be so green," the young private commented, his head shaking slightly. "So green."

That color had been stripped from the world by the blight. What remained had been erased by the rain of ash from the eruption of Mt. Hood, not quite 50 miles further east.

"It's amazing that you can make out where we are," Martin said from the back seat.

He sat between Schiavo and Genesee, supplies crammed in nearly every space around them. After he'd offered the comment, he gasped slightly, drawing a shallow, painful breath. The injury he'd suffered was wearing on him. I hoped that we'd soon reach some place where he'd be able to truly rest.

"I can almost feel my way around this city," Carter said. "There was a great Vietnamese restaurant near here, just down that street there."

He pointed to the left, and I glanced that way, seeing only darkness and the faintest hint of an intersection.

"Good pho," Carter said. "Really, really good."

The young man smiled, though only for a moment. All that he'd known and experienced and reveled in was gone, from noodle restaurants to wooded parks. I wondered if it was almost better that he couldn't lay his eyes upon the exact places bubbling up in memory. Perhaps it was best that the city was veiled in smoke and ash. In my own situation, I had no idea what I would feel were I to venture back to my home in Missoula, and I'd thought about what my own reaction would be to finding the place I'd known as home for so long just a ravaged shadow of its former self.

"Turn right coming up," Carter said.

I slowed and made the turn, taking us onto Columbia Boulevard. We continued east for just five minutes before the way forward was hopelessly blocked by a literal wall of trucks and trailers which had been piled high to create a substantial roadblock. With the drifting ash added to the barrier, it looked like something Dante might have conjured in a fevered dream.

"Someone really didn't want people going this way," I said.

"They were trying to barricade the airport," Schiavo suggested from the back seat.

Long ago, likely when the worst of the blight was ravaging Portland and the surrounding area, some functionary had come up with the bright idea to shut down travel, or restrict it severely. Denying road access to a major transportation hub had been the purpose of what rose in the swirling ash before us.

"We can cut across the golf course," Carter said. "My buddies and I used to sneak onto it at night to watch the planes. It's right at the end of the runway."

Following his directions, we turned north, then cut through the parking lot of a business whose building had been reduced to a collection of walls folded in upon a collapsed roof, all of which was being buried by the black grit falling from above. A battered wooden fence at the rear of the property gave way with a nudge of the Humvee's stout bumper. We rolled over it and drove on.

"You sure about this?" I asked Carter as I drove blindly forward.

"You can't see it, but the airport is straight ahead," he assured me. "Not far at all."

Not far, though, turned out to be too far.

Ten

The Humvee gave out as we crossed the golf course that bordered the western edge of the airport. It sputtered and lurched, then rolled to an easy stop in the foot-deep accumulation of ash, the engine finally choked of the oxygen it needed for combustion.

"The last air filter is shot," Carter said.

I looked to the private riding shotgun and nodded. We'd run through all our spare air filters, and now the fine particles of ash had worn through any protection the last one had once offered the engine. The inner workings of the motor were likely clogged by the infiltration. Our only transport was about to join the millions of other vehicles abandoned across the landscape.

"The airport is just over there," Carter said, pointing from the passenger seat to the swirling blackness cut by the still burning headlights. "Less than half a mile."

In the back seat, Schiavo looked to her husband. Genesee sat on the opposite side of Martin and was doing the same.

"I can make it," the man said, trying to allay any fears as to his wellbeing.

But it was clear that he wasn't well, and wouldn't be for some time. He needed rest. That wasn't possible where we sat, though. Only death would result from remaining in the Humvee.

"We should move," I said. "The quicker we get to the airport the quicker we can get out of this."

"The terminals should be built to hold up under this," Carter said. "This is earthquake country."

Building codes to deal with seismic dangers would dictate reinforced structures be the norm, especially in any facility open to the public. Safety, for us, lay across the once green fairways and beyond the runways we could not yet see.

*　*　*

We unloaded and geared up, carrying all that we could. As we left the Humvee behind, the twin beams of its headlights grew dimmer and dimmer, until, glancing behind, we could see them no more.

"Stay close," I reminded those trailing me, waving my flashlight to mark my position through the relentless rain of ash. "Keep in sight."

Directly behind me, Schiavo and Genesee walked, with Martin between them, each offering a supporting hand to help him through the knee-deep drifts of singeing ash. A few yards to their rear, his own flashlight sweeping left and right, Carter followed.

"Should we rope up?" Genesee asked through his dust mask.

Connecting ourselves like climbers ascending some alpine peak might be a safer way to travel, but it could very well slow us down. And we couldn't chance that. We had to get to shelter.

"No," Schiavo said, of the same mind as I was. "Just keep moving."

We pressed on, reaching the airport perimeter thirty minutes after setting out, the only marker of the boundary a breached length of chain link topped by razor wire. Beyond it lay wide concrete aprons and runways, buildings and hangars.

"They would have come in on this runway," Carter told us as we crossed a wide expanse of featureless terrain. "This is Twenty-Eight left."

I looked back and saw the private pause briefly, sweeping the piled ash clear of a spot, revealing roughened concrete beneath.

"It's eleven thousand feet," Carter said. "Longest one at PDX."

"You sure you joined the right branch of the military?" Martin asked the young soldier.

"Long before I used to sneak onto the golf course with my buddies, I'd watch planes land from our apartment when I was a kid," Carter shared as he got moving again, pointing in a generally south eastern direction. "Over that way."

"It's not here now," Genesee said. "That's for sure."

As we'd entered Portland, the understanding that Air Force One would have departed as soon as there was a threat had been accepted. The first indications of an eruption would have forced its pilots to leave the affected area behind. That didn't mean, though, that there would not be some message waiting for us. Even some personnel left behind to meet us and instruct us on what to do next.

First, though, we had to reach someplace where those individuals, or that message, might be.

The first wispy features of the terminal building became visible through the ash fall a few minutes after we'd crossed the facility's longest runway. I could make out the straight lines of walls, and openings where windows would be, though there was no guarantee that any glass remained after so many years of certain vandalism and neglect. As we drew near, I did see that there were only frames where windows had once looked out upon aircraft arriving and departing. There was also more.

Much more.

Debris. Mounds of concrete and steel filling the interior of the structures, much of it collapsed all the way to the ground, pancaking floors that lay below. We moved left, along the southern spur of the U-shaped building, our lights sweeping over burned out planes and more of the structure, its rubbled, charred interior pointing to some catastrophic fire having destroyed it long before the eruption of Mt. Hood.

"There's nothing left," Carter said.

What he was really saying was that there was nowhere that we could take refuge.

"Ma'am..."

"Yes, Private?"

Carter showed her something in his hand. A plain wall thermometer, unremarkable and common.

"I took this from the bank building," the young soldier explained. "It felt like it was getting hotter while we were there, and I wanted to see if it actually was."

"And?" Genesee asked.

"It's ninety-eight degrees at head height," Carter said. "A hundred and fifteen at our knees near the ash."

"It's only going to get hotter," Martin said.

Everything, it seemed, was trying to kill us. The air we breathed. The earth we walked on. And now we were, slowly, being baked alive. Standing there and discussing it, though, would do nothing to protect us.

"Keep going," Schiavo ordered.

Behind, I could see that Martin was moving on his own, his wife and Genesee close by, ready and willing to assist him. But he was summoning some inner strength, some deep will, so that he did not become a burden, though none of us would see him as such.

"This is getting deep," Carter pointed out.

It was. As the point person of our unit, I was trying to blaze a trail, high stepping and kicking the hot ash clear of the path as best I could. But as the gritty rain continued, doing so became more difficult, even verging on impossible. Soon, we would not be able to move at all. And even as we did push on, the heat of the freshly fallen volcanic ejecta was beginning to affect the skin beneath our thick clothing.

"There's a parking structure," Carter said. "It's beyond the terminals."

A multi-level concrete structure would certainly have held up under the ash fall, and would not have burned. That had to be our destination now that the terminals were unusable as shelter.

Five minutes later, after crawling over a jagged pile that once had been the northern end of the passenger buildings, we reached the lower level of the road that wound through the airport, the upper deck having, for some reason, pancaked down upon all that was below it. Years ago, cars and vans would have filled the lanes, picking up and dropping off. Now there were only the tops of wrecked vehicles that we crawled over to reach the parking structure.

"No..."

Martin was the one who gave voice to our collective frustration as we came within view of our destination, the nearest edge of the parking structure. But it, too, had collapsed, deck upon deck having fallen, bringing the entire mass of concrete down upon itself.

"What happened?" Carter wondered aloud.

Schiavo stepped close to the rubble, focusing on a stout support column, the rebar exposed from its failure twisted and, in some places, severed completely. She reached out and touched the incredibly strong metal with her gloved hand.

"This is blast damage," she said, looking back to us. "This was taken down."

"Why?" Genesee asked. "Who would do that? For what purpose?"

The captain shook her head.

"I don't know."

I looked past the fallen structure, a bit more visibility here in the scant shelter of the broken decks overhanging the similarly destroyed roadway. Perhaps fifty feet ahead were more cars, and more bits of the parking structure that had fallen out onto the roadway and now protruded from the drifts of ash like grey icebergs in a sea of steaming black.

"We can't stay here," I said.

"Private..."

"Yes, ma'am?"

"What's down that way?" Schiavo asked, pointing through the slightly cleared air I'd just scanned.

"Some buildings, hangars," Carter answered. "And another runway to the north. Out past that you have Marine Drive and the Columbia River."

"Buildings," Genesee said. "Maybe a hangar."

Schiavo nodded and pointed. I led off again, guiding us past rubble and over cars, some beginning to smoke in the building heat that was enveloping them up to the door handles. We passed a collection of short buildings whose walls were all that remained, the roofs having fallen from fire long ago, or collapsed in the last few days from the combined effect of earthquakes and the weight of accumulated ash. Taller hangars had been flattened, just one left with a meager, partial structure after its rear portion folded inward upon a forgotten Lear Jet.

"There has to be some shelter," Schiavo said.

"There are more buildings ahead," Carter told her. "Across a parking lot."

Schiavo squinted through her goggles toward the blacked-out sky above.

"Get us there, private."

Carter gave a quick nod and took the lead from me, high stepping through the thickening ash.

* * *

Twenty minutes later we came to a light pole rising out of the steaming black drifts. The smoking hulk of an abandoned sedan nearby confirmed that we'd reached what had, at one time, been a parking lot, presumably for airport workers.

"Private, hold up," Schiavo said.

Carter stopped, though it was doubtful he, or any of us, would have been able to press on much further in this direction. The mounds of ash, rising by the minute, were becoming too deep to navigate. Martin, too, was struggling, though he fought mightily against letting his condition show.

"You okay?" I asked him, already knowing the answer I would receive.

"Hanging in there," he assured me.

He was. That was no lie. But he would do so until he dropped, something that was bound to happen. Soon.

"I'm just going to take a breather," Martin said, taking a position next to the light pole, one arm planted against it, propping his body up like a bike's kickstand.

"The buildings should be right there," Carter said, suddenly doubting himself. "They should."

"They might have been at one time," Schiavo told him.

Implicit in her words was a fear she wasn't expressing directly—that we'd come this far for nothing. That, I knew, mirrored a greater worry that was certainly weighing on her, as it was on me—that we'd made it to Portland, to the airport, escorting Schiavo to the place she'd been instructed to be, only to find nothing. And, worse, to know that reaching our destination only cemented the act as a one-way trip.

There was no going back. Not through the hell surrounding us.

"I'm sorry, ma'am," Carter said.

Schiavo looked to the newest member of her garrison and shook her head, absolving him of any responsibility for our situation. But she said nothing. None of us did.

And it was at that moment, as the reality of our situation began tilting us toward a collective feeling of desperation, that the world around us exploded.

Eleven

The blast wave hit us just before the sound, and the shaking. It was less an earthquake than a crack of the loudest thunder one could imagine that announced a new, and more violent, eruption, the tremor seeming to roll through our bodies, not just beneath our feet. The wall of ash which blocked any direct view of the mountain swirled suddenly, rushing toward us as we struggled to stay upright on the jittering earth we stood upon.

"Watch out!"

Genesee's warning was instinctive, and pointless. The blast wave had traveled forty miles from the mountain, or what was left of the mountain, a pressurized front of air pushed away from the explosive eruption, slamming into us with the force of some unseen and angry beast taking down its prey. Martin was tossed against the light pole we'd stopped near, his face bouncing off its solid surface as he fell into the burning ash. Carter and I were knocked flat. Somehow, Schiavo and Genesee, shielded somewhat by the edge of a high drift of ash, were able to stay on their feet.

"Ahhh!"

Carter's scream drew me to him. I grabbed the young soldier and pulled him free of the scalding ash which had almost swallowed his crumpled form. He swatted at the sleeve of his thick shirt, the material torn open, the exposed skin beneath red and burned from direct contact with the simmering black drift. Genesee and Schiavo hauled Martin up from where he'd fallen, saving him from any serious burns.

"What's happening?" Genesee asked, grabbing onto the swaying light standard for support.

"The mountain blew," Martin said, his body tipping, right arm instinctively pressing against his side as a wave of pain rolled through him.

Schiavo shifted a shoulder below his arm to steady her husband, and I did the same on the opposite side, mindful of the patch job Genesee had completed less than a day earlier.

"Blew?" Carter asked, grimacing at the blistering burn on his arm. "I thought it already erupted."

"This was different," Martin said, coughing through his mask.

"Like Mt. St. Helens," I suggested.

Martin didn't have to think long on that possibility before nodding.

"We need to get to cover," Schiavo said, an urgency in her voice now.

"We're forty miles away," Martin told her. "If the west face let go completely, the pyroclastic flow could be here in ten minutes."

"There's nowhere to hide," I said.

Schiavo, though, wasn't letting those facts of geology and physics stop her search for some semblance of safety.

"What if it's the south face, or the east face?" she asked, already knowing her response to any answer. "If that's the case, we still need to get to some shelter."

Genesee let go of the light pole as the shaking stilled. He scanned the area we'd reached after traversing the runways and searching the crumbling hangars.

"That hangar," he said, seizing on structures we'd passed by less than twenty minutes earlier.

Schiavo, though, wasn't enthused about that suggestion.

"Every single one of them was rubble or close to it," she said.

She wasn't wrong. Years of decay and vandalism, weathering, ground shaking their foundations, and now hundreds of tons of volcanic ash dropped on their roofs, had brought every one of the cavernous structures down, folding once sturdy metal walls inward and collapsing steel rafters and beams upon what remained.

Every hangar but one.

"That small one with the wrecked Lear Jet," Genesee said.

"The entire back half was pancaked down on the plane," Schiavo reminded him.

"And the front could go at any second with this ash still coming down," Martin added.

"We don't have a lot of options," I said.

Almost none, I knew. The terminals and every other structure within walking distance had been burned to the ground long before our mission to Portland was even conceived. All that was even remotely close that might provide us some modest shelter from the increasing rain of burning ash was what Genesee had suggested.

"Ma'am," Carter said.

"Yes, private?"

"The temperature is up to a hundred and eight," Carter reported, wiping the grit from the thermometer in his hand.

"That's ten degrees in thirty minutes," Genesee said. "We have to get out of this."

Some decisions were made. Others were forced upon a leader. Schiavo knew the latter was the reality here.

"All right," she said. "Private, we're backtracking. Get us there."

* * *

It took us fifteen minutes to reach the remnants of the private plane hangar across the runway, trudging through feet of ash, Private Carter Laws leading us, the beam of his flashlight sweeping left and right like a blind man might wield a white cane.

"I can't see anything!" the young soldier shouted through his mask, the white filter material caked black.

"Stay on course!" Schiavo instructed him.

We'd set out on a bearing, one based upon memory and dead reckoning. Compass needles were jumping wildly with the static charge in the air, and any signal we'd hoped to receive using the GPS provided by the SEALs was hopelessly scrambled this deep in the ash fall. We had to rely upon an unseen fixed point to guide us through the hell raining down all around.

"Yes, ma'am!"

Carter kept moving, Schiavo second in line. Every minute or so she'd glance behind to see Genesee and I, with Martin between us, still on his feet. Still moving. Still fighting.

"I see it!"

Carter's excited voice drew our attention, and we were suddenly able to see what he was, the half-collapsed building looming before us, not twenty yards away. We sped up, the ash to our thighs in some places, scorching our pants, heating the boots that protected our feet to almost intolerable temperatures. We had to get out of this. And, finally, we were.

We stumbled into the shelter, a good thirty feet of the hangar's floor clear of anything more than a dusting of ash. Beyond that, the roof had settled to the ground, crushing the Lear Jet that had been abandoned within, likely stripped of anything useful long ago.

"Martin, over here," Genesee said, pulling an upturned bench clear of some debris. "Sit."

Martin did, shedding his gear and laying his weapon atop it. Schiavo came to him, stripping the mask from his face, revealing a comparatively clean oval of skin in the midst of black cheeks and a bruised eye.

"This isn't counting as the honeymoon we postponed," Schiavo told her husband.

Martin chuckled, his face twisting quickly into a pained scowl. Genesee checked his patient, lifting his shirt to adjust the shifting bandages beneath. Schiavo watched her husband wince as the doctor manipulated his battered body. After a moment she turned away, walking to where I stood near the skewed nose of the wrecked private jet. A few yards from us, Carter stood, at the hangar's wide opening, its doors pushed aside and locked in that position by the structure's shifting supports. Schiavo looked to her young recruit for a moment, watching him as he stared out into the blackness.

"There's nothing here, Fletch," she said to me, her voice stripped of even the hint of forced confidence. "We came for nothing. Because of me."

"We came because we had to," I told her.

She didn't dispute that, but she didn't embrace the statement either. The truth, in this situation, didn't matter. And it didn't assuage the guilt Schiavo was feeling.

"I'm sorry, Fletch," she said, looking to me. "I wish—"

"Ma'am," Carter said, interrupting his commander, his gloved hand raised, finger extended as he pointed out into the ash fall. "I see lights."

The reaction to his almost sheepish announcement was electric. Schiavo and I rushed to his side. Behind us, Genesee stayed by Martin, whose gaze swelled at the news.

"Where, private?"

Carter answered Schiavo's question by leaning close so she could look down the length of his outstretched arm, using it as a guide.

"I don't see anything," she said.

"The ash was blowing," Carter said. "It seemed like a wave of it thinned out for a few seconds, and that's when I saw them. Right out there."

We kept looking, even Genesee joining us now to scan the dark landscape. But there was nothing out there. Nothing at all.

Until there was.

Twelve

Carter was right. There were lights. Tiny hot specks resolving through the rain of dark, hot ash.

"That's a vehicle," Genesee said.

He was right. They were headlights, high off the ground, the transport they shone from clearly large. A truck, maybe. Something beefy enough to venture out into the hell that had spread across the land.

"What do we do, ma'am?"

Schiavo didn't immediately answer the newest member of her garrison. She wiped the fine skim of black dust from her eyes and coughed, thinking. Weighing options. Choices. Above, what remained of the hangar was groaning continually now, the weight of ash building, the structure supporting the battered roof weakened by the load and years of neglect.

"We can't stay here," she said.

Martin appeared at our side, abandoning his place of rest, something in his hand, retrieved from his pack, which lay open on the ground behind us.

"Signal them," he said, holding the road flare out to me.

"We don't know who they are," Genesee said.

"We were told to come here," Martin said. "Maybe they were, too."

I looked to Schiavo as she considered the logic. It wasn't unassailable, but, in the end, that didn't matter. Not with the hangar, our only shelter, ready to fall.

We were out of options.

"Do it, Fletch," she told me.

I put my mask back in place and lowered my goggles to cover my eyes. Then I stepped out into the volcanic rain and ignited the flare, lifting it above my head and sweeping it back and forth. The lights dimmed again, as if the vehicle was turning away from us, then grew brighter, and brighter, the twin beams seeming aimed right at me.

"They see you!" Carter shouted from the hangar.

Whoever 'they' were, he was right. The vehicle's occupant, or occupants, had zeroed in on our signal and were coming. Drawing closer with each second until we could make out plainly that it was no truck coming our way.

"It's a Stryker," Schiavo said.

A wheeled military fighting vehicle, lightly armored, meant to carry troops into battle. The variant approaching us was topped with a wide, squat turret, slender cannon protruding from it, the weapon pointed directly at me. I stepped backward until I stood with my friends again, not out of any fear, but to put our signal in proximity to the remainder of our group. Whoever was at the controls of the Stryker, I wanted them to see that part of our number were very clearly soldiers.

I lowered the flare as the vehicle stopped just short of the hangar, then tossed it outside, its burning tip smothered in the drift of ash that swallowed it. This could not be a coincidence, I knew. An Army vehicle showing up to a place Schiavo was tasked to be? No, this was a mission in and of itself. A rescue mission not unlike the one Genesee and I had set out on.

A hydraulic whine sounded, and at the back of the vehicle, visible from an angle, I could see a ramp fold down, coming to rest on the pile of ash not cleared by its eight wheels. Two figures emerged, soldiers, their faces obscured by goggles and breathing masks. Each was armed with an M4, but neither held their weapon in any hostile way as they cleared the vehicle and came toward the hangar. Once they'd reached its meager shelter, they raised their goggles and lowered their masks.

"I'm Lieutenant Roger Pell," the Stryker's commander said, rendering a salute to Schiavo. "You're Captain Angela Schiavo?"

She returned the salute and nodded, some great relief dammed within.

"I am," she said, the dam threatening to burst. "I am, lieutenant."

Pell gestured to the soldier with him, sergeant's stripes plain on his surprisingly camouflaged fatigues.

"This is Sgt. Ed Matheson," Pell said. "My wheel man is Sergeant Tommy Hammer."

Schiavo offered quick introductions of our group, ending with Genesee, both Pell and Matheson saluting the Navy commander.

"We need to get you out of here," Pell said, looking over those of us standing with Schiavo. "I wasn't told there would be anyone with you."

"This didn't turn out to be a trip I could complete alone," Schiavo told the young lieutenant.

"Of course, ma'am," Pell said. "It's not a problem. We've got room."

"Where are we going?" Martin asked.

"McChord Air Force Base," Pell said. "Air Force One had to reposition there when the mountain blew."

It was exactly as we'd expected. Almost exactly.

"McChord?" Martin asked, both curious and wary. "Just south of Seattle."

Pell nodded and Martin looked to me. I was thinking the same thing that he was—the Hordes.

"Lieutenant, we've had some trouble in the past from groups that came south from Seattle," I told him.

Trouble...

That was putting it lightly. The Seattle Hordes, drug crazed survivors who'd resorted to any and all manner of unspeakable acts to both feed their cravings and their need for sustenance, had seemed just memories for a while now. Part of our past. I'd killed a number of them as they charged across the bridge spanning the Coquille River. I didn't want to face any more.

"Seattle is a ghost town," Sgt. Matheson said.

"He would know," Pell assured us. "He was part of a patrol two days ago after everything was repositioned up north. A security check of the city."

Matheson looked to both Martin and me and shook his head.

"Just bodies," the sergeant said. "And not many of those."

The news was both welcome, and horrifically sad. An entire city depopulated. Seattle was not unique in that respect, I knew. Most of the world's major cities, if not all, would have met a similar fate in the years after the blight. Still, to imagine everyone gone bordered on impossible.

Except...

"Why was a patrol sent into the city?" I asked, seizing on the oddity of such a mission. "That seems a bit far afield from your concerns."

"When Air Force One was approaching McChord, the pilot thought he saw flashes from Seattle," Pell explained. "It was a standard patrol to rule out any ground threats while we were in the area."

"So what made the flashes if the city is empty?" Genesee asked.

Pell shrugged and shook his head.

"Reflections," he suggested. "An old gas cylinder rupturing after years of rust. Could be anything."

"Or nothing," Matheson added. "Just a pilot thinking he saw something when he didn't."

"Lieutenant," Schiavo said.

"Yes, ma'am?"

"I'd really love to keep discussing Seattle, and flashes that might not be flashes, but do you know what I'd really love to do right now?"

Pell smiled and nodded.

"Let's get you aboard and out of here," the lieutenant said.

We gathered our gear and walked through the falling ash to the back of the Stryker. After stepping onto its ramp and entering the passenger compartment, the door folded upward and sealed us inside. A quick rush of air filled the space as filters kicked in, allowing us to breathe freely for the first time in days.

"Sgt. Hammer, get us moving," Pell said as he slipped into the closed turret, the upper half of his body mostly hidden from us.

"Get comfortable," Matheson said, grinning. "As much as you can in this tin can. We've got a good ride ahead of us."

We found our spots in the cramped interior, a fuel bladder filling much of the center aisle between the seats. The motion of the vehicle was slow and unsteady as the eight wheels negotiated the drifts of ash and obstacle beneath which had been covered. Matheson moved forward to his position just behind the driver, focusing himself on his duties.

We had no duties. Not now, at least. No tasks. For the first time since the eruption, we were not fighting for our lives. All the weight of those struggles lifted instantly from me, and a tiredness like I'd never known rose within. I was not alone in the experience.

Across from me, Martin was already out, his eyes shut, head resting on his wife's shoulder, her own eyes batting slowly in a futile attempt to stay awake. To my right, Genesee was ramrod straight, except for his head, which was pitched forward, bobbing gently with the motion of the

Stryker as he slept. Just beyond him, Carter Laws had tipped fully to his right and lay in a near fetal position on the open seats next to him.

Safe...

I thought that. The relief might be temporary, but it was real, and each of us was embracing it. We were in a place of safety.

But we weren't done.

Beyond even that reality, though, was the fact that none of us had any idea what 'done' meant. I didn't even try to muse on the possibilities as I let my body relax, and felt my eyes flutter shut, slipping into a dreamless sleep.

Thirteen

I woke two hours later to the sound of wheels turning fast on pavement.

"Where are we?"

I asked the question to no one in particular, but it was Matheson who looked back from his station behind the driver and filled me in.

"We're on Interstate Five, about forty miles north of Portland," he said, adding something that I didn't process immediately. "We're in the clear."

"Clear?"

Matheson nodded.

"The weather is our friend," he said.

That could only mean that the ash cloud was behind us, the wind carrying it mostly east and south.

South...

South was home. If the weather had shifted enough, Bandon could be experiencing some of what had literally crushed the remnants of Portland, leaving the river city smoldering beneath the burning downpour of ash. That was what my mind was considering as we cruised along the interstate, slowing to maneuver around abandoned cars and damaged roadway. Across from me in the cramped passenger area of the wheeled military vehicle, Martin was still dozing, his head on Schiavo's shoulder, her hand reaching up to caress his bare, swollen cheek.

He was suffering, more than the rest of us. I had burns on my neck and shoulders from exposure to the ash after the second, cataclysmic eruption which must have devastated the mountain and everything between it and Portland. Carter's left arm had been singed severely, blisters already rising on the skin. Genesee, who'd come through the blast and what had preceded it relatively unscathed, worked on the young soldier's wound as we headed north, rebandaging it for a second time. Everyone, it seemed, had caught an hour or two of sleep. Hardly enough to restore our physical and mental health, but enough to allow some semblance of normal function to return.

"Fletch…"

Schiavo called to me from across the narrow aisle, both our feet resting on the fuel bladder that was a tactically crazy necessity. One round penetrating the vehicle's comparatively light armor could set the interior ablaze, the resulting inferno sure to end our lives in a horrible way. But without the spare fuel, the heavy personnel carrier might not have made it to Portland, or back to where it had departed from.

"Yeah?"

"Thank you," the captain said, shifting her gaze to Genesee. "Both of you. You didn't have to come."

Genesee looked up from the fresh bandage he was applying to Carter's forearm.

"Despite my obvious ambivalence to the uniform, I've never refused an order. And I never will."

Schiavo allowed a smile. She didn't seem at all surprised by Genesee's response, nor by the simple explanation he had offered as to why he was here. It was a sense of duty, something she could fully understand, and embrace. Despite his initial reluctance to accept the mission that the SEALs had brought him, due mostly, I believed, to his expectation that he was not cut out for a field assignment, he'd performed admirably, without complaint, under the hellish conditions we'd encountered.

Conditions, I suddenly realized, we would have to return through to reach our home. I turned forward and tapped Matheson on the shoulder.

"How bad is it behind us?"

"It's not good," Matheson answered.

"Have a look," the lieutenant, looking down from the vehicle's turret, told us.

Schiavo shook off the offer, and Carter was still in the midst of having his burned arm treated, leaving me alone to see what we'd left behind.

"Up there," Matheson said, pointing to a rectangular hatch above me, a similar one on Schiavo's side. "Release and rotate the handle, then push up."

I stood, hunching slightly, and completed the sequence necessary to open the hatch, the slab folding up and toward the side of the vehicle, revealing a brilliant blue sky above. That view, though, lasted just a few seconds, until I stood upright, my body straightening through the opening so I could see in all directions.

Including from where we'd come.

It was as if some hateful being had swept a brush dipped in burning night across the southern sky, the blackish gash spreading from a point roughly over the coast all the way to the eastern horizon. Every few seconds a flash would appear from the ash cloud, and jagged fingers of lightning would race across its billowing surface.

"You made it through that," Lieutenant Pell said from his position in the turret, his body from the chest up protruding from its now open hatch.

"Barely," I reminded him.

Looking back at the hell we'd come through, my thoughts again returned to Bandon. To Elaine. To Hope. What were they going through? Had the hellfire from the second eruption reached them? I could think on that continually. Could worry without any way to satisfy my wondering, one way or another. But doing so would paralyze me. And whatever we'd come through, there was that possibility, however remote, that something ahead would test us with equal ferocity.

I had no idea just how prophetic that thought of mine would be, even when the Stryker slowed suddenly and came to a stop.

"What is it?" Pell asked through his headset.

He heard it more clearly, I was certain, but even where I stood I could make out plainly that Hammer, at the vehicle's controls, was reporting a problem ahead. I turned and leaned to the side for a better view past the turret, which Pell had now dropped back into, pulling the hatch closed. I could see nothing worrisome ahead, just four lanes of blacktop and a few dozen cars scattered about, most pushed to the shoulder of the highway.

"Button it up!"

Pell's command echoed in the vehicle, and, before I could react, Sergeant Matheson was beside me, pulling me and the hatch down, sealing the vehicle up.

"What is it, Lieutenant?" Schiavo asked.

The Stryker's commander dropped down from his perch in the turret and faced the captain.

"We left our other section just up the road," Pell explained. "About five hundred yards. But they're not there."

"Dismounted?" Schiavo asked.

"No," Pell answered. "Another Stryker."

Schiavo's expression changed right then. It hardened a bit, as I'd seen it do when a battle was upon her. Upon us.

"You're not going to miss seeing that," she said.

Pell shook his head in agreement and retook his position in the turret, scanning the landscape with the advanced optics available to him.

"Martin," Schiavo said, nudging her husband awake.

"Yeah," he said. "Did I fall asleep?"

She nodded and reached to where he'd placed his AK, retrieving the weapon and handing it to him.

"You might need this," she said, looking to her new recruit next. "Private Laws."

Carter eased his arm away from Genesee and grabbed his M4.

"Ready, ma'am."

I slipped forward, taking the position Matheson had left to haul me back inside the Stryker.

"Did you have any protocol for why they would have to move?" I asked, looking up into the turret.

"Only that they should hold this position," Pell said. "Unless it became untena—"

The sudden impact on the left side of the Stryker cut off what the lieutenant was saying, and answered my question at the same time, the vehicle's reactive armor exploding to protect it from an incoming round. The vehicle rocked a full foot to the right, absorbing the impact as the engine revved, accelerating it forward.

"Contact left!" Hammer shouted from the driver's position.

"Scan right!"

Pell shouted the order, and Matheson popped a hatch on that side of the vehicle nearest the rear door, rising through it with his weapon. Schiavo did the same with a hatch just above her as the lieutenant swung the turret to the left, firing quick bursts from the 30mm cannon.

"Small arms to the west!" Pell informed us. "I need shooters on the left!"

I moved to the hatch that backed up to Schiavo, and Carter did the same with the opening nearest Sergeant Matheson, the both of us popping through the openings to a fusillade of wild fire coming at us from distant woods.

"Two hundred yards!" I called out, and quickly removed the suppressor from my AR, bringing it to bear again and firing. "I see three positions!"

Pell, though, was focused on another area of the dead woods, his 30mm cannon fire following the trail of smoke that marked where a rocket had been fired at us. Some sort of man portable anti-armor weapon, equivalent to an RPG.

"Keep it up!" Matheson directed, swinging his attention to the Stryker's rear and opening up on the firing positions as we left them behind.

"Hammer, what do you see?"

Pell's question to his driver was a simple act of trying to know what was ahead of them as they raced away from the apparent ambush. He couldn't see everything, in every direction, so he had to rely on his men to be his eyes, his ears, and sometimes, his brain, taking evasive action before he could give such a lifesaving order.

That was exactly what Sergeant Tommy Hammer did without answering his commander, swinging the Stryker severely left, almost off the road as another anti-armor rocket sailed past, having been fired from directly ahead amongst the mix of wrecked vehicles where Pell had expected to find his fellow soldiers.

For an instant, as I stayed in the fight, squeezing off bursts at positions sending fire our way, I thought that the rocket which had just missed us sounded familiar. It wasn't just some weapon like an RPG—it *was* an RPG. I'd experienced that sound on Mary Island, as the lighthouse protecting us was battered by repeated hits from the venerable Russian weapons. It was possible that some RPGs, which had become common in armies and insurgencies around the globe prior to the blight, could have made their way here, to the States. Possible.

There was another explanation, I knew, one that I had a hard time considering, much less accepting—the Russians were back. On our flank, and right in front of us.

Before Pell could slew the turret to take on the new threat dead ahead, Schiavo leaned from the hatch, over the edge of the vehicle, and began firing with her M4, directing controlled bursts into the tangle of abandoned vehicles ahead.

"Get us off this highline!" Pell ordered his driver.

Without hesitation, Hammer veered sharply right, steering the Stryker off the roadway and across the shoulder, the vehicle nosing hard over, wheels bouncing across rocks and broken guardrails as we moved into a low spot alongside the highway.

"Dismount!" Pell commanded, slipping his own body out of the turret. "Hammer, take the firing position. Everyone out!"

Pell slammed a control, and the back door folded down. With weapons in hand and geared up, we poured down the ramp, seven shooters looking for the fight.

"I'll take Martin, Fletch, and Commander Genesee," Schiavo said. "We'll push back along this side of the road and set up a strongpoint to cover the flanks and draw them out."

For an instant, Carter thought, as new guy, he'd been forgotten. He hadn't.

"Private Laws, you go with Lieutenant Pell's fire team," she ordered, and Carter gave a certain, if nervous, nod to her.

"We'll push north and clear those cars with the Stryker providing cover against any secondary assault from the east," Pell said. "Or any who breach our defense and get onto the road."

Already Hammer was slewing the turret, the height it rested just high enough that its cannon could bring fire directly onto the length of the road. Behind, across five hundred yards of open dirt, a distant patch of falling woods were the only cover that could conceal a potential rear attack. Fire and movement over that distance seemed unlikely. Our enemy, whoever they were, was to the west and north. That was where our fight was.

"Let's move," Pell said.

Matheson and Carter followed the lieutenant, staying low beyond the nearest shoulder of the road, weapons directed forward toward the collection of old wrecks that spilled off the highway two hundred yards to the north. The young private, untested in battle, was about to face death, not to mention his assigned task to kill his fellow man.

"Let's get in position," Schiavo said.

I led off, Martin behind me, struggling. He would have insisted on taking part in any action despite his wounds, and ordering him to remain at the Stryker would only waste time.

"Doc, you stay close to me," I said, and Genesee nodded, under no illusions that he was ready for this fight.

We pressed south, a hundred yards, staying just beneath the rise of the road to our right, until Schiavo signaled to stop and take our positions.

"Ten yards apart," she said.

We spread out and went to our stomachs, Martin crawling up the berm like the rest of us, pain plain on his face. Soon we were peeking over the rise, the road before us, and the woods further in the distance. Sporadic fire flashed from three points along the line of dead trees, but the volume had decreased. That might have had something to do with the bursts cracking from the Stryker's cannon, expertly aimed, rounds chewing into the enemy.

"They're not advancing," Martin commented.

I glanced and saw Schiavo nod slightly at her husband's very correct assessment of the puzzling tactics. Or no tactics at all. The enemy had us blocked from moving forward, and pinned down, but, from all we could see, they were not maneuvering for any advantage.

"Fletch, check our other section," Schiavo said.

Without acknowledging her directive, I slid down the berm, fully shielded from fire west of the highway, and looked to the north. Even without binoculars I could make out the shapes of Pell, Matheson, and Carter, reaching the area of the roadblock and disappearing into the tangle of vehicles. They were taking no fire.

What's going on?

I tried to process that very question as I turned and looked to the grey woods to the east. No threat had materialized there, meaning no ambush had been set up to hit us from three sides.

"Fletch!"

It was Schiavo, calling down to me from the top of the berm.

"No fire up there," I reported, checking one more time to verify what I'd just seen. "They're beyond the junked cars now and—wait."

I stopped, taking immediate note of the lone figure sprinting back from the element that had moved north. Without a doubt I could tell it was Carter Laws, running fast, his weapon low and ready. He reached the Stryker and continued past it, heading in our direction.

"Carter is coming," I told Schiavo.

"You two maintain cover," she instructed Martin and Genesee, before sliding down the berm to join me just as Carter reached us and dropped to his knees, winded.

"Ma'am," he gasped.

"Catch your breath, private," Schiavo said.

Carter drew a few deep gulps of air then looked to Schiavo.

"The other Stryker is up past the roadblock," he told us, steeling himself against the memory he was about to relay. "The crew is dead."

Schiavo glanced briefly to me before focusing on her new recruit again.

"They're all outside the vehicle," Carter continued. "It's all shot up. Wheels blasted away."

"Where are Lieutenant Pell and Sergeant Matheson?" Schiavo asked.

"They're pushing to the woods to the west," Carter answered. "There was no enemy near the roadblock. They sent me to tell you to watch for friendlies coming out of the woods."

"They're going to try to drive them toward us into the open," I said.

Schiavo nodded, then shook her head.

"What is it?" I asked her.

"It's not a bad tactical move," she said. "But if they're letting vengeance drive them..."

I knew what she meant. That very desire for retribution, to avenge Neil's murder, had pushed me into a conflict with Olin that could have ended badly. Very badly. For me. Pell and Matheson, I hoped, were only letting that blood lust fuel a decision made of sound mind.

"Private, go to our Stryker and tell Sergeant Hammer what you just told us," Schiavo ordered. "Then cover our north flank from that position."

"You think they may pop up at the roadblock again?" I asked.

"Sounds like they did once before," Schiavo said. "And people died."

She was right. We had a plan, but the enemy might have their own which would turn ours into a disaster. It was more than prudent to prepare for any eventuality.

"Get moving, private," Schiavo ordered.

Carter took off, racing back to our Stryker. Schiavo and I returned to the top of the berm.

"Eyes on that tree line," she told Martin and Genesee. "Shooters may be bolting from it. And watch your background—friendlies will be in the woods."

Martin looked to me, seeking some explanation.

"The Stryker they left here was taken out," I told him, then shared the rest of the plan.

"I haven't done any serious shooting since basic," Genesee said.

"Only shoot at what you can hit," Schiavo said, the directive mostly for Genesee's benefit. "Get ready."

We made sure we were spread out where the berm crested and the highway's shoulder began. I focused my attention on the northern part of the woods, where Pell and Matheson would have entered, trying to gauge the progress they would have made. Two hundred yards south, I thought, and shifted my aim to that point.

Almost immediately a fusillade of fire erupted, just glimpses of muzzle flashes visible through the distant trees. The sounds of battle rose, and it was odd to be able to tell which pieces of the firefight belonged to our side, and to theirs. Quick, short bursts signaled Pell and Matheson zeroing in on our enemy. More wild, full automatic spraying indicated that enemy returning fire, their resistance desperate. Undisciplined.

"Movement," Martin said.

I saw his weapon shift to the south as he began to fire, taking single shots at a figure in dark camouflage bolting from cover. Within seconds another fighter followed, and another, each clutching weapons that they would swing toward the woods they'd fled and loose wild rounds. Schiavo began firing bursts from her M4, and I followed with my AR. Genesee might have been firing, but I could not tell. My concern was fully on the enemy fleeing across the open. One fell, then another, but to replace them a half dozen more spilled from the woods.

"Keep it up!" Schiavo ordered.

To my right I could hear the Stryker's cannon begin to open up, its retort both sound and sensation, like a jackhammer on steroids. One of the enemy soldiers dropped to a knee and seemed to fix his attention in our direction.

"RPG!" Genesee shouted.

The warning was spot on, as the soldier I'd noticed fired off the rocket before a burst from the Stryker ripped his body to shreds, pieces tossed into the air like wet red rags as the RPG sailed harmlessly high over the armored vehicle. Two more of his brethren dropped, then three, and, in less than two minutes, the last movement across the open ceased. Our weapons quieted quickly.

"Reloading," I said.

As I dropped my empty and inserted a fresh magazine, I caught a glimpse of Genesee, his bare hands holding his M4 in a death grip, knuckles white and skin red. He breathed fast, air rushing in and out of his lungs, and his attention was fixed on the scene past the smoking muzzle of his rifle.

"Clay..."

His head angled slowly toward me, eyes almost slack, as if he was inhabiting some dream state.

"It's over," I told him.

He nodded slightly. His grip on his weapon eased and his breathing slowed as he stared at me.

"I've never..."

He couldn't say it, but I know what the completed statement would have been. He'd never shot at anyone. Never used his weapon in anger. He was a doctor, a healer, sworn to treat patients, not create them. If he'd hesitated, or expressed any overt doubt about what role he could play in a firefight, I would have reminded him that medics and corpsman in the military carried weapons, and would use them to defend themselves and their patients. With Martin just a few yards away, Genesee might not have realized it, but he'd just done both of those things.

To our right, Carter approached, running from his position near the Stryker. He hurried to a spot on the berm near Schiavo.

"Ma'am, Sergeant Hammer wants to know what we should do?"

Carter had come through this first test of his combat skills well. As a young man, a teenager, actually, he'd participated in the defense of Bandon against the Unified Government forces. This, though, was his baptism by fire while in service to his country, not his town. It seemed, though, that the two were synonymous with each other. None of us knew exactly how far beyond Bandon any semblance of the United States even existed.

"Hold your position and your fire," Schiavo told her new recruit, raising a clenched fist above her where Hammer would see it, the signal telling him to sit tight. "Pell and Matheson are out there somewhere."

We heard no more shooting as we waited, scanning the woods beyond the killing field we'd created.

"That wasn't much of a fight," Martin commented.

I looked to him, knowing he was right. We hadn't come up against troops of any quality. Nothing to compare to what we'd faced on Mary Island, or in the pit in Skagway, or those fighters aligned with the Unified Government. The people we'd taken out were running away, fleeing the maneuver Pell had initiated to drive the enemy from the woods.

"Movement," Schiavo said.

We focused in on the tree line and saw what she did, a figure between the dead pines, holding a rifle above his head one handed, creating a T.

"It's Pell," Schiavo said.

He was giving us the signal that all was clear. We rose from the berm and crossed the highway to the field, Pell and Matheson emerging from the woods to meet us near the scene of the carnage we'd created. To the north, the Stryker began to move, positioning itself on the road to better cover us in all directions.

"That was worse than a turkey shoot," Martin said.

"There are six more we took out in the woods," Pell said, crouching next to one of the dead men and gripping his uniform coat in his gloved hand. "Russian."

It was a uniform like we'd seen before. But others who were strewn across the field wore different clothing and gear, from various units and branches of the Russian military.

"An ad hoc unit," Schiavo said.

Pell stood, nodding.

"This was thrown together," the lieutenant said, scanning the landscape and shaking his head. "Why? And why here?"

"I don't know," Schiavo said, unable to comprehend the almost futile attempt at blocking the highway.

Almost...

"How did they get your other troops?" Schiavo asked.

Pell glanced back toward the roadblock, imagining what he'd seen beyond it, then faced the captain again.

"It looks like they caught our guys outside their vehicle," he explained, shaking his head once again. "That's just bad tactics in an area that hasn't been cleared."

The three troopers, equivalents to Pell, Matheson, and Hammer, had likely been taking a break from the confines of their Stryker. Maybe gazing at the blackened southern sky in awe. Even an untrained small unit could do damage to seasoned troops when their guard was down.

"A waste," Pell said. "A damn waste."

A hand rested suddenly on my shoulder. Not a gentle touch to announce one's presence or offer of comfort, but with the weight of one seeking support. I looked to see Martin struggling, the distress plain in his eyes.

"There's nothing more to do here," I said, slipping an arm under Martin's. "Let's load up."

Genesee stepped close and added his help in assisting our friend. Pell raised a hand and signaled the Stryker. Thirty seconds later the beefy vehicle was next to our position, the back ramp down. We filled its interior again and drove to a point past the road block and stopped there, watching and waiting as the lieutenant and his men left the

Stryker and buried their fellow soldiers in a patch of barren earth next to the highway.

Fourteen

The drive north from where we'd been ambushed by what could generously be termed a unit of Russian irregulars was uneventful. Genesee took the opportunity to rebandage Martin's ribs and put a fresh dressing over the wound where he'd inserted the chest tube.

"I have pain medication," he told Bandon's former leader.

Martin shook off the offer and slipped back into his shirt and jacket.

"I'm not doping up," he told the doctor. "You'd have to drag me through the next firefight."

"You sure there's going to be another one?" Genesee pressed him.

"You sure there's not?"

There was no adequate answer Genesee could offer to Martin's retort. And he was right. Despite that, though, I felt at ease. I sensed that, for now, we were safe. As safe as one could be in our world.

Free of dread, though, did not mean my thoughts were completely settled.

"Angela..."

Schiavo looked to me from her place next to Martin.

"Yeah, Fletch?"

"What was that back there?"

She thought for a moment, the vagueness of my question clear enough for her.

"I'm not sure," she said. "They didn't have much fight in them."

"Exactly," I agreed. "So why were they here? If it was a land grab by Russia, or what's left of Russia, they didn't put much effort into it. Those troops were fodder."

"I know," she said, shaking her head. "That worries me."

"Why?"

"Because if their command is treating them as expendable, there might be more."

Matheson, who'd heard our conversation from his place near the turret, looked back toward us.

"There was no sign of them in Seattle," the sergeant said. "That would seem a logical place for them to go if they were here to plant their flag. Take a big American city without firing a shot."

He wasn't wrong. But that didn't add any clarity as to the Russians' motive, or their mission.

"Maybe their focus is to the south," Martin suggested, joining the exchange now.

"Bandon?" Schiavo challenged him mildly.

He shrugged slightly, wincing through the gesture.

"Kuratov had enough intelligence from us in Skagway to know exactly where we were from," Martin said.

"But Kuratov is dead," I said. "And he was rogue. He wasn't operating on any orders but his own."

"Maybe some of his men had a deeper connection to the Motherland than to him," Martin suggested.

"His men died, too," Schiavo reminded her husband.

"Maybe not," Carter said. "Ma'am."

"What are you saying, private?"

Carter Laws had sat in silence next to me, taking in the discussion. Something in what we'd said, though, had obviously struck a nerve, if only mildly.

"I was young, but not that young, when we were taken to Skagway," he said. "I wasn't in the pit with the little kids. I was out with the adults. And I was watching."

What had begun with the forced evacuation of Bandon, along with other survivor colonies the government had identified, had turned into a capture through force of Skagway and the Subterranean Survivor Complex by Kuratov and his elite troops. All of whom we'd taken out.

Or so we'd thought.

"Kuratov kept his infiltrator among us in town," Carter reminded us. "I think he may have had someone outside of town, too. Hidden."

"You saw something," Schiavo said, sensing where the young man was going with this.

"I saw lights," Carter confirmed. "They were dim and red. Like you use at night to read maps."

"Lights," I said. "More than one."

Schiavo eyed Carter, puzzled.

"Why didn't you say anything about this?"

"I did, ma'am. I told Mr. Perkins."

Earl Perkins. Leader of the Yuma survivor colony and, if our past radio communications were correct, a traitor to the nation who'd thrown in with the Unified Government.

"And he kept that to himself," I said.

Schiavo, though, despite the path Perkins had taken after being returned to Yuma with his people, didn't necessarily think that his lack of action in Skagway was damning.

"I don't know, Fletch," she said. "With going on right then, a man like Perkins hears something from a kid, does he act on it or dismiss it?"

"Or forget it," Martin said. "In one ear and out the other."

"I was looking for you, Martin," Carter said. "I found Mr. Perkins first and he said he'd look into it."

There was no blame to be attached to this bit of information that had been lost in the tumult of the situation in Skagway. But there was consideration that had to be given to it now.

"So, we're thinking now that at least one of Kuratov's men remained when we left Skagway," I said.

"They hang around, make their way back to Mother Russia, and report on what Kuratov did, and on what he learned," Martin said.

"What they learned about us," I said. "About Bandon."

Schiavo leaned back against the Stryker's stiff passenger seat, processing what we'd just learned, long after the fact.

"The truth is, we don't know what they know," she said. "Or what they were doing here. What we do know is that one group is not going to cause anyone any grief."

"Damn straight, ma'am," Matheson commented.

The Stryker slowed and made a turn, shifting as it rolled over a short obstacle.

"We're here," Lieutenant Pell said, looking down from the turret. "Have a look."

We opened the top hatches and stood, taking in the sights around us, an expansive apron and torched hangars. Anarchy and looting had been visited upon McChord Air Force Base in the wake of the blight, leaving the facility a shadow of its former self.

One thing, though, stood out as a symbol that, in some part, our once great nation still endured.

"Would you look at that," Genesee said.

I did, we all did, until our individual and collective attention was focused fully on the beautiful blue and white fuselage in the distance.

"Air Force One," Carter said.

We'd done it. Reached our destination, a bit farther than any of us had planned or expected, and through conditions that should have stopped us. But they didn't.

"Good," Schiavo said, an unexpected tightness to her expression, I thought, as she looked to me. "Because I want some answers."

Fifteen

The aircraft sat at the southern end of Runway 34, nose pointed north, its engines spinning at idle. A half dozen troops stood around it, facing outward. In the old world, the number might have been fifty, or a hundred. Now, this was what could be mustered. But mustered against what?

I feared we all knew what the answer to that might be.

"You'll be wheels up in five minutes," Lieutenant Pell told us as he returned from inside the gleaming 747. "A member of the staff will be out to get you in just a moment."

We stood off to the side of the Stryker, its engine off, Matheson and Hammer seated on the open rear ramp.

"To where?" Martin asked.

He gave a half chuckle, a tired reaction to a question with no answer that mattered.

"I was just supposed to deliver you," Pell said, shifting his gaze to Schiavo to correct his answer. "To deliver her."

Schiavo was instantly uncomfortable with the focus Pell's innocent words had put on her.

"I don't suppose your Stryker will fit on this bird," she said to the lieutenant.

"No, ma'am. We came in on a transport. It's supposed to be back to get us. Soon."

He offered the information with a glance at the sky, still blue except for the wall of putrid ash just skimming the horizon to the south. There was hope in what he said, but no certainty. Their ride, a C-17, most likely, was supposed to come. Supposed to.

"We'll be heading back light," Pell said, referencing the vehicle and men they'd lost.

"Where is 'back' for you?" Schiavo asked the young lieutenant. "Where is home?"

"There really isn't any home," Pell said. "Just where they move us to when something needs cleaning up."

"You've seen more action than just today," Schiavo said.

Pell nodded and ran a hand through his damp and dirty hair.

"I think we'll be seeing more," the lieutenant said, glancing back the way we'd come. "No, I'm actually sure of it."

The exchange between the Army officers ended when a man in, of all things, a crisp blue suit with complimentary striped tie, trotted down the stairs at the rear of the plane and jogged over toward us.

"We're ready," the man said.

He wasn't young, maybe fifty, but had the air and energy of one driven to prove he could keep up with those half his age. His hair was grey at the edges, and neatly trimmed. All about him said that he'd lived well, even in the world torn apart by the blight.

"And you are?" Schiavo asked.

"Carl MacDowell," he answered, holding off adding any more until the captain's silence suggested he probably should. "I work with the president."

Schiavo looked past the man, to the entrance to Air Force One.

"Is he in there?" she asked.

MacDowell looked momentarily surprised by the question.

"The president? No. No."

His answer was emphatic. Almost too much so.

"Then why are we here?" Schiavo challenged the man.

He snickered lightly, his brow furrowing at the lack of understanding.

"Miss, the—"

"Captain," she corrected him, forcefully. "Captain Angela Schiavo, United States Army."

MacDowell accepted the dressing down without comment and continued.

"Captain, the president doesn't come to you. You come to the president."

Despite the man's off-putting demeanor, Schiavo knew that he spoke the truth, in both a governing and a security sense. This was no place for the leader of the nation to be, particularly if, as seemed logical, he was in a place both protected and well supplied.

"All right," Schiavo said. "We're ready."

Once more, MacDowell reacted with mild amusement at her words.

"We?" he repeated. "Captain, you're the only one the president wants to see. Your friends can head home from here."

"Wait just a—"

Schiavo raised a hand and cut me off, her stare laser-focused on MacDowell.

"The message we received said to send a delegation. This is our delegation."

MacDowell gave us a quick look, four more bodies than, apparently, he'd expected he'd have to deal with.

"Right, I know. We didn't expect you to make the trip alone. But you're here, and—"

"I'm here," Schiavo interrupted, "with my delegation. Who will accompany me."

"That's not the protocol," MacDowell said.

"It's our protocol," Genesee said.

Schiavo gave the Navy man an approving glance, then eyed MacDowell again.

"You could be telling us a nice story," Schiavo said. "The reality is, I don't know who you represent, only who you *say* you represent."

"Once she's on that plane," I began, "she's at your mercy."

"That's not going to happen," Martin said.

MacDowell absorbed the revolt he was facing, looking to Carter, the only one of us who hadn't voiced an opinion.

"You have anything to say, young man?"

Carter straightened, his commander's gaze shifting sideways in his direction.

"I go where my captain tells me to go," Carter told the bureaucrat. "And she wants me with her, so that's where I'll be."

MacDowell shook his head, frustrated.

"Look, Mr. MacDowell," Schiavo said. "You can either fly back alone and tell the president I was unable to meet with him because I refused to abandon the people who'd gotten me here, or you can let us aboard so we can see what this is all about."

It wasn't an offer—it was an ultimatum. MacDowell knew this. For an instant he glanced behind, to the small array of soldiers surrounding the plane.

"Don't," Schiavo said, sensing what scenario might be unfolding in his head. "You're not here to force anything. You're here to facilitate a meeting. That's all you have to do. Any heat that comes because I'm bringing an entourage, well, that's heat on me. Not you. Understand?"

MacDowell knew he had little choice in the matter now. Forcing Schiavo to go alone might very well instigate an armed standoff...at best. His desire to imagine what might be the worst faded very quickly after Schiavo spoke.

"All right," MacDowell said, acquiescing. "Captain Borenstein will get you all situated."

The bureaucrat turned smartly and returned to the plane, nodding quickly to an Army officer who stood nearest the rear stairs. The man approached us, his attention fixing on Martin for a moment where he leaned awkwardly against the jagged front of the Stryker.

"Captain Wallace Borenstein," he said, introducing himself. "Are you injured, sir?"

"I'm okay," Martin assured him.

"We have a medic in our unit," Borenstein said.

"We have a doctor," Martin one-upped him, tossing a thumb toward Genesee.

"All right then," the captain said, an almost southern manner about him, minus the accent. "Let's get you all aboard."

Martin started off, walking on his own, his gait almost normal, though I couldn't tell if that was through force of will, or if he was actually beginning to feel better. Genesee stayed close behind, with Carter just to his right, both seeming ready to provide any support should Martin stumble. Borenstein headed back toward the plane as well, signaling his men to pull in the perimeter they'd set up around the aircraft. Schiavo and I hung back, just for a moment, as she looked to Lieutenant Pell a final time.

"Thank you again, lieutenant, for getting us out of that hell," she said, offering her hand.

"Just glad we were able to locate you," Pell said, taking Schiavo's hand in his and shaking it.

"You take care," Schiavo said, looking next to me. "You ready for this, Fletch?"

"If I knew what *this* was, I could give you an answer."

She looked toward the aircraft and I could see in her eyes that she shared my sentiment. It was uncertainty, not doubt, which informed our reaction right then. Then again, little that we'd faced had been presented in clear cut terms. This was no different.

Except, it was. Everything about it was. Particularly the part about being taken to meet with the President of the United States of America.

Sixteen

No one disarmed us or searched us. We'd simply boarded the beautiful 747 with our weapons and gear and took seats near the middle of the aircraft as directed.

"We're flying east," Martin said.

He was comfortable, sitting next to his wife. Every so often he'd shift, searching for the optimum position in the surprisingly pedestrian airplane seats. Simply being out of all the gear we'd worn for days was comfort enough, but, when one added in that we were no longer on our feet in foot deep ash, and the quick opportunity to wash ourselves in one of the aircraft's bathrooms, it would have been more than conceivable that we should have fallen fast asleep.

None of us did.

"East is a big destination," Genesee said.

To that fact of ambiguity, Schiavo nodded, no relief in the affirmation.

"It sure as hell is," she said, then rose from her seat.

Martin reached out and put his hand on hers where it now rested atop the seat back just ahead.

"What are you doing?" he asked.

"I want some answers," Schiavo told her husband.

"That Army captain looked fairly serious when he said to stay right here," Martin reminded her.

Borenstein was his name. Wallace Borenstein. That and his rank was all we'd gotten from the man as he'd escorted us to our designated seating area. Neither he, nor any of his heavily armed troops, offered any explanation, all disappearing forward with MacDowell once we were situated. We were in the air in five minutes, and had been flying for nearly half an hour, glances out the right side of the plane showing the distant ash cloud, still well south of us, and vast swaths of dead woods creeping up mountain slopes. Our destination was a mystery. Maybe a secret.

Schiavo wasn't satisfied with that. At all.

"There's no conceivable reason why we can't be told where we're flying," she said.

"Actually, there is."

The response came from just beyond her. We looked and saw Borenstein. Schiavo turned to face her fellow captain.

"We're in the air," Schiavo said. "We'll know our destination when we land, so why keep it from us now."

Borenstein, who'd left his rifle forward and come to us with just his sidearm riding in a low thigh holster, took a position half sitting against a short conference table that was just forward of the seats we'd been led to.

"This is the staff section," he told us, motioning to the small but serviceable space. "Was, I guess. Not much staff anymore."

"Captain Borenstein, we've traveled through a fair bit of hell to get to where we are," Schiavo said. "So excuse me for not giving a damn who sat where on this plane."

Borenstein smiled lightly and pointed past Schiavo, toward the back of the aircraft.

"Guests have a little spot just back there, and then we come to the press section," he said, continuing with his seated tour of the aircraft despite Schiavo's protest. "The press. Journalists. What did some people call them? The Fourth Estate? I don't even know what that means. I probably would if I'd paid more attention in college, but, I didn't."

"What's the reason, captain?" I asked.

Borenstein looked to me, his smile still there, but a touch of darkness finding its way into the expression now. A shadow. One cast by memory. By reality.

"There were two of these, you know," he said. "Two Air Force Ones. Not anymore. There's just this one because one day, six months after everything started to fall apart, one of those fine people back there got a signal out to people on the ground and when that plane landed it was hit."

"Hit," Schiavo repeated.

"Attacked," Borenstein clarified. "No one knows if it was that Foreign Legion nut, or if it was the first stirrings of the Unified Government. It didn't matter much, because the end result was that the president died, along with a lot of good people."

He was referencing Borgier, the nom de guerre of American Gray Jensen. His fight, an opportunistic power grab which might have included actually releasing the blight, had been superseded by the inception of the Unified Government. One of them, if Borenstein was to be believed, had killed the president after being tipped to his arrival on Air Force One.

There was one problem with that, though.

"You said a signal," I reminded him. "By radio?"

Borenstein nodded, knowing where I was going with my questioning.

"All this happened maybe an hour after the Red Signal was shut off," he said. "By our people."

The pieces of what he was suggesting came together now.

"It was an inside job," Genesee said. "Someone who knew the airwaves would be clear tips the reporter, and the reporter gets word out where they're heading."

"The protocol after the chaos of the blight was not to release any destination until the aircraft was off the ground," Borenstein said. "That's the reason you're in the dark."

Schiavo studied the captain for a moment, her posture relaxing, the determination which had prompted her to push for some answer now quelled by a simple realization.

"You don't protect the president," she said. "You protect this plane."

"It's one of the last symbols that project some continuity of government," Borenstein said. 'That's important, now more than ever."

"Why?" Martin asked.

"Any other time before the blight, what happened would have been called an assassination," Borenstein said. "But the attack on Air Force One was the beginning of a coup. One that's been going on to this very day."

Borenstein stood again and looked to each of us.

"So you'll know where we're going when we get there," he said. "I hope that's enough for you."

The Army captain smiled and left us, heading forward to rejoin his troops and MacDowell.

"Angela," I said.

She looked to me.

"When we were in Skagway, and you talked to Washington, who did you actually talk to?"

Two years it had been since the event about which I was questioning her. Still, she summoned an answer from memory.

"Not the president," she answered me.

"That would have been well after this attack Borenstein talked about," Martin pointed out.

Schiavo thought for a moment, then took the spot Borenstein had vacated, half leaning against the conference table.

"We're being told the president was killed, and we're being taken to see the new president," Schiavo said.

"Or whoever's in that position right now," Carter suggested.

The private had sat in silence, listening, which, to his credit, was a skill too few possessed. Particularly those in his age group. Somewhere, though, in something he'd heard, a point worth interjecting had come to him.

"If there really is some endless coup happening, who's to say what the office even means anymore," Carter said.

"That's a bold statement," Martin told the private.

Carter accepted the challenge, but didn't back down from the possibility he'd shared.

"You can't kill the presidency," he explained. "You have to take the man out. Or the woman."

"Borenstein didn't say anything about who the president is, or how long he's been in office," Genesee said, bolstering Carter's suggestion.

"The office is reduced to a series of placeholders," Schiavo said, thinking for a moment before shaking her head. "We're not there yet. We don't know anything about the person in the office at this moment."

"What would it even mean?" I asked. "To us? To the country?"

"We're not there, Fletch," Schiavo reiterated. "Okay? Let's wait and see what this is all about."

I could do that. I could wait. We all could. But it was a sobering possibility to contemplate that the actual leader of our country might be less crucial than maintaining a warm body in the office. In a way, Borenstein's mission, protecting the image that was Air Force One, hinted that such a thought might not be too far off the mark. If it was at all.

Schiavo sat again, saying nothing. But I could sense it from her—she was entertaining the same thoughts that I was. Playing the same scenario out in her head. Gaming the possibilities. I tried not to get into her head, but failed. She had to be wondering, I knew, now more than ever, why the president, whoever that was, had summoned her. Who was she to him? To the office he inhabited? That she couldn't fathom any logical answer troubled her. This I could see and sense as she stared at the seatback before her and held her husband's hand. Whatever truth awaited her would be known soon enough.

But every truth, we'd all learned, was often not an end, but a beginning of some new endeavor. Some new journey.

Some new unknown.

Seventeen

"There's a good chance you'll have a bit of a hot trip to meet the president," Captain Borenstein said.

He'd come back again from forward. In a time past, Secret Service agents would have inhabited that space as they served as the defenders aboard Air Force One. Now it was Wallace Borenstein and a handful of troops cobbled together from units which had survived the blight, as well as the chaos and conflict that followed.

"Wait," Schiavo said. "We're going to take fire on landing? This is a big target, captain."

Borenstein nodded and leaned on the seatback just ahead of Schiavo.

"It is, but we're not setting down anywhere near the man. You'll push from where we land on other transport. That's where things may get hairy."

"We?" Martin asked, noting the language of separation the officer had used. "You're not coming with us?"

Borenstein shook his head.

"My job isn't to protect you," he reminded us, referencing what he'd shared about securing the symbol of power we were passengers on.

"How hairy?" I asked.

Borenstein looked to my AR, resting on the seat next to me.

"Hairy enough that I hope you're good with that."

The Army captain turned and left us. I looked to Schiavo, and to Martin, his back straight against the seat as he attempted some position to minimize his discomfort.

"Sorry about this, Fletch," she said. "I know you were supposed to be all done with this sort of thing."

"What am I going to do?" I asked. "Leave you out there?"

"It didn't have to be you," she said.

"Yes, it did," Martin said, and we both looked to him.

I smiled at the man, and he smiled at me. He knew me, and he understood the situation that had existed back in Bandon after the eruption, even if he hadn't been there to experience it first-hand. There would be a million things to do, and little time to accomplish what was necessary to protect the town from the effects of Mt. Hood's violent awakening. Others could do those things. But I was suited for the task that had fallen to me, and to Genesee. It was a moment of necessity. Each would have to do not just their part, but the part which they could uniquely handle.

"Yes," I agreed. "It did."

* * *

I was not seated where I could directly look out a window to see where we were descending to land, and no one who was in the know had shared that particular bit of information. By the flight time and imagined speed of the aircraft, and the certainty that we were traveling east, I was fairly certain we'd crossed the Mississippi River, putting us into the eastern portion of the country. In the country behind us to the west, ash would be building, and spreading, a slow-motion rain of black creeping eastward across the land.

The main gear screeched upon touchdown, wheels spinning fast on concrete as the nose of the big aircraft settled toward the runway, nose wheel letting out a fast scream as it, too, grabbed pavement. We slowed and taxied, turning left toward a grouping of hangars.

"Wright-Patterson," Genesee said, noting our gazes converging on him. "I flew out of here on my way to Hawaii."

"We're in Ohio," I said.

Schiavo nodded, and gestured out the window.

"And we're not alone," she said.

I looked and saw a pair of Blackhawk helicopters, their rotors turning, a single crewman standing outside each near open side doors, miniguns mounted just forward of them.

"They look like they've seen some action," Carter commented.

He was more than right. Both birds bore the marks of battle damage. Hasty patches on their fuselage. A spider web crack one window where an incoming round had been deflected. Holes in inconsequential areas which hadn't been repaired yet.

Schiavo stared out the window at the pair of aircraft for a moment as Air Force One's taxi roll slowed, then she stood just before the plane came to a gentle stop and looked to us.

"We'd better gear up," she said.

No sooner had she spoken the directive than Borenstein and his men moved quickly past us, MacDowell right behind, the bureaucrat stopping where we were hurriedly getting back into our filthy tactical vests and taking our weapons in hand.

"Captain Borenstein told you we might come under fire?"

"He did," Schiavo told MacDowell.

"One time a few weeks ago one of the helicopters had to set down after taking fire," MacDowell said. "The crew had to demo the bird and fight their way into the city."

The bureaucrat's skills at reassurance left much to be desired, if he'd had any at all to begin with.

"We're ready," Schiavo assured him.

"I hope so," MacDowell said. "Since I'll be riding with you."

* * *

We left the big 747 and boarded the second Blackhawk, slipping into headsets as the rotors spun up. Just across the apron, Borenstein had his men back aboard Air Force One, the aircraft already moving fast along the taxiway. When it reached the end of the runway it wasted no time, the pilot executing a sharp, quick turn to line it up, the throttles firewalled as we held position. With a roar that penetrated our headsets, the president's plane, minus the president, leapt into the sky and climbed toward the thin clouds high above.

"Stay sharp," our pilot said over the intercom. "We're on the move."

The lead Blackhawk began to roll forward as its turbines throttled up. Our bird followed, maintaining a fifty-yard separation. In thirty seconds both helicopters were in the air, noses pitched down as they gained speed. I sat at the rear of the cabin, facing forward, Martin to my right and Schiavo next to him. Genesee and Carter faced us, MacDowell between them, and visible just beyond were the left and right door gunners, each situated a few feet aft of the pilot and co-pilot. Each had both hands on the miniguns mounted at their stations.

Miniguns...

I recalled with perfect clarity what those weapons could do. A flying gunship not unlike what we were riding in had attacked my Montana refuge, nearly killing Neil and me. Were it not for an incredible shot fired by Grace, the chopper, which had been fielded by Borgier's rogue legionnaire force, would have annihilated the both of us, just as it had the buildings on my property.

"You think we'll be lucky and slip through?" Genesee asked over the intercom.

Before any of us could reply, the left door gunner looked back and provided the answer none of us wanted to hear.

"Half the time one of the birds gets hit," he said.

Genesee twisted in his seat and looked to the helmeted soldier.

"The other half, both birds get hit," the door gunner added, then returned to scanning the earth below.

Genesee faced rearward again, looking to me. After a few seconds he brought his M4 up and readied it, keeping the muzzle directed downward as we flew low over fields that once helped feed the nation, and the world. They were brown and grey now, with a likelihood that, if winds from the west behaved as they should, a coating of black ash would settle upon them.

"Right turn," the pilot said, as if issuing a warning.

We were belted in, but instinctively I grabbed the canvas seat's crossbar beneath my knees, just in time to steady myself as the Blackhawk banked severely right, taking our course from generally northeast to due east.

"Interstate below," Schiavo said, scanning the terrain through the door's window on her side.

"I Seventy," Genesee said. "Heads straight to Columbus."

Columbus, Ohio. Was that our destination? Or someplace before or after the state's capital city? We would know soon enough, I thought.

"They see us."

The report over the intercom was delivered calmly by the left gunner. Glancing his way I saw two things—a thin trail of smoke tracing an arc into the sky to the north, glowing red spot at its top, and his gloved hands swivel the minigun toward a point on the earth where the obvious projectile had originated.

"Flares," MacDowell said. "That's one of their observation posts signaling that we're inbound to the city."

It had to be Columbus. That was solidifying in my thoughts now, just as the left gunner opened up, the minigun screaming, a lance of fiery lead pouring down into a collection of farm houses and outbuildings just off the interstate. The structures disappeared for a moment in a cloud of smoke and dust, but as we passed the position the carnage became fully visible, structures shattered and afire. The gunner checked his fire after a few bursts, the damage done, and complete.

But we were no longer some covert mission to deliver Schiavo to the president. We were two big black warbirds screaming low over dead earth toward the city.

Eighteen

There was no warning in advance of what happened next. As the land below shifted from desolate farms to densifying neighborhoods, with the tall buildings of Columbus growing larger out the windows, the Blackhawk carrying us dove and turned hard left all at once, the awful sound of rounds striking metal audible above the roaring turbines.

"Fire right!"

The right door gunner called out the threat, a fusillade of fire erupting from the built-up area just to the south. He began firing, the minigun whining like a maniacal buzzsaw, spitting fire and 7.62 millimeter projectiles toward those trying to kill us.

"Have your weapons ready if we have to set down."

The directive came from one of the two pilots, though it was impossible to know which as the world outside the Blackhawk's windows erupted in streams of tracer fire and smoke trails. What unnerved me most, though, was the coolness with which one of the two men in the cockpit had passed along the warning, and the very fact that he'd thought it necessary.

BAM!

The Blackhawk shook as the right door gunner's weapon slammed upward, some sort of round from below striking the multi-barreled muzzle that was exposed outside the aircraft. The impact tossed him backward, but he recovered quickly, checking his minigun and shaking his head.

"Right side is down!" he reported.

The Blackhawk leveled off, skimming low over houses and trees, still more fire tracing across the sky toward us. Just ahead, through the port where the out of commission minigun hung useless now, I saw the lead Blackhawk execute a tight turn, swinging completely to our right and disappearing behind.

"They're drawing fire," Schiavo said, taking note of the same maneuver I'd seen.

That was exactly what was happening. The other bird, which had been leading the way, was now circling behind us, its gunners laying indiscriminate fire upon the buildings below. The majority of fire shifted from our Blackhawk to it as our pilot increased his evasive maneuvers, the helicopter banking sharply left, and then right, as we continued forward through a series of tight 'S' turns. It was during one of these that Schiavo called out to me over the intercom.

"Fletch."

I looked past Martin and saw her motioning out the right-side window, to a spot on the earth below where a house had been caved in and burned, the charred tail of a wrecked helicopter lying next to the rubbled crash site. As we swung back to the left, blocking our view of the site, I looked to Schiavo and found that she was laying an unsettled stare upon me. She didn't say anything, which, to me, was an indication that I should not either, since any exchange was certain to be heard over the intercom. She did, however, glance to MacDowell after her gaze left me. That was a signal, too, but of what, and about what, I didn't know.

Not yet.

"What is it?" MacDowell asked, noticing the attention now being focused on him.

"This route is more than hot," Schiavo said, her words both truthful and misdirection away from whatever was truly on her mind.

"It'll cool down in a minute," MacDowell assured her. "Their numbers thin out here."

Schiavo nodded, accepting the man's word. But it was also a gesture of realization, I thought, as if, with that promise just given, some confirmation had come for a suspicion she held. I wanted to press her on what was working on her, or troubling her outright, but I knew she preferred silence on the matter for now.

"Martin, how are you holding up?" Genesee asked.

Martin gave the doctor sitting across from him a thumbs up.

"How about you, private?" Schiavo asked.

"Ready for anything, ma'am," Carter answered her, a cocky nervousness clear in both his words, and his delivery.

"You've done fine so far," Schiavo told the young man. "Rely on your training."

They were wise words. Ones that had been given from countless commanders to their troops in conflicts with names never to be forgotten—Normandy, Khe Sanh, Gettysburg, Inchon, Fallujah. I suspected, though, that Lorenzen hadn't imagined a battle of Columbus when he'd put Carter Laws through a rigorous and accelerated training regimen.

"Five minutes."

The callout of our time to touchdown again came from one of the two men in the cockpit as the fire directed against us trailed off and the craft they piloted leveled out, gaining altitude to clear the rising buildings nearer the city center. Five minutes until some answer to what this was all about. Some justification for what we've been through.

Whether any of that mattered, I suspected, depended on just one thing—what the President of the United States had to say to Captain Angela Schiavo.

Part Three

The President

Nineteen

"Welcome to Columbus," MacDowell said, confirming our destination as the Blackhawk banked sharply to the left, crossing over a river below.

"Scioto River," Genesee said through the headset. "If my high school geography is correct."

"It is," MacDowell confirmed.

Glancing left as we turned, I could see the trailing Blackhawk still following us, its side doors open now, the feet of shooters dangling. The soldiers aboard were ready for action. Or more action, to be accurate.

"We expecting more of a fight?" I asked.

"Hopefully not," MacDowell said. "We've got the northern approach to the city clear."

"Then why didn't we take that route all the way in?" Schiavo challenged the man.

MacDowell looked to her, not smiling, not registering any reaction at all. Just offering stony silence.

"On the ground in one," the pilot reported over the intercom.

As soon as his words ended, the Blackhawk leveled out and nosed down, threading itself between two buildings and following a road for a few blocks before slowing and making a severely sharp right. Glancing ahead as I held on to the straps which secured me to the seat, I could see past the left gunner a circular stone projection rising from an older building.

"The Ohio Statehouse," MacDowell said, noticing my attention.

"Hang on," the left gunner said. "You're bailing fast when we touch down."

The helicopter slowed quickly, its nose rising as it glided over a pair of irregular patches of dirt in front of the statehouse.

"I want everybody out in five seconds," the pilot instructed. "We're down in three...two...one...GO!"

The Blackhawk's right side gunner threw that door open, his gloved hand stabbing toward the exit as MacDowell removed his headset and hopped out first. Schiavo and Genesee helped Martin down and away from the bird, Carter and me following, weapons at the ready.

"Across the street!" MacDowell shouted as we jogged away from the Blackhawk, his destination appearing to be the base of a tall building on the corner. "Hurry."

We'd barely cleared the Blackhawk when it lifted off, joining the bird that had trailed it but hadn't landed, circling instead, providing cover. But from what?

"They're heading north," Carter said, noting the Blackhawks' choice of route away from the capital.

That was an oddity. If MacDowell was being truthful, and parts north were free of fire, then using that route for transports without passengers made little sense. Or little sense to *us*.

"Just stay focused," I told the young private, and he looked away from the departing choppers.

Just ahead of us, Martin was keeping up well, waving off any further assistance as we reached the street. Across it, where glass doors and windows had once enclosed the tall building, there were only openings to a dark interior. But not dark enough that we could not see a dozen soldiers in full battle dress waiting, most on one knee, their weapons trained at the world outside. And at us.

"Just keep your weapons down," MacDowell cautioned.

We did just that, even when, halfway across the street, a shot rang out, and chips of the hard road surface erupted from a bullet striking just short of us.

"Sniper!"

The warning was shouted from inside the building, just before a pair of troopers emerged and scanned the buildings to the east through optics mounted atop their rifles. As we quickly crossed the sidewalk, each of the soldiers who'd exposed themselves to cover us opened up, squeezing off individual shots, the report of the dozen or so rounds echoing sharp behind us.

"Hold up," a bearded soldier instructed after we were all safely inside the building, in what had once been the lobby of some commercial tower, stripped now to its bare essentials of floor, walls, and ceiling. "All weapons on safe. You'll surrender them on the second floor."

Schiavo looked to Martin, and then to me, before eyeing the soldier again.

"And you are?" she asked.

"Captain Michael Robertson, head of the president's protective detail."

"You're not Secret Service," Martin said.

The captain shifted his attention to the man who'd challenged him.

"There is no Secret Service," Robertson said. "Not anymore."

"Just listen to him," MacDowell urged us. "This isn't some violation of your rights. They're protecting the president, all right?"

There was little to gain by resisting any request or order now that we were here. Schiavo had already played that hand with MacDowell as we waited to board Air Force One. Now, though, in apparent proximity to the man who'd summoned her, playing along was the order of the day.

"All right," Schiavo said.

* * *

We followed MacDowell and Captain Robertson up a flight of stairs to a makeshift command post, two dozen more troopers filling the space, most settled into old hotel couches as they cleaned their weapons and prepared their gear.

"Patrol heading out," MacDowell said, explaining the activity.

"That sniper who missed on your way in isn't alone," Robertson said, flashing a grim look at the bureaucrat who'd accompanied us. "They're probing us hard."

"It won't be long, captain," MacDowell told the officer, offering some vague reassurance.

Too vague for Schiavo.

"What won't be long?" she pressed MacDowell.

He didn't answer, holding still more back from the woman who'd been summoned here, and from those of us who'd accompanied her.

"You can put your weapons over here," MacDowell said, pointing to a large conference table where Robertson had stopped.

"There's food right through that door," the captain said, pointing to a space some trooper with a sense of humor had labeled *'Chow?'* with a crudely made sign. "You all can eat while Captain Schiavo heads upstairs."

Schiavo was first to shed her weapons and gear, placing them on the table before laying a determined look on both MacDowell and Robertson.

"I'm not going anywhere alone," she said.

"Captain..."

MacDowell's exasperation was mild, but openly expressed now.

"We brought your friends with you," the suited bureaucrat said. "We did that. But you are here to see the President of the United States. *You.* Not your entourage."

Schiavo shook her head at the man's resistance.

"Not everyone," she told him. "Just Mr. Fletcher."

Gazes angled toward me, while mine naturally shifted to Schiavo. She'd given no indication that this was a move she was making, but I wasn't taken completely by surprise. From the point that Genesee and I had joined her on this journey, she'd made it clear that, though this was ultimately about her, we were all stakeholders in not just the outcome, but also in the process. This insistence she'd just voiced was only a continuation of that.

"Captain," MacDowell repeated, though the wind was clearly leaving his sails.

Schiavo seized the initiative and nodded past the man, toward a pair of armed troopers standing guard at the base of an open staircase leading to a landing barely visible in the din above.

"Is that the way?" she asked and suggested at the same time. "We should get moving."

MacDowell drew a breath and gave in, nodding.

"Let's go," he said.

Schiavo gave the others in our group a quick look, then focused on me.

"You ready, Fletch?"

I was and I wasn't. But that in no way meant that I wasn't going to see this through. Whatever came of it.

Twenty

MacDowell stopped us at a door down a wide hallway on the second floor, two more troopers stationed outside this space.

"Wait here for a moment," he instructed, then opened the door and stepped through, closing it quickly.

"Do you have even the foggiest idea where this might be going?" I asked Schiavo in a quiet voice, the troopers a few yards away ignoring our conversation in a practiced manner.

"None," she said, quieting for a moment before a bare, sly smile spread briefly upon her lips. "Maybe he just wants to tell me my enlistment is up and shake my hand."

I could have laughed, mostly because expressions of humor were not natural to Captain Angela Schiavo. That she was letting something like that out now spoke either to her nervousness, or to the confidence she was feeling after steering the interaction away from MacDowell's desired protocol.

"Again, Fletch, thank you. It seems like every step of the way, no matter what we're facing, you're there. For me. For all of us."

"I can say the same about you," I reminded her.

"I'm in a uniform," she said. "You're not."

"From the day the blight hit, we've all had a bit of soldier in us. We're all fighting for something, for someone. To survive."

She seemed to consider that for a moment, then nodded, accepting my premise just as the door opened and stayed that way, MacDowell stepping out and standing just clear of it.

"The president will see you now," he said.

If any moment was worthy of some hesitation, this was it. But Schiavo didn't. She strode straight for the door. I moved quickly to catch up, and a few seconds later we were inside, the door closing behind, MacDowell and the troopers remaining in the hallway.

* * *

It was a medium size meeting room on a floor that seemed designated for such things, no guest rooms on the level. Mostly it was empty, just a large conference table pushed against one wall with a half dozen chairs arranged in a semi-circle near the far end of the space. Then there was the man walking toward us, smiling.

"Thank you for coming," he said as he reached us.

Schiavo hesitated only briefly at the sight of the man, the *young* man, the crisp blue suit he wore acting to amplify the appearance that this was some stage play where children performed as adults. Then, as expected, she saluted the man who was, apparently, her Commander in Chief.

"Sir."

He returned the salute, then extended his hand. Schiavo shook it, then I did, the man giving us each an approving once over.

"You've come a long way," the president said. "Been through a lot."

Schiavo could have confirmed what he'd obviously been briefed on, but she didn't. She offered not a tip of the head, nor a word of agreement. Instead she considered the man for a moment, some wariness creeping into her demeanor.

"I don't recognize you," she said.

"I wouldn't either," the president said. "The line of succession was obliterated by the chaos after the blight, and then in a series of Unified Government attacks. Eventually, the buck stopped with me. Assistant Secretary of the Interior for Land and Minerals. My name is Kenneth Stone."

"Stone," I said.

The president nodded and grinned.

"Appropriate for Land and Minerals," he said, the brief flourish of joy fading after a few seconds. "Maybe for all this, too. We can hope."

Schiavo, though, didn't say anything. She made no comment. Just regarded the man with continued and obvious skepticism.

"I understand this is a bit much for you to process," the president said. "Maybe even difficult to accept. Two others came before me. Both are dead. The simple truth is, I'm what's left, and I'm doing what I think is right. Part of that includes bringing you here."

Finally, Schiavo's concern seemed to ebb. Her posture, still straight and respectful in the presence of the nation's leader, became less rigid. She was not facing an enemy, nor an unknown, she realized, but a man trying to do what we all were, only on a grander scale.

"The eruption of Mt. Hood has obviously complicated things," the president said. "We may be seeing some effects from the ash cloud here in a day, maybe two."

"Do you have the ability to track its progress?" Schiavo asked. "Any satellite imagery?"

"We do still have some of that capability," the president confirmed. "But it's limited, as well as sporadic."

"What about the west coast?" I asked. "Has there been any information on the ash cloud out our way?"

The president nodded.

"It began clearing two days ago when the wind shifted onshore."

I actually let out a breath right then, one that felt as though I'd been holding it since leaving my wife and my daughter.

"That's wonderful news," I said, knowing how much easier that would make life for all those we'd left behind in Bandon.

The president, though, didn't register the same relief that I did.

"I didn't bring you here to discuss weather or natural disasters," the president said, looking to Schiavo.

"Why did you bring me here?" she pressed him.

The president hesitated for just a moment, shifting his attention to me in his own expression of concern. Schiavo, though, almost instantaneously quelled any resistance the man might be feeling now because of my presence.

"Sir, without Mr. Fletcher, we'd all be dead. He and two others were the ones who discovered the process to defeat the blight."

"I know that," the president said.

"There is no issue of trust where he is concerned," Schiavo assured the man.

"I'm certain there isn't. But this is…different. Very different."

"How so?" she asked.

I remained silent and watched as the president looked away from me and fixed fully on Schiavo. He slipped a hand into the inside pocket of his suit coat.

"You want to know why I brought you here," the president prompted, and Schiavo nodded. "I brought you here for this."

Twenty One

The president held out the small object he'd retrieved from his pocket. It was a card, no larger than one which might come from a collection of Queens and Aces and Twos. It was thicker, though, and seemed more of a sleeve, with another, thinner, card sandwiched within.

"You'll need this," the president said. "Colonel Schiavo."

Colonel...

Until a moment before she'd been *Captain* Angela Schiavo. But, with a word from the Commander in Chief, she'd apparently vaulted past the ranks of major and lieutenant colonel to what she was now.

"Colonel?"

The president nodded.

"The few generals we have left would skewer me if I handed this responsibility off to a captain."

Schiavo absorbed what had just happened, her gaze fixed on the card still in the president's outstretched hand.

"Responsibility, sir?"

"Your responsibility," the president said, nodding toward the card. "Many consider it a burden. The greatest burden a leader possesses."

The woman I'd come to respect immensely as a leader, and as a friend, looked to me, as if to seek some reassurance that this was all real. I managed something that approximated a smile, enough, it seemed, to encourage her to take what the president was offering her.

"Guard that with your life," the president said, his gaze shifting to me. "With all your lives."

Schiavo studied the small sleeve, sliding the contents out for inspection, a series of letters and numbers printed in bold upon it, and beneath it a number with a single decimal place, which looked like a radio frequency to me as I glimpsed the contents.

"That is the master code, Colonel Schiavo," the president said.

"Sir?"

"With that you can authorize the launch of any strategic weapon that remains in our arsenal," the president told her. "I have one, and now you do, as well."

"The football," I said, recalling the man we'd met on our journey to and from Cheyenne.

"Not exactly," the president corrected. "The football is more of a communication device that allows encryption and transmission of launch orders contained within. This is more than that."

I couldn't recall Colonel Ben Michaels saying anything about a master code, and one in his position, the human equivalent of the football, would have known of such a thing. At least he should have.

But there were secrets to be kept from everyone, I imagined. Even from the man standing before us, who was giving to Schiavo the ability to destroy what remained of the world.

"Reaching any unit with strategic weapons and using the call sign Viper Diamond Nine will give you immediate access to their launch officer," the president explained. "Giving them a target and that code will initiate a strategic strike against that target, destroying it."

Schiavo eyed the code for a moment before slipping it back into the sleeve and sliding it into her shirt pocket. She then fixed a hard look on the Commander in Chief. *Her* Commander in Chief.

"One of our surviving missile subs has been tasked with staying on station in the Pacific," the president said. "Their orders are to monitor the frequency on that card at three a.m. and three p.m. every day for any transmission from you."

"Sir, why do I need the capability you've just given me?" she asked, considering her own question for a moment before emphasizing its focus. "Why do *I* need that authority?"

The president didn't answer quickly, though it was clear he could have. He seemed to take a moment to choose his words. To temper them with only as much reality as was necessary.

"Because there is every chance I will not survive what's to come," he said.

"Just what is to come?" I asked, interjecting myself into this sobering, delicate exchange. "If you don't mind me asking."

"The final battle," the president answered without a hint of melodrama. "We have some reconnaissance ability, limited, but enough in this instance to know that the Unified Government forces in the east are massing and maneuvering."

"Maneuvering in this direction," Schiavo said.

The president nodded and led us to the conference table. A map of the continental United States was spread upon it.

"We hold Hawaii," he said. "An ocean protects it. I believe you were initially deployed from there, colonel, yes?"

"When I was a lowly lieutenant, sir," Schiavo confirmed.

The president pointed to a spot near the border between Kansas and Colorado.

"Remnants of the Second MEF hold a position at Colby, Kansas," he said.

"Marine Expeditionary Force," Schiavo said.

"Their expedition is Kansas, now," the president said. "What's left of them. They were our blocking force east of the Rockies."

His finger shifted to the area where we were, Middle America, blocks from the Scioto River in Columbus, Ohio.

"And we hold this city," he said.

There was a very obvious locale he'd left out.

"Washington?" Schiavo asked.

He shook his head.

"D.C. is gone. Burned and bulldozed."

"What?" I prodded, unclear as to whether he was being dramatic or literal in his description. "Bulldozed?"

"You heard correctly," the president said. "When they drove our forces out, they set everything that would burn afire and took the wrecking ball to every last gleaming monument."

I took a moment to imagine what the man had just told us, but could not. For all the faults of the men and women who'd inhabited the political class occupying that great city, it was a beacon, to those fortunate enough to inhabit the land between the shining seas, and to those beyond our borders who dreamed of the same thing that made our very nation possible—freedom.

"We also hold this," the president continued, his finger pressed directly where Bandon lay on the map. "And by 'we' I mean 'you'."

"We're one country, sir," Schiavo told him.

"For now," he said, his finger shifting to the south along the California coast. "The Unified Government forces have moved north again after taking Yuma and San Diego. They've halted near the border between California and Oregon."

I understood, finally, why the man hadn't reacted with some glee when sharing the news of the ash fall shifting away from the coast.

"The way is clear for them to move north again," the president said. "They feel emboldened after their success in San Diego. Your BA-Four Twelve gambit had an expiration date, it would seem."

"How do you know about that?" I asked.

The president managed a smile. Some small reaction to one success in a string of failures.

"You don't believe our enemies are the only ones who've mastered the art of infiltration..."

"We have someone inside the Unified Government," Schiavo said.

"We do," the president confirmed. "And from that person we know that the leadership no longer feels that the biological agent Mr. Moore stole is a viable threat."

Neil had taken the deadly virus to prevent its use against the very people our government had let down. That was his fear, and, recalling those dark days as the blight exploded across the globe, and across our nation, I could understand the wrenching worry that must have weighed upon him. He was a lone man striking out to prevent a catastrophe which might have dwarfed what the blight had done. It had killed the plants, and the animals which fed upon them, and the predators which preyed upon those herbivores. But we'd survived that. If Four-Twelve had been unleashed, a virus which targeted humanity directly, it was unlikely any of us would be standing here discussing the continuing survival of our species.

We would have gone extinct.

"We no longer have instantaneous and reliable communication, Colonel Schiavo," the president said. "If there is a grave threat on the west coast, I need a commander with the experience and judgement to deal with it. You've exhibited both of those qualities. Bandon exists today because of you."

"It exists because everyone refused to give up," she told the Commander in Chief.

He didn't take her correction as insubordinate, smiling and nodding instead, acknowledging her humility. But to a large degree the president was right. Lieutenant, then Captain, and now Colonel Angela Schiavo, onetime piano player for Army dignitaries, had demonstrated extraordinary leadership at places like Mary Island, and Skagway, and during the Unified Government siege of Bandon.

Still, in light of recent contacts we'd had, a question remained. At least in my mind.

"Sir…"

The president looked to me.

"You have an admiral in the west," I said, recalling what the SEALs who'd come ashore had implied. "I can't remember his—"

"Adamson," the president said. "Lionel Adamson."

"Adamson, yes," I said, remembering now. "With no offense to you or Cap…I mean Colonel Schiavo and her accomplishments, shouldn't this responsibility you're handing off more logically belong to him? Or to some general you could dispatch?"

"I don't have spare generals lying around, Mr. Fletcher. And even if I did, my decision would be the same."

I sensed that even Schiavo was having difficulty with the explanation the president had offered to my question. As it was, the man had no problem going further with his reasoning.

"If I give to a warfighter what I've just given to you, they'll fight a war. But it will be a war of conquest, not the kind that you've been fighting."

"What kind is that?" I asked.

"A war for survival," the president said. "I've given you access to a weapon of last resort. I'd expect that you will see it as such, Colonel Schiavo, and wield it accordingly."

Schiavo reflexively brought a hand to the shirt pocket where she'd placed the code card, touching the spot with reverence. And with a hint of fear. Obvious fear.

"It's good to be afraid of it," the president said, noticing her reaction. "That you express such an emotion tells me I made the right decision. You've spent enough time trying to build the world back up that the idea of destroying it turns your stomach."

"A bit, sir," she confirmed.

The president nodded, satisfied. But that state of contentment was only momentary.

"I wish I could say the Unified Government is the only military threat you may face," he told us, pointing to a place on the west coast north of Bandon, along the coast of Washington state. "We have some intelligence reports that a Russian force may have landed here. Your encounter on the way to Air Force One would seem to confirm that."

A report from the Stryker crew had clearly reached the man in advance of our arrival. But what they'd seen, what we'd all seen, was thin in the area of confirmation.

"We only saw a handful of troops," Schiavo reported. "None were quality fighters. Nothing like Kuratov's men in Skagway."

The president nodded, not disputing her assessment.

"They could be twenty in number, or two hundred," the president said. "What's most troubling, though, is why they've apparently come ashore."

"Why is that?" I asked.

"We have reason to believe that the Unified Government has secured some kind of agreement with the surviving Russian forces in the east of their country."

"What sort of agreement?" Schiavo asked.

"A treacherous quid pro quo," the president answered. "The Russians have been promised Alaska if they help the Unified Government eliminate our forces on the west coast."

"You mean eliminate *us*," I said.

Again, the president nodded.

"I doubt the Russians will be spoiling for a fight on their own, however," the president suggested.

Schiavo innately knew what he was saying.

"Defeat the Unified Government forces to Bandon's south, and the Russians will pull out."

"That's the assumption," the president confirmed.

For a moment, the discussion paused, all that needed to be shared complete. But not all questions had been answered.

"Sir, why do you feel you won't survive?" Schiavo asked her commander in chief. "You can be evacuated. If we can get in, you can get out."

"Yes, I can. But if I go, the reason for our enemies to attack this city goes away."

Both Schiavo and I puzzled at the man's reasoning for a moment. But just for a moment.

"You're the bait," I said.

"I'm the bait," the president confirmed. "Their lead elements have penetrated the city perimeter already."

"The snipers," I said, recalling the shots taken at us just after landing.

"Precisely," he said. "We have the northern approach to the city relatively clear. It's our planned escape route."

"You didn't bring us in that way," Schiavo said, understanding now. "You brought us through the gauntlet."

"If the Unified Government suspected that we have a way out, they'd move to shut it down," the president explained. "They would shift forces and have us truly encircled."

Giving the enemy targets of opportunity, as we had clearly been, was a necessity, the man was saying.

"I'm sorry you had to come through that," he told us, true sincerity in his apology. "But we need their forces concentrated."

"Why?"

He considered my very simple and straightforward question for a few seconds.

"I'll show you why," he said.

Twenty Two

We climbed the building's stairs with members of the president's security detail ahead of and behind us. On the landing just outside the door to the 28th floor we came face to face with two soldiers guarding the way forward, armed to the teeth, their weapons at the ready even when they saw their commander in chief approaching.

"Open it," the president instructed.

"Yes, sir," one of the guards said.

His partner stepped away from the door, allowing us to see right then a large chain and padlock securing it, several additional layers of reinforcement welded and bolted to the barrier and the frame that contained it. Great effort had been expended on securing whatever lay beyond.

Twenty seconds after he'd begun to remove the lock, the guard had it off and several sliding bolts around the door edge thrown. At that point he took hold of a levered handle and twisted it upward. A slight push inward allowed just a sliver of a view beyond.

The space I saw looked as black as night.

"Sir," the guard who'd stood back from the door said, his hand held out, a flashlight in it.

"Thank you," the president said, taking the device and activating the beam. "Let's go."

The nation's leader pushed the door fully open and stepped through. Schiavo followed without hesitation. I did, however, hold back for just an instant, an almost imperceptible pause while images from old movies flashed in my head. Ones where some Mafioso would step into a room and have a bullet put into his head from behind.

* * *

"This way," the president said.

He kept the flashlight aimed low, brightening a path on the bare concrete floor ahead of us. We'd landed in daylight, and it was certainly still that outside, but whatever windows there'd been in this space had been covered completely. Not a hint of the sunlight shining outside was apparent anywhere in the darkness.

"You covered the windows," I said.

"We sandbagged the windows," the president corrected me, shifting the beam briefly to illuminate a continuous wall of sandbags stretching from floor to the exposed concrete ceiling above. "The entire floor is ringed with them. They're stacked six feet thick. The floors directly above and below are fully filled with loose sand and stone blocks."

He wasn't saying it, but what he was describing was a bunker in the sky. One which we'd just been led into.

"You're protecting something," Schiavo said.

"Very astute," the president said. "You didn't say some*one.*"

Doing so wouldn't have been out of the realm of possibilities. Providing a safe space for the commander in chief would have been a logical act. But so would evacuating him from a city supposedly being targeted by a large enemy force. Schiavo was right—something precious was being kept in this space.

"Right here," the president said, stopping finally, his flashlight directed at the reason for our visit to the makeshift bunker.

"Jesus..."

The exclamation was mine. Schiavo stood silently next to me and stared at the object, which, most appropriately, rested on a pedestal, as if on display. Two thick cables snaked from its conical body and ran to a large plastic tub, the size of a child's coffin, which sat on the floor a few yards away.

"A W-Eighty Eight warhead," the president said, staring at the device as we were, reverence and fear in his gaze. "Removed from a Trident missile off one of our subs before she was scuttled near Norfolk."

I knew what we were looking at now. The thing had a designation, and an origin, though its lineage rightly stretched all the way to a New Mexico desert where the first of its kind had been detonated more than seventy years earlier. This descendant of that city killer looked to be a bit over five feet tall, and not quite two feet across at its widest part near its base. In that relatively compact package was more power than the armies of Genghis Khan or Napoleon could have dreamed of. It was the power that the president had just given Schiavo the ability, and the authorization, to deploy.

But that would come from a different delivery system. This destroyer sat here, landlocked. It was going nowhere. That, I suspected now, was by design.

"You can see now why we want the Unified Government forces here," the president said, gesturing with the flashlight to the box connected to the warhead by the stout wiring. "The timer mechanism is in there. Once I give the word and that's activated, I'll leave with the last of our troops. We'll have forty-five minutes to reach a safe distance to the north."

He redirected the beam of light back to the warhead.

"If all goes right, a four hundred kiloton blast will wipe out our enemy on this side of the country once and for all."

We stared at the warhead for a moment, the quiet breaking only when Schiavo turned toward the commander in chief and spoke.

"I wasn't your first choice."

The president eyed her, not with surprise at her statement, but with an unexpected admiration at her prescience. He smiled, and I thought, even in the dim light cast only by the man's flashlight, that, for the first time since we'd met him, the blood of a politician flowed freely through his veins.

"Mr. MacDowell said a bird had to be destroyed after its crew landed not long ago," Schiavo told him. "But on our way in we saw a crash site. A Blackhawk went down into a house."

I understood now why she'd directed my attention to the place where the helicopter had gone down. She was sending me a quiet signal that MacDowell might be telling the truth, but he wasn't telling the entire truth. Or all truths.

And neither, Schiavo was implying, was the president.

"I think a bird getting shot down is worthy of a mention over one landing," Schiavo continued. "Unless you're not keen on letting on just who went down with it."

The president nodded, some faux contemplation in the gesture.

"Colonel, I've just given you the ability to destroy what's left of the world. Does it matter if others never got the chance to wield that power?"

"With all due respect, sir, that's not my concern," she said.

"This isn't a high school dance, Colonel Schiavo," the president said. "Your two prettier friends didn't turn me down, leaving you as my only hope for a date. This is cold, hard reality. This is about the survival or the destruction of what's left of humanity. I chose you, and whether I chose anyone before you shouldn't matter, because you're on the dance floor now and the music is about to start."

She accepted his metaphorical explanation. Most of it.

"Sir, we've been lied to," she said. "We've been kept in the dark. When pieces of the truth bubble up I begin to wonder about that truth. And about motives."

"You can wonder all you want, Colonel Schiavo. Just keep those codes safe and your mind right when it comes to our enemies, because, in the event that you ever need to make the call, everyone will be wondering about *your* motives. That's what comes with the responsibility I've just given you—eternal second guessing. Constant doubt. As long as you're not the one engaged in that pointless reflection, then I've made the right decision."

He let that hang there for a moment, then motioned with the flashlight, directing us toward the door. Schiavo didn't, but I gave the warhead a last look before moving toward the exit. It was dull and unimpressive. The wires snaking from a port on its side looked like lines keeping a patient on life support. In a short time, if what the president expected came to pass, a simple electrical signal, maybe five volts of current, would set it off. Seconds later the capital of the state of Ohio, and all those within ten miles, would be dead or dying. The war that was never meant to be would be over in this part of our once great nation. I wondered—no, I feared—that the same cataclysmic act might be necessary to save those of us clinging to life on the west coast.

"Mr. Fletcher..."

I turned toward the president, the man standing halfway between the warhead and the door, waiting for me as Schiavo made her way out.

"Time for you to go home," he said.

* * *

We were back in the lobby, geared up, troops all around us, only MacDowell unarmed as he walked us toward where we'd dashed into the building not an hour earlier.

"Helicopters are on their way in," he told us. "You'll be taking the northern route out to get you back to Air Force One."

"You're not worried about tipping your hand on your escape route anymore," I said.

"The moment is at hand," MacDowell said, unintentionally theatric in his choice of words, a thinly confident smile on his face. "We'll be following the same route in a few hours, I suspect."

The Unified Government forces had to be massed close. Closer, maybe, than either he or the president wanted to believe.

"Good luck," MacDowell said.

Captain Robertson and his troops took up positions near the outer support columns that defined the lobby as the windy roar of the Blackhawks rose, dust kicking up on the street as one of the helicopters settled toward the earth precisely where it had dropped us off.

"Angela," Martin said, putting a hand on his wife's shoulder. "What happened up there?"

She looked to him, just looked, signaling very clearly in some marital shorthand—*not now*. Martin understood and didn't push it. I did wonder, though, if '*not now*' in her mind actually meant '*not ever*'. If she thought that what she'd been told, and what I'd been privy to, was a secret she would not share, even with the man closest to her.

But after a few seconds of consideration, I realized that she was almost certainly being truthful in her response to Martin. The time would come, I thought, for him to bear the secret alongside her. And me.

"Ten seconds!" Captain Robertson shouted.

Seventy-five yards away the Blackhawk touched down and its left door slid open. Four of Robertson's troopers dashed into the street and took up positions, covering both east and west.

"Go!"

We reacted to the captain's direction and dashed out of the building, jogging quickly across the street and onto the dirt field in front of the capitol building, rotor wash throwing clods of earth and debris at us. Martin was first to reach the helicopter, the rest of us piling in, taking the same seats we'd occupied on the flight in and slipping back into our headsets as we buckled in. The door slid shut and the turbine's roar rose, the bird rising and tipping forward, gaining altitude and banking sharply right, heading north.

Before we flew beyond the domed statehouse building I was able to glimpse out the right-side window three of Robertson's troopers dragging the fourth back toward the building, two squeezing off shots to the west, firing at a point we'd just flown over.

"Enemies to the west now," I said.

"We took sniper fire from the east when we arrived," Schiavo said.

I nodded, knowing what that meant.

"The Unified Government is closing in," I said.

The president had called it the final battle. It seemed that the ultimate conflict he'd envisioned was arriving sooner than anyone had expected.

Twenty Three

We were no more than two miles north of the capital building when the folly of a safe escape from Columbus became apparent.

"Fire right!"

It was the pilot, I thought, taking note of a sudden burst of heavy machinegun fire rising up from the city on his side of the aircraft.

"Fire left!"

The copilot announced what he was seeing from his vantage point, the Blackhawk taking immediate evasive maneuvers which tossed us back and forth, testing the fabric belts which held us in our seats. The left door gunner began firing, laying streams of red hot lead on the buildings below from his minigun, his partner on the right doing what he could, firing an M4 past the disabled gun hanging uselessly from its mount.

"This is supposed to be clear!" the left gunner shouted over the intercom.

If the northern route had been clear, it wasn't anymore, a fact made abundantly clear by the line of impact holes that appeared on the left side door, rounds tearing through the metal and ricocheting off the bulkhead just behind and above me.

"We're taking hits!"

It might have been the right door gunner announcing the obvious, but I wasn't sure. In the growing chaos, I tried to focus, readying my AR for use should we need to open the side doors and add something to the defense of our aircraft.

"Get us out of here!" the right door gunner nearly screamed over the intercom. "We're getting butchered on the right!"

Incoming rounds shattered the window in the door on that side of the aircraft, as if to emphasize his point.

"Hang on!"

The warning came from the cockpit just before we nosed severely down, losing altitude, the bottom of the Blackhawk skimming the tops of dead trees and rooftops and church steeples. Just visible off to the left, maybe a hundred yards distant, the other helicopter, which had been leading us out of the city, was now dropping back, smoke trailing from it as puffs of rich orange fire pulsed from the exhaust of one of its turbines.

"Zeke Four is hit," the co-pilot announced.

"He's going down," Schiavo said.

She was right. Though the ground fire had slacked off, there was no escape for the Blackhawk which had absorbed the brunt of the fire as we punched through the gauntlet which had, for all intents and purposes, closed the northern escape route which had been counted on. The dying bird slowed and turned, wobbling as the crew tried to maintain control, a dangerously narrow space between buildings in an industrial area the only spot possible for it to set down.

"They'll be sitting ducks on the ground," Genesee said.

But as the wounded Blackhawk touched down, its main rotor clipping an old telephone wire, we continued on. Leaving them behind.

"What's going on?" Schiavo said over the intercom, unbuckling and moving toward the left door, dragging the intercom cable with her as she scanned the earth below and behind through the window. "Pilot, what are you doing?"

"Getting you out of here," the reply came, short and to the point.

"You have people on the ground back there," Schiavo said. "They're alive."

"My orders are clear," the pilot said. "Getting you back to Air Force One is my only mission."

"Not anymore," Schiavo said. "Turn this helicopter around and set down so we can pick up the other crew."

"Ma'am, my orders—"

"You have new orders...what is your rank?"

"I'm a captain, ma'am."

"I hope you're aware that I was promoted by the president himself, to full bird," Schiavo told the officer. "So, with that in mind, I'm giving you a direct order to put your aircraft on the ground and effect a rescue. Is that understood? We're not leaving anyone behind!"

There was silence for a moment, then the Blackhawk began a sweeping turn. Schiavo steadied herself with a hold on the center seat support as the pilot lined up for a landing on the same avenue where the other helicopter had set down. Already the fire was picking up again, from elements of the Unified Government force which had completely encircled Columbus.

"That's a hornet's nest down there," Martin said.

"Martin, you help the doc," Schiavo said. "Get to the downed bird and help them back to ours. Fletch, Private Laws, and I will set up a perimeter. Everyone clear."

A quick flurry of nods signaled that we were.

"Gunners, you back us up," Schiavo ordered. "Keep this bird intact."

"Yes, ma'am," the gunners said in unison.

"Ten seconds," the co-pilot reported.

Already we were below the tops of nearby buildings, the hot whoosh of red tracer fire arcing over our shifting position. If the enemy wasn't already on top of us, they would be in short order.

"Five seconds."

Schiavo threw the left door open. Carter did the same to the right. The sound of ground fire poured clearly into the cabin now. Shooters were only blocks away.

"Ready," Schiavo said.

We unbelted and shed our headsets. The pilot flared his approach as the Blackhawk descended between a pair of old warehouses, the main rotors seeming to have almost zero clearance, the tips spinning just feet from the abandoned structures. The tail wheel touched down first, an instant before the main gear, the aircraft rolling forward a dozen yards or so before coming to a full stop.

"Go!"

We moved on Schiavo's command, exiting from both sides of the Blackhawk. Genesee and Martin moved quickly forward to the other helicopter, its nose pointing at ours, fifty yards separating each. I took the north side of the street, while Carter took the south. Schiavo shifted to a position just aft of the spinning tail rotor, covering the western approach to the landing site.

I looked toward the downed helicopter and saw Martin just outside the right door, covering to the east as Genesee climbed into the cabin. There was no more flame from the engine, but heavy smoke billowed skyward, marking our exact position for anyone who was paying attention. Many obviously were, as the sudden eruption of cannon fire just beyond the warehouses signaled.

"That's mounted weaponry!" the left gunner shouted out to me.

I moved a bit forward to get a better vantage to the south, peering down an alleyway that ran between the old buildings, the walls of one structure collapsed, rubble blocking the narrow passage. But not enough to obscure the trio of enemy fighters creeping along toward our position.

"Contact south!"

I shouted the warning and began firing, the right gunner doing the same with his M4 from inside the

Blackhawk as the rotors spun fast above us. The fighters took cover behind mounds of bricks and twisted steel.

"Cover!"

The directive came not from inside the helicopter, nor from Schiavo, who was holding position fifty feet to the west. Instead it came from Carter, who dashed across the open space in front of the alley, ducking beneath fire from the door gunner's M4 to take a position at the very beginning of the single lane passage between buildings. Rounds from the enemy ripped into the corner of the wall where he'd found cover, but Carter didn't take the bait and lean into the open when the fighters paused for a few seconds. He had another plan.

The grenade was already in his hand when he reached the corner, and the pin out. When the lull in fire began he expertly lobbed the explosive device at an angle down the alley, its hard shell bouncing off the partially intact wall of the building on the western side and rolling just past the pile of rubble where it exploded.

In a flash and a puff of smoke a fast rush of screams sounded, then quieted, Carter's aim either true or very, very lucky. He looked to me and I gave him a thumbs up as he held position, still covering his side of the street.

"Here they come!"

It was the left gunner announcing what we'd waited for, Genesee and Martin returning with the crew of the downed helicopter. Not everyone, though, was approaching on their own. Three of the downed chopper's crew were carrying their fourth member, one of the door gunners, it appeared to me. His limbs hung lifeless and a thin trickle of blood left a red trail from their abandoned aircraft. Genesee stayed at the man's side, holding pressure on at least one obvious chest wound, while Martin brought up the rear, covering them as he ignored his own injuries.

"GO! GO! GO!"

The left gunner again urged haste as the others reached the Blackhawk. Schiavo pulled in her position from the west, and Carter from the south. I covered the alley from my position just forward of the nose, holding it until the rotors spun up and the co-pilot, through the windshield, gave me a very emphatic gesture which signaled that the helicopter was leaving, with or without me. A final look down the alley satisfied me that we had this moment, and this moment only, to leave our landing zone before it turned hot.

"Fletch!"

I heeded Schiavo's call, now, and climbed into the helicopter's cabin, both doors sliding shut as I did. Genesee knelt on the floor over the wounded soldier, a sergeant his uniform insignia indicated. The rest of us filled the seats and held on as the Blackhawk rose quickly into the air.

"Left gunner, we're turning right outbound," the pilot said. "Hose that bird."

As we performed a very shallow turn just above the buildings, the left door gunner fired multiple bursts from his minigun, shredding the downed Blackhawk. Its fuel tanks ignited and ruptured, sending a column of boiling fire into the narrow space between old manufacturing and industrial buildings. It was a necessary move to deny the enemy anything useful from the damaged aircraft. But it also marked our position before we'd even climbed high enough to be seen by the swarming Unified Government forces.

"Right! Right! Right!"

The gunner on that side yelled frantically over the intercom, forgetting the discipline which had been drilled into him—don't just announce a threat, *identify* it. Before he could correct his mistake, the rocket he'd spotted launching sailed dangerously close, just missing the outer edge of the main rotors chopping through the smoke-filled air. He began firing as the pilot completed his turn, staying insanely low on a due west heading.

"There's no safe route out," the pilot told us. "So we're taking the shortest."

He jerked the helicopter left and right in unevenly spaced maneuvers meant to keep any fire from the ground from zeroing in on us. The motion, though, made Genesee's job all the harder as he struggled to stabilize the wounded sergeant.

"Is there any plasma on this bird?" he asked, but he'd not bothered to put on his headset.

"Is there any plasma on board?" I asked, passing the question on to the crew. "Any medical supplies at all?"

"Just basic trauma kits," the co-pilot answered.

Genesee already had that, and more, in the gear he'd brought along. But we'd had to leave a substantial amount of what had been in the Humvee when abandoning it near Portland International Airport became a necessity. Including the lifesaving fluid he needed at the moment.

"Clay," I called to him, and when he looked I shook my head.

"Keep the pressure on," Genesee said to the pilot of the downed chopper, redirecting his attention to his patient. "Hard. Right on that wound."

The thick bandages he'd stuffed into the pair of gaping wounds apparent in the bloodied front of the sergeant's shirt were soaking through. Still, the man was hanging on, breathing on his own, his chest rising and falling with each raspy gulp of air he took.

"Fire left!"

The door gunner sprayed the tower of an old brick building, returning the fire that was coming from it, the upper part of the structure disintegrating in a shower of smoke and stone.

"It's easing up," the co-pilot reported, signaling that the path ahead bore less resistance than what we were leaving behind. "We'll be wheels down in—"

"Does the president ever ride on Air Force One anymore?"

The question that interrupted the report from the cockpit came urgently from Genesee, who'd slipped partially into a headset, just one ear covered and the boom mic askew below his chin.

"Who is that?" the pilot challenged.

"Commander Genesee. Now answer the question. Does the man ever fly on that aircraft or is it just for show?"

"Sir, I'm not at liberty to—"

"Screw the security protocols!" Genesee exploded. "Is he ever on board the damn plane!"

Silence hummed over the intercom. For just a moment.

"Captain, answer him," Schiavo said, backing up the man who had very likely saved her husband's life. "Now."

"All right," the pilot said. "Yes. He's flown on it."

"Recently?" Genesee pressed.

"Two weeks ago."

Genesee pulled the headset off and looked to Schiavo, shouting over the painful whine of the engines.

"He's coming with us," Genesee said.

"Who?" Schiavo asked.

Genesee pointed to the gravely wounded sergeant. Schiavo puzzled at his statement, as did I, but not for very long, both of us quickly making the connection between what was necessary and where that need could be met.

"All right, commander," she said.

Genesee took a calming breath, then looked to the sergeant. The man didn't have long. One didn't have to be a Navy trained doctor to see that.

"Captain," Schiavo called out into the pilot.

"Yes, ma'am."

"Wheels down in how long?"

"Fifteen," the pilot answered.

Schiavo looked to me. Fifteen wasn't good enough.

"Firewall those throttles, captain," Schiavo said.

Ten seconds later we were screaming over the western outskirts of the city. Carter looked to me, confused.

"He needs a hospital," I said.

"I thought we were going to Air Force One," Carter said.

"Exactly," I told him.

Twenty Four

The Blackhawk hadn't even stopped rolling when the left side door slid open. As soon as its wheels stilled, the sergeant's fellow crewmembers carried him off the Blackhawk with Genesee and Carter jogging alongside toward the stairs already lowered near the tail of Air Force One. Captain Borenstein stood near that entrance to the aircraft, his small contingent of troops arrayed near him, not surrounding the plane as had been their stated mission.

Something had happened.

"Angela," I said as I left the Blackhawk, shouldering Genesee's gear for him.

"What?"

I gestured toward what I was seeing and Schiavo looked, just as Borenstein came jogging our way with his men.

"What's going on?" Martin asked as he stepped out of the helicopter, surprised that we hadn't begun to move toward our ride home.

"I think we're about to find out," I said.

Borenstein stopped, facing us, but his men continued past and boarded the Blackhawk.

"Colonel Schiavo," he said, greeting his now superior officer with a salute.

Schiavo returned it, but was both puzzled and wary.

"You know about my promotion," she said.

"We received word from Columbus," Borenstein explained. "Along with orders."

Past the Army captain there was more movement. The crew of the downed Blackhawk, minus their wounded comrade, came fast down the stairs and raced toward the helicopter just behind us, passing us at a dead run and joining Borenstein's troops aboard the bird.

"Captain..."

Borenstein hesitated briefly at Schiavo's prompting, his mood verging on grim.

"We've been ordered to Columbus to help with the evacuation of the president. The route they had secured out of the city is no longer safe."

"We know," Schiavo said. "We came through it."

"Colonel Pedigrew and Major Handley will get you home," Borenstein said, gesturing toward Air Force One. "They're flyboys, but they get the job done."

Schiavo nodded at the mild poke at the Air Force officers who would be flying us back across the country.

"We won't give them any trouble," I said.

"The Stryker unit will meet you at McChord to take you the last leg home," Borenstein said, an obvious sense of finality to what he was sharing.

Behind us, the Blackhawk's rotors spun at speed, just a bit more throttle necessary to get it into the air. Borenstein and the others would be on their way to face their destiny in no time. To me it seemed that he was not reluctant to perform the duty he'd sworn an oath to fulfill, but, rather, that he knew that this might be the last moment of his life which would exist without some form of death racing at him.

"Captain," Schiavo said, locking her gaze with Borenstein's, "you give them hell. And then some."

"Will do, ma'am," the man said, allowing a smile.

Schiavo nodded, and Borenstein moved past us, joining his men and the others. The Blackhawk's doors slid shut and it rolled forward, rising into the sky, nose low as it sped fast over the runway and dead fields beyond. It was heading east, straight for the city.

"They're not going to make it," Martin said.

"We did," I told my friend.

He turned to me, grave reality hardening his face.

"We were running away," he reminded me. "They're heading into it."

I couldn't argue with the cold logic he had thrown at me.

"Hey!"

The call came from an unfamiliar voice. A man's voice. We looked and saw an Air Force major running our way from the aft stairs, ducking slightly against the jet wash from Air Force One's idling engines.

"Major Handley?" Schiavo asked as the man reached us.

He tossed her a quick salute and nodded.

"We need to get you aboard, Colonel Schiavo," Handley said. "The doctor with you needs assistance on the quick."

There was no more discussion. We ran to the plane and climbed the stairs. Handley followed, the steps folding up as soon as he activated the controls to retract them. Air Force One began to roll almost immediately, its four engines spinning up.

Our journey home had begun.

Twenty Five

The mighty white and blue 747 rose sharply into the sky, nose coming up at a severe angle. A few seconds after we were airborne, the sound of the massive landing gear assemblies retracting rumbled through the aircraft.

We were nowhere that allowed any view of the scenery outside. Nor were we inclined to care. Instead both Schiavo and I stood with Genesee in the surgical suite near the nose of the aircraft, Martin and Carter just outside, bracing themselves, the aircraft gaining altitude as we fought to save the wounded sergeant. The space around us was equipped with every device and instrument necessary to keep the President of the United States alive, no matter the health crises that faced the Commander in Chief. Genesee had realized that getting his patient to this airborne medical facility was his only chance to save the anonymous sergeant.

"We don't even know his name," I said.

"Lyons," Genesee said as he cut away the man's camouflaged shirt, his name stitched above the breast pocket.

"Sergeant Lyons, can you hear me?" Schiavo asked.

The man's open eyes stared blankly at the sterile ceiling above, harsh lights glaring down at him as his chest heaved irregularly, every breath pushing spurts of blood from two gaping wounds in his abdomen that the doctor worked furiously to wipe away

"Hang on, Lyons," Schiavo said, taking wads of gauze from Genesee as each became soaked with blood.

Genesee probed the wounds with bare hands, the protocols of a sterile environment negated by time and situation.

"Roll him on his side," Genesee instructed.

Schiavo and I did that, pulling the back side of his shirt that hadn't been cut away clear, revealing one massive exit wound where both rounds had left his body.

"Jesus," Genesee said. "It had to be a fifty."

Lyons coughed, blood pouring from his nose and mouth.

"Keep him on his side," Genesee said. "I need to get an IV started."

The doctor turned away and pulled open cabinets in the unfamiliar space, finding a bag of saline and most of the implements needed to get an intravenous line flowing.

"Where are the damn needles?"

Genesee searched frantically. To my left, though, Schiavo was calm. More so than just a second earlier. She eased her hand from where it had supported Sergeant Lyons' body and shook her head at me. I let go as well, and we let him roll gently back until he was flat on the mounted gurney.

"Commander," Schiavo said, trying to get Genesee's attention.

"Give me a second."

"Clay," she said, hoping that the familiar would draw him from what he was focused on. "Clay."

As if he knew what her choice of words, and her tone, meant, Genesee stopped his search and turned back toward his patient, his arms bloodied to the elbows.

"He's gone," Schiavo said.

Genesee said nothing. He just stood there. Behind me I sensed movement, and a second later Martin stepped past both me and his wife, a sheet retrieved from a shelf in hand.

He opened it and spread it over the lifeless form in front of us as the plane leveled off, climbing at a more gentle angle now.

"Hello."

The voice behind us was unfamiliar, but the uniform, crisp blue, was not. It was an Air Force officer in shirtsleeves, insignia on his collar showing his rank as equivalent with Schiavo.

"I'm Colonel Martin Pedigrew," he said, looking past to the bloody mess in the surgical suite. "Major Handley said we had a patient aboard but..."

"His wounds were too severe," Schiavo said.

Pedigrew nodded, looking to Genesee, the doctor still focused on the shrouded body before him, crimson stains soaking through the stark white linen.

"Commander," Pedigrew said, and Genesee looked up, finally. "You should wash up. You did what you could."

"I didn't even get a chance to try," Genesee said. "There was no time."

"There isn't always time," Pedigrew told him. "And even if there is, it might be too late. Now get cleaned up, all of you. We'll see to this soldier's proper burial when we land."

Silence filled the space for a moment as Schiavo handed Genesee a large towel. He wiped his arms and stared down at the shrouded body. At the patient we'd lost.

"I'll show you to your seats," Pedigrew said.

* * *

A few minutes later we sat in a section of the aircraft most recently occupied by Captain Borenstein and his small unit. It still bore evidence of their presence. Simple things. An empty paper cup that had very recently been filled with coffee. A smear of mud on the once pristine carpet, left there by a boot which was more at home on a field of battle than in the flying office of the President of the United States.

"We're going home," Genesee said from his seat across the space, looking to me. "Almost all of us."

I knew why the emphasis was so important to him. I'd stood next to him on the ash choked interstate on our way to find our friends, right after the crash which had given him a glimpse into a kind of death he hadn't known to that point. Desperate death. Hopeless death. A family gone together in a broken-down van so long ago that they were little more than mummified horrors. Shortly after that, he'd saved Martin, and had nursed the man along through the events which had followed.

Then he'd been faced with Sergeant Lyons. A combat death. The first that Genesee had truly faced with bullets flying. His first loss of this kind.

"No one was going to save him," Martin said. "No doctor. No ten doctors. It was his time."

Genesee knew that. Probably more than any of us. I suspected the unfairness of that had begun to gnaw at him. As he'd said, we were all going home. To our families. Our friends. And, in his case, to a new future. To a new love.

"Grace will be glad that you're coming home," I told him.

A quiet shift of attention happened, both Schiavo and Martin, and, to a lesser extent, Carter, looking to me, then to our doctor friend. Clearly the feelings that had developed between him and Grace were not public knowledge yet. She'd admitted their quiet relationship to me, as had Genesee on our trek to reach our friends, and now I was very plainly hinting at it, openly, for his own sake.

"Grace said Elaine and I are invited for dinner when we get back," I told him. "I want to see what you're capable of putting on the table."

Genesee considered my words for a moment as he absorbed the approving looks from the others, then he smiled lightly.

"I can burn any piece of meat on the grill that you want," he said. "Grace will probably insist on actually making something edible."

And there was that flash of humor the man was capable of, according to Grace. It looked good on him. The ability to express joy had been one trait lacking in Clay Genesee. It had contributed to the perception, for a time, that his defining quality was aloofness. If my friend's widow was moving past her grief to a place where she could love again, and bring out the better person in the town's doctor, then what we were witnessing right now could only be seen as a sign of the world righting itself for two people.

If only the remainder of humanity could experience the same, we'd be on a better path toward a truly sustainable time of surviving.

That, though, was only a hope. A wish. And one that would not be granted for us on this trip home.

Twenty Six

"We've got a problem."

It was the co-pilot, Major Handley, delivering the news as we sat in the spacious cabin, not quite thirty minutes after moving there from the surgical suite. That he had come back from his place in the cockpit was worrisome enough.

"What kind of problem," Schiavo asked the Air Force officer.

"We've lost control," he said.

"What do you mean 'lost control'?" Schiavo pressed.

Handley gave each of us a brief look, his uncertain gaze returning quickly to Schiavo.

"You'd better come see for yourself," he told her.

Schiavo stood. As if on cue to put an exclamation point on what Handley was hinting at, the aircraft bucked slightly, shuddering for a moment until the stillness of flight enveloped us again.

"Turbulence?" Martin asked.

The co-pilot didn't answer. Or couldn't.

"Let's go," Handley said.

Schiavo looked to me.

"You, too, Fletch."

I wasn't sure if Handley would disapprove of the invitation I was being offered, but I didn't care. I rose from my seat and stepped into the wide aisle.

"Major..."

Handley hesitated only briefly at Schiavo's gentle prodding, then he gave a quick nod and led us forward.

* * *

We stepped through the cockpit door, Handley leaving it open behind us. Gone were the days of security procedures, it seemed. As were the days of a fully crewed presidential aircraft, I thought, watching Handley take the right seat as Colonel Pedigrew looked back to us from the left seat. A third crew member should fill the empty position to our right, facing an array of instruments on the electronic wall before them. To our left and just behind, opposite the entry door, another station sat empty. The president was not aboard, but I had the impression that, like all things in this new world, Air Force One had been forced to operate with less.

"Colonel Schiavo," Pedigrew said, a slack discomfort to his face.

"There's a problem?" she asked.

"We no longer have control of Air Force One," Pedigrew said.

I looked past the pilots, to the myriad of gauges and displays that told them everything about the aircraft, and about the world around it. Weather radars. Radios. Engine thrust settings. And dozens more bits of information at their fingertips, not to mention the yokes, the plane's equivalent to a car's steering wheel, each one rising from the cockpit floor between their feet. With those, and with sophisticated flight management systems, the pilots could guide the aircraft to any place on the planet.

Or so it had seemed until just a minute ago.

"We're still flying," Schiavo said, pointing out the obvious to signal her confusion as to the statement.

"We are," Pedigrew confirmed. "But we have no control over the aircraft."

"Both you and Major Handley have told us that now," I said. "That doesn't explain anything that we're seeing out the windshield."

A bank of clouds in the distance blotted out the sky, but glimpses of the earth below still peeked through. Fields that once had been green. The breadbasket of the world and the Great Plains.

"Air Force One has every defensive measure possible," Pedigrew said. "We can blind radars, jam missiles, confuse our enemies. Those are all external threats. But in the years after September Eleventh, a new countermeasure was designed and implemented. One that could deal with a different kind of threat. One from inside the aircraft."

"A rogue pilot," Handley explained. "Or two."

Pedigrew gestured back toward the instrument cluster which would normally inform the decisions he made while flying

"What you're seeing is not us flying the aircraft," the pilot said.

Schiavo took just a few seconds to process the information.

"You're telling us that someone else is in control of Air Force One?"

Pedigrew shook his head.

"No, just that we aren't."

The pilot's hand extended, a finger pointing to a small red triangle in the upper corner of the central display.

"That tells us that step one has been activated," Pedigrew said.

"Step one?" I asked.

"It's a two-step countermeasure," Handley explained. "A signal relayed by satellite first cuts all pilot input, leaving the aircraft flying straight and level. That signal can be sent from any number of stations. A second signal then instructs the flight computers to accept only inputs from an external control station, which would maneuver Air Force One to a safe landing at a secure airfield. Except..."

"Except that station doesn't exist anymore," Pedigrew told us.

"It was taken out in a Unified Government attack on Cheyenne Mountain," Handley said.

"NORAD," I said, using the acronym for the North American Aerospace Defense Command, a complex located in the heart of a Colorado mountain. "They control that?"

"They destroyed it," Handley said.

"They used infiltrators," Pedigrew explained. "Opened up the mountain to a direct assault."

"It was still operating?" Schiavo asked, puzzled by the fact that such an installation would still be staffed for effective use so long after the blight took its toll on the world.

"Barely," Pedigrew said. "It was deemed a vital facility after the state of emergency was declared."

"Wait," Schiavo said. "They destroyed it? They didn't capture it? Occupy it?"

"There's no indication of that," Pedigrew answered. "If they had control of the station, they could just fly us into the ground."

Handley glanced out the windshield, the wall of storm clouds drawing near.

"So you're saying that someone knew enough to put this protocol into action," I said.

"The codes to do so are as highly guarded as the ones the president would use to launch a nuclear strike," Pedigrew confirmed.

I'd traveled across the wastelands with a man, an Air Force officer, who'd used one of those codes to launch a Minuteman ICBM that saved my life, along with Elaine's and Neil's. It was a sledgehammer killing a flea, to be certain, but that incident showed, if anything, that those codes were only as secure as the men and women who were entrusted with them. Both good and evil could result from their use. Or misuse.

We, based only on our perspective, were bearing witness to the latter.

"If they had infiltrators in NORAD," Schiavo said, the suggestion implicit in her statement.

"Yeah," Pedigrew agreed.

If the government had been penetrated at that level, it was hard to imagine how anyone could be trusted. Anyone.

"So what can be done?" I asked. "How do you regain control?"

Handley glanced to his commander, then back to us and shook his head.

"If I had a dozen computer programmers and equipment and ten years, I might be able to crack the security that has locked us out of our own aircraft," the co-pilot said. "But I don't."

"There has to be something," I said. "Some failsafe. Some override."

Pedigrew smiled at me and shook his head.

"Mr. Fletcher, I fly the President of the United States," he said. "If there was an override, I'd be the one to know."

There was silence for a moment. Schiavo drew a breath and shook her head.

"You can't get any help through the radio," she said, more stating a fact than inquiring as to any possibility.

"The protocol locks us out of communications," Handley said. "Only the ground station can speak to us, but..."

"They no longer exist," I said.

Schiavo looked past the pilots and over the instruments, to the white wall beyond.

"The protocol should have been disabled when we lost NORAD," Pedigrew said. "But it wasn't."

"You're telling us we're going to crash," she said.

Pedigrew nodded.

"Under normal circumstances we'd fly on this heading until we ran out of fuel," Pedigrew said. "Somewhere just east of Japan, I'd guess, considering our fuel load and heading."

"But we're not in normal circumstances," I said.

"That's not what I'm talking about," Pedigrew said, then pointed to a display showing green and yellow and red bands. "That's what's ahead of us."

"Thunderstorms?" Schiavo asked.

Before Pedigrew could answer, the aircraft sailed into a world of white, clouds surrounding us.

"That dark purple area beyond this bit of clouds we're in," Pedigrew said. "That's ash."

The eruption of Mt. Hood had spread catastrophic amounts of volcanic ash across the landscape, ejecting it tens of thousands of feet into the air. That it was reaching the heartland of America in appreciable amounts wasn't a surprise. The weather radar was confirming that very fact.

"We won't make it through that," Pedigrew informed us.

"Those ash crystals will wear down the turbine blades in the engines, choke the systems that depend upon air for combustion, for sensing," Handley said.

Schiavo nodded somberly.

"So we don't have hours left," she said.

"No," Pedigrew confirmed. "We have minutes."

Schiavo looked to me, some attempt at a smile twisting her lips. A grin of futility.

"I need to be with Martin," she said.

I nodded. She gave the pilots a last look, then left the cockpit. Were there any way I could be with Elaine, and with our daughter, I would. But there wasn't. In this situation, it seemed, the well of hope that had sustained me through the trials and tribulations since the blight took hold had run dry.

"There's nothing?" I pressed the pilots, my question incomplete, but not indecipherable.

"Nothing we can do," Pedigrew told me.

I lowered myself into the seat facing the wall of instruments. The navigator's station, I thought, though that was only a guess. I swiveled the seat to face forward as the pilots stared out the windshield at the clouds that veiled the sky ahead.

But soon, just seconds after I'd taken the seat, the world beyond the window began to change. White slid toward grey, light from the sun settling lower in the western sky suddenly muted.

"Here we go," Handley said.

Pedigrew took hold of the yoke, an instinctual move. He was a pilot, and his plane was about to be tested, to and beyond its limits. There was nothing he could do to prevent what was about to happen, but to feel the controls of the 747 in his hands was, I thought, some comfort.

"It's been an honor to fly with you, Jeff," Pedigrew told his co-pilot.

"And an honor to fly with you, Marty," Handley said.

Two warriors were saying their goodbyes to each other through expressions of respect. I supposed I could be back with those I'd come aboard with, my friends from Bandon. It would be right to share these final moments with them.

But I did not want to.

"I love you, Elaine," I said softly, neither pilot reacting to my words. "I love you, Hope."

Then, through the windshield, I saw the blackness.

I'd wanted to glimpse something before the horror. Some sliver of glorious blue sky. But that did not happen. All outside was suddenly erased as if the world had been dipped in perpetual, stinging night.

The aircraft began to shudder, vibrating unnaturally around us. I thought for an instant about my friends just a dozen yards behind and below me on the 747's lower deck.

We were all facing the same fate. A fate which connected us in these final moments of our lives, which made my absence from their presence inconsequential. I wanted to bear witness to what was to come, as it happened, even if that only meant staring into some blackness as we plummeted from the foul skies.

"One and two are shutting down," Handley reported.

Our left side engines were failing, behaving exactly as the crew had warned, bits of the abrasive volcanic ash tearing at the fine mechanical workings. The aircraft began banking slowly to the left, its right-side power pushing the lumbering plane in that direction.

BANG!

The sound was a true explosion, one that seemed to envelope the aircraft as a pulse of the brightest light I'd ever experienced filled the cockpit for a split second.

"Lightning," Pedigrew said. "Generated by the—"

"We've got control!" Handley shouted, interrupting his commander.

The aircraft shuddered violently, just the flickering glow of failing instruments lighting the pilots, all outside still blacker than the darkest night. Pedigrew grabbed the yoke with his left hand and the throttle levers with his right.

"Engines are responding," Pedigrew said, maintaining as calm a voice as possible under the circumstances.

"Numbers one and two are gone now," Handley reported, no chance to restart the damaged turbofans.

The 747 was banking to the left, severely now, the pilot struggling to get his plane back to level flight.

"What happened?"

Neither pilot looked back as Pedigrew answered me.

"I don't know. Static charge overloaded the system when that lightning bolt burst. Maybe reset the computers internally."

"We're flying," Handley said, relating the simplest of descriptions as to what the technical failures had made possible.

"I don't know how long that's gonna be possible," Pedigrew said.

The aircraft began pitching forward.

"Number three is shutting down," Handley said.

On the instrument panel, red and yellow lights were flashing as the crisp displays continued to flicker and skew, not every effect from the almost explosive bolt of lightning a positive development. The ash which had spawned it had killed two big turbofans already, and was about to destroy another.

"You'd better get to the back," Pedigrew told me. "All the way to the press section in back. Get everyone back there. We're going down. It's gonna be a hard one."

Black volcanic grit scraped at the windshield, racing past like a wind blowing straight from the depths of hell. Through this the men before me were flying, piloting their dying aircraft toward some ending that, with more luck than I could imagine, might end with not everyone aboard dead.

"Good luck," I said.

They were grossly inadequate words to leave the men with, but there was no time for any deeper consideration of a parting thanks. I stood from the seat I'd taken and left the cockpit, racing to the stairs which would take me down to the main deck. There was hope in the pilots' words, and in their determined actions, and even if was indicative of only a scant chance at survival. But any chance to be with my wife and daughter again was a chance I would seize and hang onto until my dying breath.

I struggled for balance on the stairs, and again as I reached the main deck, the aircraft's severe bank not lessening, and its dive growing more steep. If this was what the pilots thought of as 'in control', I wanted no part of whatever the opposite of that state was.

"We have to move," I told my friends as I reached them in the forward section of the cabin, in the area that senior staff had once occupied, when there were things such as senior staff. "Back of the plane. Now!"

"Fletch, what happened?" Schiavo asked as she and Genesee helped Martin up from his seat. "I thought we were going down."

"We are, but they have some control back."

Another loud *BANG* sounded from outside the aircraft, and the engine noise increased in pitch, becoming an almost painful whine as the huge 747 shook violently, floor and walls and ceiling vibrating like a tuning fork.

"Go!" I urged. "Grab your gear!"

Carter led the way, fighting against the incline of the steep descent as he pulled himself along the aisle, gripping seatbacks like a climber would take hold of rocks in a tricky ascent, his weapon and pack hanging off one shoulder.

"How did they get control?" Schiavo asked as made our way aft.

"Some sort of static buildup from flying through the ash," I told her.

"The lightning," Martin said, doing his best to help those helping him toward the rear of the aircraft. "It burst right around the fuselage."

"It did something to the electronics," I said.

"Are they going to be able to land?" Genesee asked.

I shook my head.

"I don't think so," I told him.

The aircraft leveled slightly, its nose down attitude less severe than a moment before. Perhaps Pedigrew and Handley were getting a handle on their plane. But one look through the windows next to us as the aisle hugged the left side of the 747 quashed any true hope that we were out of the woods. Everything outside was black. The ash cloud still held us in its grip.

Another *BANG* shook the aircraft, tossing us against the windows. Almost immediately the irregular whine of the engines stopped, the last of the dying powerplants spinning down.

"Hurry," Schiavo said.

Carter rushed aft, the rest of us behind him, until there was no further we could go. We tossed our packs aside and took seats, buckling in. I strapped my AR across my chest and looked to the right, where my friends had positioned themselves as the aircraft descended rapidly, tipping back and forth, some intense struggle for control of the huge plane going on in the cockpit. There was no engine noise, just a screaming whine of the plane slicing through the ash-filled atmosphere outside.

BANGBANGBANG!

The jolts shook the cabin around us, our backpacks flying upward.

"We're on fire," Carter said, pointing past me.

I looked out the left side window and saw swirling orange and black, flames and smoke blotting out the ash which had doomed our flight. Something had happened to one of the dead engines. A fuel leak, maybe. Or a fan blade shattered by collisions with millions of grains of volcanic grit. Whatever it was, the world outside was no longer a veil of ash—it was flame.

"We're going to be okay," Martin said.

I looked away from the window to my friend, one of his hand's clasped tightly with Schiavo's.

"We are," he said.

I didn't nod any acknowledgement, because I didn't believe him. Hope had been my mantra for so long.

There's always hope...

That had been the gift Neil had given me. Had left me with. My daughter bore the concept as her name. But this that we were facing...

BANG!

"It's like it's coming apart," Carter said about the terrible sounds penetrating the cabin.

He was right. The aircraft rocked back and forth, no power to propel it, Pedigrew and Handley doing what they could to control what was essentially a four-hundred-ton glider.

"This is it," Genesee said.

I looked to my right, past the others, and saw him clutching the arms of his seat, pulling up on them out of some instinctive response to the sensation of falling. The thought of some flight attendant giving instructions to survive a crash landing flashed suddenly, but I wondered how much good tucking my head between my knees would do. And, still, I wanted to be witness to...

Blue sky...

It was just a flash of it. A glimpse that lasted less than a second, but past the swirling flame and smoke outside my window I did see it. That could only mean one thing—that we were free of the ash cloud.

But not free of its effects. That fact became abundantly clear as the nose of the aircraft pitched slowly upward, more than leveling out, reaching what many pilots would consider a stall angle—the point at which the speed of the aircraft had reduced so much that not enough air was flowing over the wings to maintain lift. All this, though, mattered for just a second or two.

The instant after that, our fall from the sky ended with a horrific impact that was filled with tumbling and fire and screaming and smoke. And then...

Silence.

Part Four

Our Final Battle

Twenty Seven

I hadn't been knocked unconscious, but as my eyes opened and my senses recovered, it felt as though I'd come out of a dream, my waking self dragged up from some dark precipice where sleep and death mingled perilously.

But I was alive.

Smoke...

Waves of acrid stench rolled over me and stung my eyes. I coughed, feeling a dull pain in my right side. Everything else was sore, but I noted no sharp discomfort that would indicate more serious injuries from the crash.

We crashed...

And we lived. Or, at least, I had. I looked around and saw only twisted metal and hanging tangles of wire and insulation. My seat still seemed anchored to the cabin floor, and me to it with the seatbelt, but those where my friends had been secured were gone entirely. Just a jagged rupture in the floor to my right remained, precisely where they had been.

Light...

The beam flashed across my face through a hole in the smoke. It was familiar light. Daylight. From the sun. But how could that be? The ash cloud we'd flown into had been total. A blinding blackness.

Blue sky...

I remembered what I'd glimpsed just before the impact. That flash of clear day beyond the windows. Somehow, we'd made it out of the ash cloud. Perhaps we'd just been on its edge when the lightning burst had given the pilots back some modicum of control. Enough, maybe, that they'd been able to guide their dying craft toward clear air.

Another cough. But it wasn't mine. The sound came from somewhere to my right. I released my seatbelt, the angle of the wreckage almost sending me tumbling. I grabbed the seatback to steady myself and rose up, looking back through the thin veil of smoke drifting through what remained of the cabin.

That was when I saw my friends.

They were alive, still belted in their seats as I was. A gentle gust of wind, glorious fresh air, rolled in through the torn fuselage, casting the smoke aside, revealing a glimpse of that wondrous blue sky above.

"Fletch!"

Carter's urgent shout snapped me out of the brief savoring of the clear daylight. I clawed my way through severed cables and buckled floor panels to the spot where my friends were, all secured to their seats, still. All alive, if somewhat stunned.

"Are you all right?" I asked.

Schiavo responded first with a look, her gaze fixed on the AR still strapped across my chest.

"Always ready, Fletch, huh?"

She laughed softly after that, drawing quick breaths of clean air, then turned to Martin.

"I'm fine," he told her, and me. "Better than I expected to be."

Genesee and Carter both unbuckled their seatbelts and stood, crouching below a crushed section of overhead bins.

"No one's hurt?" Genesee asked, almost incredulous.

"I'm okay," Carter said.

Schiavo pulled herself up from her seat and surveyed our surroundings. Small licks of flame burned a few yards forward, and the smoke drifting through the ruptured cabin was almost overwhelming at times, but there seemed no imminent risk of being overtaken by either. Still, this wasn't a place we needed, or wanted, to be.

"Is our gear close?" Schiavo asked.

"I don't see any," Genesee answered, scanning the mangled space.

"Over there," Martin directed, pointing.

Our backpacks and weapons had been tossed about, but remained in the same general area as us, only Martin's AK taking some extra effort to retrieve from the space it had fallen into beneath the shredded cabin floor. Within two minutes we had almost everything back in our possession, minus a few inconsequential items.

One thing, though, was more important than all the rest.

"Do you have it?" I asked Schiavo quietly as the others were occupied gathering our gear.

She checked her shirt pocket and nodded. The code card, the apparent reason for our entire journey, was still in her possession.

"Let's clear out," Schiavo ordered.

We worked our way over buckled floors and broken seats, toward a massive gash where the fuselage had been torn open during our crash landing. Emerging from the wreckage of the aircraft we could see that the once beautiful 747 had been broken into three major sections, not counting the wings which had been ripped fully off as the plane tumbled and came apart, each mangled and mixed with the center section, fuel from internal tanks spilled and blazing.

"That's where we were," Genesee said. "If we hadn't moved aft..."

We would be dead. That reality, which hadn't come to pass, didn't need to be spoken for all of us to realize how fortunate we were.

"The cockpit," Carter said.

I looked and saw that he was pointing to a spot in a dirt field a couple hundred yards from where we stood, near a bend in the highway the pilots had clearly aimed for as some substitute for a runway. The blunt forward end of the aircraft, with its distinctive hump, was still recognizable, even on its side and ripped apart from the fuselage it had left behind in a blazing pile.

"Let's move," Schiavo said.

That we could was a miracle, I thought. But it would take that and then some to believe that the men who'd brought the dying plane down were still alive, considering the damage that was becoming more and more apparent as we crossed the distance to reach the severed front section of the plane. When we reached the twisted and battered nose, it became clear that we would be finding no survivors. Genesee and I climbed atop the wreckage and peered through a yard-wide gash in the aircraft's skin, both of us seeing the same thing—Pedigrew and Handley still belted in their seats, the cockpit compressed around them. There would be no burial for the men who'd saved our lives. Removing them from the tangle of steel and aluminum would be a futile effort. The place where they'd done their best work, served their last full measure, would be their tomb.

The doctor and I climbed down. Neither of us needed to confirm anything. Once again, we were on our own.

* * *

"Does anyone have any idea where we are?" Martin asked.

We'd moved a good half mile from the smoldering wreckage, to a spot in the flat, open expanse of dirt that, at one point, must have been fields of wheat. Or corn. Or some staple vital in nourishing the masses. Now, it was nothing. The last evidence of dead and dried vegetation was long gone, rotted through spring rains and swept away by winter winds.

"Middle America," I said. "East of the Rockies."

"Thanks, Fletch," Martin said, acknowledging my purposely vague estimation. "At least you didn't say 'earth'."

I smiled at my friend's mild jab. But his question was an important one to answer. Before we could decide our direction of travel, it would help to know where we were, hopefully with some specificity. Unfortunately, that wasn't possible.

"We know home is to the west," Genesee said. "Why not just start off in that direction."

Schiavo pointed toward the horizon where the sun was slowly settling lower in the sky.

"A hundred miles that way could be swamp," she said. "Or impassable mountains."

"Wait..."

It was Carter interrupting the discussion, suddenly energized.

"The GPS," he said. "It wouldn't work in the ash, but we're not in the ash anymore."

I'd forgotten about the device provided by the SEALs in Bandon. We all had. Until now. I dug through my pack and found the handheld unit at the bottom.

In pieces.

"Sorry," I said, retrieving what was left of the device, shattered plastic and circuit boards. "It didn't take to that landing too well."

Schiavo didn't dwell on the setback, because we were no worse off than just a moment before.

"All right," she said. "We have a decision to make. Which way do we start walking?"

It was quiet for a moment as those she'd posed the question to pondered what the best answer would be, most, I thought, gravitating toward the obvious choice that Genesee had already voiced.

I had another suggestion entirely.

Twenty Eight

"North," I said.

"What?" Genesee asked, scanning the barren landscape of dead farm fields that surrounded the smoking debris.

"North," I repeated.

Schiavo looked that direction. Hanging in the darkening sky was a still darker cloud, stretching from west to east. Thousands of tons of ash, the volcanic grit that had brought down Air Force One, drifted there, much of it settling to the earth below.

"Fletch, we've done our time in the ash," Schiavo said. "Now I'm not sold on moving due west like Commander Genesee suggests, but I'm less inclined to repeat the past."

"That ash cloud is twenty miles away," I said. "Maybe thirty. We glided from twenty thousand feet. Pedigrew and Handley put us a good distance south of it. Besides, we're not heading north to find home—we're heading north to find the way home."

Schiavo puzzled at my explanation. Carter, though, did not.

"A road," the private said.

"Exactly," I confirmed, nodding. "We head north until we find an east-west road, hopefully a highway with signage, and then we hang a left. There's got to be something substantial between us and the ash cloud."

Schiavo looked north again. In the waning daylight the cloud, with its origins not far from what had become our home, looked more ominous than it possibly was. But it had done damage far and wide, and was due some deference in how we approached it.

"We're losing daylight," Martin said. "At the very least we should get moving and see if there's someplace we can shelter for the night."

"This is farm country," Genesee said. "There's got to be a house or a barn or something within a few miles."

Carter spun slowly, scanning the landscape in every direction. When he was facing us again he drew a breath and shook his head.

"Maybe more than a few miles," the private said.

"All the more reason to get moving," Martin said. "In *some* direction."

Schiavo considered the input for a moment, then looked to me.

"North it is," she said.

I picked my pack up from where I'd rested it on the dry earth and slipped into its straps.

"I'll take lead," I said.

My offer wasn't akin to some soldier volunteering for duty on the point of a tactical column. The chance that we'd face any threat out here was remote. It was my idea, and I felt compelled to be the one at the front of our group, just in case some obstacle presented itself.

* * *

Twenty minutes later, nearly a mile north of the crash site, something did present itself. Not a threat, but the rusted hulk of a car on a what had been a dirt road, its shell rusted and interior empty but for shredded upholstery and empty soda cans. Every window was broken and all four tires were flat.

It did, however, hold some value to us.

"Kansas," Carter said, crouching at the bumper of the abandoned Chevy and brushing dirt off the license plate. "We're in Kansas."

"Or that car drove here from Kansas," Genesee said.

Schiavo, though, wasn't ready to dismiss the information we'd just stumbled upon.

"It's reasonable to assume we're standing in Kansas," she said, looking to me. "But this is just a north-south dirt road."

I nodded and started walking again. Heading north.

* * *

Night came, just a hint of daylight left, the twilight landscape that surrounded us appearing almost unsullied by years of blight. The world looked better in shadow. This part of it, at least.

"A building," Carter said.

He was pointing northeast, his youthfully sharp eyes having spotted the angular shape that was darker than the sky that silhouetted it. A half mile away at most, I thought. I shifted direction and led us there.

* * *

It was a farmhouse, validating Genesee's supposition about the area we'd crashed in. A classic two story home, with a barn out back that had been flattened by years of snow load and lack of maintenance. The structure where we'd chosen to stop for the night had fared better, with nearly half of its windows intact and a collection of furniture which was covered with layers of dust, but still supported our weight as we sat and laid upon it.

"How's your water?" I asked Schiavo.

She shook her head. I handed her the clear bottle from my pack, about half full. She took a sip and handed it back.

"We're not going to find any here," she said.

"No," I agreed.

Just across the living room, Martin had broken up some vintage side tables and had the beginnings of a fire going in the hearth. Genesee and Carter were upstairs, scouting and scavenging.

"We've covered six miles," Schiavo said. "Maybe seven."

I knew that. Glancing behind as we'd walked, when there was still enough light in the sky, I'd been able to make out the smoke column from the crash site until just before Carter had spotted the farmhouse. And in that distance we'd found a dirt road and a car, but no thoroughfare that would lead us west.

"There's something else to consider," Martin said, joining us, the wood blazing in the fireplace now.

"What's that?" Schiavo asked her husband.

"The actual act of crossing half the country on foot," he said, looking to me next. "Fletch has done that, and from what he's shared about it, I don't know how we approach a journey like that."

There was some odd symmetry to the trek he was referencing. The first leg of it, from Bandon to Cheyenne, had begun by plane, then continued when we'd been forced to land after mechanical trouble. Continuing on foot, we almost immediately lost one of our number, Burke Stovich, leaving Elaine, Neil, and I to push on through the wasteland. The return trip from Cheyenne, though, had been what had truly tested us. And almost bested us.

"We put one foot in front of the other," Schiavo said. "That's how we do it. We scavenge and supply ourselves, and we keep moving. If some abandoned bus or pickup truck will start, we'll use that. One way or the other, we're getting home."

Martin didn't doubt his wife at all. And he hadn't been dismissive of our chances to reach Bandon again. He was simply reminding us that we were about to set out on a journey that would require all that we had within us. And maybe more.

"Ma'am," Carter said, coming down the stairs, Genesee right behind.

"What is it, private?"

"I'm pretty sure I see something in the distance," Carter said. "Through binoculars."

"I looked, and I can't see anything," Genesee said, countering the private's restrained excitement.

"There is something there," Carter said, his confidence unshaken. "I'm sure."

"What sort of something?" I asked.

"Some terrain feature," he explained. "Like a low hill. It is hard to make out, but just north of us the ground isn't all flat."

"Are there many hills in Kansas?" Martin wondered aloud.

"There are hills everywhere," Schiavo said.

"Maybe," Martin mostly agreed. "It could just be an aberration in the dark. Your eyes playing tricks on you."

Carter wasn't buying that. And he wasn't backing down.

"Ma'am, permission to go scout that area."

Schiavo thought for only a second on his request, then shook her head.

"In the morning we'll be able to see clearly," she said. "With rested eyes."

Disappointment showed mild upon Carter's face, but the feeling was real. I could see it in his eyes—he really believed that something was out there.

*   *   *

"Fletch…"

I woke to sunlight streaming through the downstairs windows and Martin standing over me.

"Come look at this," he said in a hushed tone.

I brushed the sleep from my eyes and sat up on the couch where I'd drifted off. Across from me, near the fireplace where just embers remained, Schiavo still slept, curled up in an overstuffed chair.

"Where are Carter and Clay?"

"Doc is in a bedroom down the hall," Martin said. "The kid is upstairs standing at the window waiting to say 'I told you so'."

It took only a minute to reach the bedroom upstairs where Carter stood at the window, his gear already packed on the bed he'd slept in.

"I told you I saw something," he said.

Martin smiled at me, the both of us joining Carter at the window, no binoculars necessary to make out what lay in the distance to the north.

"Man made berm," Martin said. "Railroad tracks on top."

"Running east and west," I said, putting a hand on Carter's shoulder. "We're going to start calling you eagle eye."

Martin nodded, smiling as he turned away from the window.

"I'm going to wake the others," he said.

He left the room, Carter right behind with his gear in hand, eager to get to the feature he'd spotted in the dark. I was, as well, but even though I knew it was close to what we'd been looking for, it still meant we'd be on foot, trudging west, low on food and, more importantly, water. And what Martin had referenced the night before, my time trekking from Cheyenne to Bandon, bubbled up again in memory right then as I stared out at the steel rails cutting across the prairie. They seemed to stretch endlessly in both directions, and I remembered the feeling that the road ahead of us would just go on, and on, and on, until we either reached home, or died trying.

This was no different, I was realizing, and the thought of reliving that ordeal was weighing on me. As was the case in that past journey, I had to keep at the forefront of my thoughts what lay at the end of the road. That would keep me going. It had to.

Twenty Nine

We reached the train tracks we'd seen in the distance and stood on the manmade rise that supported them. Without a map, or GPS, or some innate recollection of geography, we could only be reasonably certain, based upon the rusting license plate on an abandoned car which we'd passed, that we were in Kansas.

"West or keep pushing north?" Schiavo wondered aloud, requesting opinions.

To the north, across the flat landscape that bore only a skim of volcanic grit, the dissipating ash cloud still hung thousands of feet in the sky. But there was sky to be seen, blue and beautiful.

"This isn't exactly a road," Genesee said. "Tracks like these can run through the middle of nowhere. Just like they are here. We're bound to hit a real road if we keep pushing north, like Fletch originally said."

The ash cloud had lessened since we'd risen, the event that had created it almost certainly waning. That would match up with what the president had suggested about the west coast clearing somewhat. That was both a blessing and a curse, considering the reported advance of Unified Government forces moving north. Here, though, we had to take it as a sign that our way home might not be fraught with as many environmental obstacles as we'd feared. So, we could continue north in search of a highway.

But that was not what we needed to do, I suddenly realized.

"West," I said.

"Why West?" Schiavo asked.

"Because Colorado is that way," I said.

"Colorado," Schiavo said, realizing where I was going with my suggestion. "Colorado."

"There were Unified Government forces in Colorado," I told those members of our group who hadn't been privy to the president's briefing. "They attacked NORAD."

"There are also Marines on the border," Schiavo said.

"Marines?" Genesee asked. "You're sure about this?"

"The Second Marine Expeditionary Force is holding a position near the border between Kansas and Colorado," I said.

"Second MEF," Genesee said, energized slightly by what he was learning.

"If we can reach the Marines, we have a better shot at getting home," I said. "At the very least they'll have supplies."

Whether they'd be inclined to part with food and water was an open question, but that destination, and the hope it made possible, was our best move. At least to me.

"Tell me you remember the name of the town, Fletch," Schiavo said.

I nodded.

"Colby."

Schiavo scanned the landscape. The tracks appeared to follow a mostly western course ahead, deviating slightly north in the distance. Somewhere along them there had to be a town where we could search for supplies. And information.

"Get us moving, private," Schiavo said.

Carter nodded and began walking, leading us west.

* * *

Two hours later, with the sun rising higher over the parched, windy landscape, Genesee tapped Schiavo on the shoulder.

"We should stop," he said, motioning to Martin.

Schiavo looked to her husband. Our injured friend had kept up, pressing on through pain that he denied, but that was, nonetheless, real. With Carter setting the pace, Martin had been right behind him. When we'd spotted streams near the tracks he was first to hustle down the berm to check the waters, all of which had been very clearly fouled beyond any filtering we were capable of performing.

Now, though, it was obvious that he was hurting, his arm tucked close to his injured side, the bandage that Genesee had continually tended to only capable of doing so much to relieve the discomfort and limitations on his motion. Having survived a violent plane crash hadn't helped his situation any, and yet he was pushing on. Pushing himself.

We had to force a rest.

"Hold up, private," Schiavo said.

I moved forward and handed my water bottle to Martin as he stopped. He eyed the meager contents and waved off the offer. His canteen was dry, as was Schiavo's. Genesee had less than I did, and Carter just a bit more.

"I'm okay," Martin assured me.

"I'd feel better if you took a drink," I told him.

He bent forward, planting his hand on his thighs to rest, and eyed me.

"This stop better not be for me," he said.

A few yards ahead, Carter lowered himself to the tracks, taking a seat on one of the rails.

"We all need a break, Martin," I said, holding the water bottle out to him again. "So just take a swig and get moving again in a bit."

This time he considered the offer, but still hesitated.

"Look," I said, "if you take the drink, your wife's not going to be concerned. If you try to play the superhero, that's going to be exactly what happens."

He knew my logic was unassailable, and finally he straightened and took the container from me, draining about half of what remained in a quick swallow. When he handed it back, I drank what remained, then put the empty back in its pocket on the side of my pack.

"Happy now?" he asked.

"Joyful beyond all description," I told him.

"Ma'am," Carter said.

I looked and saw that he'd moved, from sitting to a position on all fours, one hand planted solidly on one of the thick rails.

"What is it, private?"

"I feel something," Carter said. "The rail is...vibrating."

Schiavo walked to where the young man was hunched over between the tracks, crouching to put her own hand on the rail near his. She held it there, eyes widening just before she bolted upright and looked west, then east.

"I feel something," she said.

"You've gotta be kidding me," Genesee said, scanning the same directions that Schiavo had. "A train? Are you serious?"

I looked to the rails, noticing something that should have been apparent as we walked along them.

"These rails are shiny," I said.

Martin, too, was making the same judgment that I was.

"They should be rusted," he said. "Completely rusted. The only thing that would keep that from happening is..."

Schiavo took a few steps to the east down the tracks and pointed.

"Train wheels," she said, smiling.

Maybe a half mile away and drawing closer at slow speed was the unmistakable blunt front end of a locomotive, its single headlight blazing through the daylight, a shroud of heat shimmer hovering over its throbbing diesels.

"Everyone off the tracks," Schiavo said.

Carter was first to follow her orders, taking a position on the north side of the tracks. Genesee joined him, while Martin and I climbed down the berm to set ourselves on the south side. Schiavo, though, didn't move. She took her M4 in hand and held it low and ready as she faced the oncoming train.

"Angela, what are you doing?" Martin asked.

"Making sure whoever's driving can't miss us," she said.

The sound of the locomotive rose now, and as it passed a slight bend in the tracks we were able to see that it was pulling three cars behind it, two of which were bulbous tank cars.

"Those could be filled with anything," I told Martin, recalling what Major Layton had planned to do with strategically placed tank cars brimming with flammable liquid.

"You think shooting might not be wise?" Martin asked.

"No one's shooting," Schiavo said from atop the berm. "Unless I do."

The train drew nearer, the sound of its engines changing, growling low now, whoever was at the controls throttling down. Its shape and structure also became more defined, and it resembled no ordinary locomotive. Steel plates had been welded around its cab area, with only small slits where wider windshields should be. The front door to the cab, reached by steps that split to both the left and right, was covered by a large slab of rusted steel, with crude hinges attached to one side.

Someone had taken the time to turn the beast into a rolling bunker.

Atop the berm, Schiavo raised her rifle in one hand, holding it over her head, signaling her presence and that she was a friendly. Whether those aboard the train were was an unknow.

"Be ready," Schiavo said. "But keep your weapons down."

She was taking a chance. A big one. And so were we all by heeding her orders. But I suspected that all she was thinking of at that moment was what the train could provide—a way to travel further west. How far we had no idea. But, if things worked as she was planning, we would know soon enough.

The locomotive groaned to a stop, its brakes squealing slightly, the cars in tow stacking up, the couplings between each sounding a racket they came together. The car immediately behind the engine was some sort of modified flat car, I could see now, the business end of a John Deere backhoe fixed to its structure, menacing jaws mounted where a bucket would usually be.

"Hello!" Schiavo shouted.

There was no reply, and it wasn't even certain that anyone within the barricaded cab could have heard her over the idling diesels. But from the side of the tracks where Martin and I stood, I saw movement, and so did my friend. Just a shifting of light and shadow through a vision slit in the makeshift armor on our side.

"Fletch," Martin said.

"Got it," I acknowledged, my finger sliding from just above the trigger to rest upon it, my AR's selector already set to burst. "Be ready to—"

My directive to move right was never fully delivered as a heavy steel plate which covered the locomotive's side window dropped suddenly, folding down on a hinge with a loud CLANG as it slapped against the welded armor below. Behind it, where there should have been glass, there was none, just a bearded face peering out at us.

"What the hell are you's all doing out here?!"

The challenge was directed at Martin and me first, then at Schiavo as the man's head poked fully out the hole where the cab's side window was missing. The surprise of seeing him, of seeing a seemingly whole human being, stuttered any reply we might offer for a moment.

"Are you's all deaf?!" the man asked, chewing on something beyond the hole through his beard. "I ain't got all day!"

"I'm Colonel Angela Schiavo, United States Army. We're low on supplies. Especially water."

The man eyed us for a few seconds, still chewing behind the bush of knotted brown and gray facial hair.

"I's got some water," he finally said. "You's all can have some."

"Good," Schiavo said, then walked straight to the front of the locomotive and climbed the steps, winding past the front armor and along the side until she was standing on the narrow catwalk next to the man. "I'd also like to talk to you."

The man considered this, his attention shifting to the rifle Schiavo held low and casual, in the least threatening manner she could while still being ready. Because the improbable appearance of a working train on the Kansas prairie necessitated at least that modicum of readiness until we were satisfied that the stranger at the controls was no threat to us.

"Talk?"

Schiavo nodded and peered past him into the dim cab. "Are you alone?"

"I am," the man answered through more chewing.

"Are you armed?"

"I sure as hell am," he told her, and all of us, his response loud and proud.

Schiavo smiled at his expression of bravado and independence.

"And do you have a name?"

"I do," the man said.

Thirty

His name was Ivan Heckerford. He told us this, and his life story, while filling our canteens and water bottles from a tank mounted just inside the cramped cab. Schiavo and I remained inside with him while Martin, Genesee, and Carter took positions outside, relaxing on or near the tracks.

"Railroad was a good job, I tell ya," Heckerford said, shifting past Schiavo and me to reach a cabinet high on the cab's back wall. "Layin' rail in the middle of God's country, a man couldn't ask for more than that."

He opened the cabinet and retrieved a clear bottle, some smoky liquid swishing within.

"Good pay," he said, twisting the cap off, the glass spout disappearing through his beard as he took a fast swig. "Good people."

He offered us a drink from the bottle. Both Schiavo and I declined. Heckerford laughed at our hesitance.

"I felt the same when the Salinites offered me some in trade a few months back. But I took a chance and, boy, am I glad I did."

"Salinites?" I asked.

"Salina, Kansas," Heckerford said. "That's what this clan of scavengers there call themselves. Sounds almost biblical, don't it? Salinites."

He smiled and capped the bottle, returning it to its cabinet.

"Said they make it from old dead wood and bone and who knows what else. It sure do hit the spot."

Heckerford plopped himself down in the engineer's seat and swiveled it to face us. As he did I could see behind it, a trio of weapons there—an AR like mine, a Remington pump shotgun, and a compact anti-tank weapon, its tube collapsed but ready for fire in seconds.

"Yeah, I tolds you I was armed," Heckerford said, noticing the attention I was paying to his small arsenal. "You look under this armor you's goona see plenty of scars, I tell ya."

He pointed to the wall of the cab, and to the roof, clear penetrations apparent.

"'Course, that was a while back now," he said. "Ain't many left who try to take what ain't theirs. Ain't many, but there's a few. So I's ready."

He grabbed the shotgun and held it before him like a knight might wield a shield.

"I's ready."

Schiavo nodded at the man and waited while he put the weapon down and faced us again.

"You's all wanted to talk," he said, fixing on Schiavo.

"I do," she said, leaning her M4 against the control panel. "We're traveling to Oregon."

Heckerford burst out laughing, slapping his knees, just a glimpse of yellowed teeth flashing through the mouth hole in his beard.

"There ain't nothin' out there," he said. "That's UG territory."

"You know about the Unified Government," Schiavo said.

"Ah," Heckerford reacted, swatting the air before him dismissively. "The UGs tried to come through the backside here, but they got swatted good by the Salinites. Poisoned them with bad swill. Can you beat that? Ha!"

It was hard to tell if the man was describing an actual move by the Unified Government to bypass any Marine force which might remain in Colby, or if he was recalling some small unit skirmish. In either case, he seemed to have knowledge of both the area, and of its happenings.

"What about the Marines?" I asked.

Heckerford quieted and sat back in his chair, swinging it slowly left and right for a moment.

"You's all know about them?" he asked.

"They're in Colby," I said. "Second MEF."

The man was genuinely surprised that we knew about the military presence in Kansas.

"How do you's all know about them?"

"How far are they from here?" Schiavo asked, cutting of Heckerford's curiosity.

"Not too far," he said, brightening a few seconds later. "I's got an arrangement with them, you know. You see, they all needs gas for their birds."

"They have aircraft?" Schiavo asked.

"Oh, yeah, those big weird looking ones with the propellers that go all which ways. Takes off like a helicopter and flies like a plane."

"Ospreys," I said.

The tilt-rotor aircraft was a primary transport for the Marines. We'd seen them in Skagway, when they'd been tasked with transporting the Edmonton survivors back home. I wondered, as Schiavo did, I was certain, if the Marines in Colby might be accommodating and get us back to Bandon.

"I brings them in the raw crude from some abandoned tanks out by Fort Riley, and they process it right where they's at into whatever those weird whirlybirds fly on."

At home we'd learned to make our own diesel from what a few inland wells produced. Making jet fuel, which is what I assumed the Ospreys ran on, was a whole different animal. But they'd found a way, just as we had. All survivors were part Marine, I thought. Adapting, improvising, and overcoming.

"And they keep you stocked up with MREs," I said, eyeing the collection of empty pouches scattered about the engine's cab.

"Bartering," Heckerford said, beaming through the hole in his salt and pepper beard. "Ain't it a wonderful world?"

Schiavo glanced outside to Martin and Genesee, sitting next to each other on the gravel slope next to the tracks. A few yards away, Carter stood on the tracks just ahead of the train, his M4 held low and ready as he scanned the landscape, his vigilance inspiring.

"You can get us to Colby, then?"

Heckerford shook his head.

"Tracks to Colby are shot. Haven't been able to repair those yet. Been too busy keeping the rails open between Fort Riley and Oakley. The Marines offload what I's carrying into some tanker trucks they have and haul it all up to their base."

Schiavo looked to me.

"If we can get to Oakley," I said.

"They have to take us the rest of the way," she suggested.

"They have to take you," I corrected her.

"They won't know squat about me or...anything, Fletch."

She was right about that. What the president had told her, and given her, could not have been shared with any far-flung outposts. Not in our world. Nor would there be any reason for a unit of Marines in western Kansas to need that information.

"We'll all be going to Colby," Schiavo said, her willingness to suffer through any hesitance at a minimum. "Mr. Heckerford, you'll take us to the fuel convoy at Oakley."

The man ran a hand over his beard where it lay against the front of his shirt, thinking.

"This isn't really a request," Schiavo added when Heckerford didn't immediately respond.

"I's got a good thing going with the Marines," he said.

"And you still will," Schiavo assured him. "I'll let them know I ordered you to take us along."

Heckerford thought for a moment, then smiled through the hole in his beard, a mouthful of stained, broken teeth showing.

"Mission of mercy!" he shouted giddily. "Mission of mercy! That's what it is. That's what I'll tell 'em. I's had to pick you up. Couldn't leave you all to die out here. That's my story."

Schiavo nodded, allowing a smile at the man's exuberance.

* * *

We were underway five minutes later, moving along the tracks at what felt like a snail's pace.

"Gotta keep it under twenty," Heckerford said, scanning the way ahead through the narrow slit in the armor that covered the windshield. "I's gotta be able to stop this baby if the track looks bad."

The side armor had been folded up again, sealing Heckerford and me in the cab as the others rode on the catwalks outside, taking in the sights of the grey prairie like hobos traveling through some apocalyptic landscape. Which, I supposed, we all were to some extent.

"I's got spare rails on my fixer car between us all and the tank cars."

"I saw the crane you rigged up," I told him.

"Snagged that all from a farm back Fort Riley way. Makes gettin' the rails off the fixer pretty easy, but I's still gotta manhandle them into place."

The man flexed his left arm for me, pumping his bicep to an impressive fullness. He was hardened by the landscape and the life, to be sure, and I couldn't truly tell if he was forty or sixty years old. What mattered was that he'd not only survived, but that he'd found a way to be useful.

"Were you an engineer for a long time before the blight?"

Heckerford shook his head as we rolled past a dead town, its flattened and charred buildings barely visible through the vision slit on the side armor.

"I didn't start running this beauty until after it all," he told me. "Just kept the rails up before that. Laid 'em, fixed 'em. But this..."

He reached out and placed his palm gently on the control panel.

"This is in my blood."

We cleared the abandoned town and passed a siding switch that Heckerford warned could be sketchy.

"Fixed that one last week," he said. "But I's gotta fee-ness it a bit still, ya know?"

"Are you from Kansas originally?" I asked.

"No, no, not even close," Heckerford answered. "Up Maine way. That's where I's was born and growed up. My daddy was lobster man. And a mean man, ya know? When I's was fifteen I ran my bee-hind outta there and down to Alabama. That's where I's got started workin' on the railroad. Long time ago. I's just headed out Kansas way when things turned all crazy like after the bug hit."

The blight was that, I knew. A bug, albeit a manmade one.

"Folks here needed movin', so I's moved em. Fired up every engine I came across and drove it until it wouldn't run no more. Then...then I found this beauty right near Fort Riley. That was right abouts the time a Marine patrol came through there lookin' for fuel. A few negotiations, a handshake, and I had's myself a job."

I wondered if Ivan Heckerford realized that he was little different than a pioneer wagon driver, steering a train of mules and supplies across the prairie to far flung outposts. If nothing else, he was an entrepreneur. The world needed more like him.

"You might wanna tell your lady commander that we's fixin' to pull into Oakley just up a piece."

I looked through the slit on my side of the front window and could just make out shapes in the distance. Vehicles and people.

"Will do," I said.

Thirty One

Schiavo was standing at the front of the engine, outside the cab, as we pulled up to the end of the line in Oakley, the rest of us on the catwalks outside the cab. A half dozen Marines were waiting, M-16s up and ready, all aimed directly at her as the short train hissed to a full stop.

"Keep your hands away from your weapon!"

The command came from a lieutenant, shouting past his rifle. Behind him and his men were a trio of tanker trucks, civilian versions that had once delivered fuel to gas stations. Each had been painted a tawny brown, a coating which might have been perfect had the world not up and turned grey. There was no recovery yet in this area. No replanting. Green fields which once had turned brown in winter were little more than endless stretches of dirt that had recently been dusted with a sprinkling of black.

"I'm Colonel Angela Schiavo. I have more people on the train."

As she finished speaking, Heckerford dropped the side armor and stuck his head out.

"Lieutenant Mason! Don't shoot 'em! It's a mission of mercy!"

The lieutenant considered the explanation, then lowered his rifle. His men did not, keeping their weapons zeroed in on Schiavo and the rest of us.

"They's friendly, lieutenant! They's good people! They're not UGs!"

"That's enough, Ivan," the lieutenant said, silencing Heckerford.

"All of what he said is true," Schiavo reiterated. "You're Second MEF?"

The lieutenant nodded, looking past Schiavo, down both sides of the engine, taking stock of the rest of us. He had us outnumbered, almost two to one if the crew of the tanker trucks were taken into account. Those Marines stood nearer those beefy vehicles, sidearms their only weapons, though I suspected each would have rifles in the cabs of their trucks. In any case, we weren't about to start a fight with the very people who could be instrumental in getting us home.

"Are you in command?" Schiavo asked.

I thought her question had a bit of psychology attached to it, some quiet flattery that she might think a lowly lieutenant would be the ranking officer of a sizeable Marine fighting force. In a small way, it appeared to work, the lieutenant shaking his head and slinging his rifle over one shoulder, notching the aggressiveness he'd greeted us with down further still.

"Major James is commander," Mason told her. "Stan James."

"Okay Lieutenant Mason," Schiavo said. "I need you to take us to him."

Mason thought for a moment, then looked back to his troops and motioned to them. Their weapons lowered.

"We've gotta load up here first," he told her. "Should take thirty minutes."

"We appreciate your help, lieutenant," Schiavo said, then waved us forward.

She led Martin, Genesee, and Carter down the steps and off the locomotive. I hung back for a moment.

"Heckerford," I said.

The man poked his head out the window hole and looked to me.

"The west coast isn't Unified Government territory," I said. "Not now, not ever. You ever get out to Oregon, you'll see that."

I held my hand out and up to Heckerford. He reached out and shook it.

"Goodspeed to yous all," the man said.

I moved along the catwalk and down the front steps, a short leap putting me on the gravel bed that supported the tracks.

"Do these guys look friendly to you?" Carter asked me as we walked toward the transport that had accompanied the tanker trucks.

"No," I answered. "They look tired."

There was an exhaustion about each and every one of the Marines we could see, from lieutenant to private. But it was not from any lack of sleep. That sort of tiredness showed in the eyes. This lack of energy I saw in their posture. In their speech. It was more what one might see in a person who'd given up. An expression of futility.

As we watched them transfer oil from the train cars to their own tankers, it became more apparent, at least to me, that the Marines were just going through the motions. They were warriors, it seemed, left out of the war.

* * *

We drank water and washed up in a halved steel barrel the Marines set up for us as the transfer from Heckerford's train progressed, diesel pumps chugging as the thick oil was pulled from the tanker cars. It was more water than we needed, but the clear, cool liquid splashed upon our faces and soaking our shirts felt wonderful. One of Mason's men explained that they had a trio of wells in Colby that produced more water than they needed, and that if they ever received some of the seeds rumored to exist that were immune to the blight, they could turn the whole area into one massive farming operation.

"They're real," Martin told the young corporal. "We've seen them grow."

The corporal nodded, but seemed to draw no joy from what he'd just learned.

"Send some our way if you can," he said. "Everyone else has forgotten about us."

He walked away, leaving Martin and I alone, sitting on a low wall near the transport. Schiavo stood not far away with Genesee and Lieutenant Mason, discussing something that likely involved logistics and possible arrangements to get us home. Carter sat on the ground in the shade of the transport, stripping and cleaning his M4.

"That reminds me," I said, gesturing toward the young private and tapping the AR leaning next to me. "Mine could use some TLC soon."

"Carter is gung ho enough to do yours if you ask him," Martin said.

"You're saying I'm not gung ho?"

"You're just like me, Fletch—a civilian draftee."

It was a peculiar status that had been thrust upon us. No need to wear a uniform, and no desire to do so, yet we fought alongside those who had made that commitment. Ours was conscription by happenstance.

"You know why she's leaning on you, right?" Martin asked.

"What do you mean?"

"You and Angela with the president, with the pilots on Air Force One, with our bearded friend in the train."

I knew she had her reasons. It would have been just as easy for her to have Genesee be her second in the interactions that Martin had just catalogued. But she'd chosen me. I'd suspected it was she wanted a civilian present. Someone who could report back to the Defense Council regarding and decisions she made, or actions she initiated, while we were away from Bandon.

I was wrong.

"She hasn't told me anything that happened with the president," Martin said. "She probably will at some point. Right now, though, she can't be seen using her husband as some civilian adjutant."

"Martin, no one would care if she did that," I said.

"She would," he told me. "She's the straightest arrow I've ever known. Appearances matter to her. She wants to be beyond reproach."

I knew some had faulted her for decisions made during the siege by the Unified Government. She'd even wished she'd handled some things differently, I thought. But there was little to no doubt that whatever Angela Schiavo did, she did for the good of the people she served.

"I know you don't mind, Fletch, but I just wanted you to be clear on why this is your burden as well as hers."

I nodded, understanding more now than I had a few moments ago. Whatever the reasons, I was there for Schiavo. And for Martin. More than ever, even a thousand miles from those I loved the most, I knew how much I was connected to the fabric of people that made up Bandon. I only wished that all who had survived this long after the blight could have what we all had.

Thirty Two

The trip to Colby from Oakley, both towns just off of I-70, took almost exactly an hour, the three vehicle convoy skirting bad patches of highway and navigating piles of abandoned wrecks which had been bulldozed to the shoulder of the interstate. We pulled into the base on the western edge of town, through a control point manned by a pair of bleary-eyed Marines armed with their personal weapons and a machinegun atop a mound of sandbags, barrel resting on its bipod.

A few minutes after we stopped, with the tankers continuing on, presumably to the processing facility the Marines had in place, Lieutenant Mason led the five of us into town. Only Schiavo and I followed the junior officer into what served as the command center for all military activities in the central United States.

Headquarters for the 2nd MEF was an old furniture store, the inventory long ago carried away, leaving just an open space with folding tables and chairs, maps tacked to one wall, and a weary looking Marine standing alone, watching us as Lieutenant Mason led us in.

"Major James, these are the people we radioed about Heckerford picking up."

Mason stepped back as soon as he'd offered the brief and vague introduction. His superior gave a quick nod toward the door and the lieutenant was gone.

"Major Stan James, Second Marine Expeditionary Force," he said, his tone matching the tired posture that made it seem his body was about to slouch to the floor.

"Colonel Angela Schiavo," she said. "This is Eric Fletcher."

"Colonel, Mr. Fletcher, welcome to Colby, jewel of the plains."

There was no discernable sarcasm in the major's voice. I suspected any inflection there might have been had been swallowed by the overt exhaustion that was the man's defining characteristic. Still, it wasn't a physical tiredness, I knew. It came of something deeper. That same thing which had bled down from him to his troops—a complete abandonment of hope.

"We need your help, major," Schiavo said. "You have transport aircraft, I understand."

"I do," the major confirmed.

"Is there enough range in one of them to get us to the coast of Oregon?"

James considered the question he'd been posed, though nothing about his demeanor indicated he was concerned with offering the answer she wanted.

"Colonel, I have two Ospreys. When command planted us here over a year ago, I had eight. Six have either crashed or broken down and been cannibalized to keep what remains flying. Except God only knows what I would fly them for, or where. We haven't so much as sniffed an enemy since we got here."

"Mr. Heckerford told us there was some action in Salina," Schiavo said.

"We heard the same," James said. "Heard. That's all. Apparently some locals did a number on a Unified Government unit trying to flank us. When we went looking after the fact, there wasn't a body or a drag mark left for us to find."

"You've had no contact?" I asked. "None."

"Mr. Fletcher, we get supply drops every six or eight weeks. I'm told they come all the way from Hawaii. We get ammunition, food, equipment from some list a bureaucrat somewhere came up with. No spares for my Ospreys. No replacement Marines. And sure as hell no information on just what it is I'm supposed to do here now that it's clear the enemy doesn't give a damn about this part of the country."

The man wore his frustration on his sleeve, and didn't apologize for it. Under circumstances more normal than this, he would have thought twice about complaining in front of a superior, even one from a different branch. But, like his men, Major Stan James was about at the end of his rope.

"I've got enough supplies to fight World War Three, Mr. Fletcher, if someone somewhere hasn't already done so. But there's no one to fight, and nothing to fight over. I'm not even sure there's anything left to fight for."

Schiavo had heard enough.

"There is, major," she told him. "I assure you of that. There are people, survivors, who would trade what you have for what they have in a heartbeat. You've lost men, major? Well so have I. I didn't ask for the command I've been given, but I'm executing my orders to the best of my ability, and right now those orders come from the President of the United States."

James took that in for a moment, then gave me a quick look.

"I'm supposed to believe this?" James challenged me.

"You don't have much of a choice," I said.

"Right now, major, the enemy you're not facing here is making their way up the California coast toward my area of operations. The president summoned me to a meeting, and now I'm needed back in case our enemy decides to close in on our home."

"Home..."

James spoke the word as if it were some alien utterance. Incomprehensible. Lacking meaning.

"Where is home for you?" he asked.

"Bandon, Oregon," Schiavo answered.

The officer drew a breath and ran a hand over his head, thinking.

"We can put auxiliary tanks in the cabin," he said, thinking aloud. "That would get us there. But unless you have a bunch of JP-Five available in your town, we'd be stuck. And I can't chance that."

"So you need a gas station," Schiavo said.

"I do."

"It just so happens we have one right off our coast," she said. "Unless you mind topping off with Navy gas."

"I can't send a bird that far west without knowing for sure, ma'am," James said.

"Fair enough," Schiavo said. "I presume you have satellite communications capability."

"We do," James confirmed.

"Let's put a call in and reserve you some fuel," Schiavo said.

Thirty Three

Just before dark we walked across a dirt field toward one of the 2nd MEF's serviceable Ospreys, its wings tilted to the vertical, huge propellers spinning at the end of each. Schiavo's call to the *Rushmore* had allowed our trip to happen, and she'd briefed the two pilots, Captain Jules Hogan and Lieutenant Arthur Grendel, on what to expect once we reached our destination, and on a suggested flight route to avoid known concentrations of Unified Government forces. We had a four-and-a-half-hour flight ahead of us, barring any complications.

The first surprise, though, occurred before we'd even taken off.

"Everyone secured?" Major James asked as he came up the aft cargo ramp, pistol strapped across the chest of his flight suit and helmet under one arm.

"Major..."

Schiavo's tone expressed her curiosity at his presence, if not outright confusion.

"This flight needs a crew chief," James explained. "And I'd like to have a few minutes to talk to this admiral who authorized fuel for my bird. Maybe he can give me some answers about this pointless use of resources I'm in charge of."

James slipped into his helmet and plugged into the wireless communications system clipped to his belt and moved past us to the cockpit. The rest of us slipped into headsets wired to the aircraft's intercom. Less than a minute later the major was back, positioned at a panel near the rear of the fuselage. He activated a series of controls and the sloped ramp tipped upward, sealing us in the aircraft as its engines spun up.

"Cabin secure," James reported over his link to the intercom, then took a seat across the cabin, the auxiliary fuel tanks between us.

The aircraft lifted straight into the air, wobbling a bit before its nose swung around, stopping when we were pointing just north of due west, the nose dipping slightly as we began to move forward and accelerate, gaining altitude fast.

"It's unnatural," Genesee said. "First time I flew in one of these I lost my lunch. You think you're in a plane, then it acts like a helicopter."

"Was it a good lunch?" I asked him.

"It was a Navy lunch," Genesee said. "So yes."

Martin laughed, grimacing after the expression. He was hurting, and I wondered if the sense of relief that we were actually going home had finally erased whatever adrenalin reserve his body had tapped into to counter the injury he'd suffered.

I wasn't the only one to notice.

"When we get home," Genesee said, pointing to Martin. "You're on rest in a hospital bed for a few days."

"You're the doc," Martin said, no need to offer any resistance now.

The lights dimmed in the cabin until there was just the bare minimum to move if necessary. James stood again, and headed to the cockpit. I noticed Schiavo watch him, intensely, as if she was pondering some greater truth about the man. Or about something.

"Angela..."

She looked to me, realizing I'd taken in the sight of her interest in the Marine major. She thought for a moment, then unplugged her headset and motioned for me to do the same, shifting the gear so that one of her ears was uncovered. I followed her lead, the pitched roar of the engines immediately surrounding us, making any conversation difficult. Sitting to my left, Schiavo leaned close.

"I'm worried, Fletch."

"About what?"

Just past Schiavo, I could plainly see Martin purposely giver her space. Not paying attention to our exchange. He was living up to the standard she'd set, allowing her to cut him out of her thoughts. For now, at least.

"Everyone we've come in contact with on this excursion has been military. Or beholden to them. Heckerford, MacDowell, they'd be bones by the side of the road if they hadn't hooked up somehow with the guys with guns."

"Or the girls," I said. "You could put me in that category, couldn't you?"

Schiavo shook her head, true concern about her.

"You're not the same. Bandon's not the same, Fletch. I'm talking about a survival structure built entirely around wearing the uniform."

"There are others," I told her.

"I know there are, but they're the ones not getting air drops of supplies. Bandon wouldn't have offloads from the *Rushmore* if I and my guys weren't garrisoned there."

"It's a necessity," I said. "Until things stabilize."

She heard what I said, but couldn't quite accept it.

"We're effectively living in a military dictatorship," she said. "Not under, but *in*. That's what really concerns me. Especially after seeing the pieces of it at every point of our journey. It seems so...normal. But it shouldn't, because what happens when this stability you see coming actually arrives? Do the people like me in uniforms, with the bigger guns, do they step aside and let civilians like you take over again? Do they cede power?"

I hadn't felt any of what Schiavo was stating. No concern at all. To be certain, we were in a world where might ruled, or could rule, if those who wielded it saw fit to impose some will upon others. That was the conflict playing out with the Unified Government right now. As it had played out between me and Major Layton in Whitefish. And between more of us and Borgier.

As those events swirled in my thoughts, I shifted without warning toward the state of worry that Schiavo had adopted. I'd faced off against those who saw themselves as some military strongman. Dictator. Ruler. Was all we were doing to build our world back up going to lead to that exact state of governance by force on a grander scale?

No...

"We're different," I told Schiavo. "We're better than that."

"If the president had thought so he would have given the card in my pocket to Admiral Adamson," Schiavo said. "He fears it, too, Fletch."

I shook my head.

"You, Adamson, Major James, none of you would abuse power. Harker didn't roll his Stryker unit into Bandon instead of rescuing us, and he could have. He could have raised hell with his weapons. Instead, he followed orders. He respected the chain of command. As long as the person at the top has the right mind about things, we'll be okay."

"And if they don't?" Schiavo challenged me.

"Then I imagine enough people in uniform who are just like you will put them in their place."

She considered my expression of confidence for a moment.

"You have a lot of faith in the system that let us all down in the first place," she said.

"No," I corrected her. "Not in the system—in the people. Like you, me, Martin, everyone. Uniform or no uniform."

After a moment Schiavo allowed a small smile.

"We the people..."

"Exactly," I said. "We started right a couple hundred years ago. There's nothing saying we can't do that again. Or even better."

"You really believe that, Fletch?"

I'd had my doubts about many things since the blight appeared. Doubts about my government, my friends, my place in what the world became. Even in myself. But at every turn, things worked out. Not without some heavy price being paid at times, but somehow, because we'd stayed true to something innate in our nature, we'd prevailed.

Right had triumphed.

"I do," I told her. "I absolutely do."

Thirty Four

The choreography had all been worked out in satellite communications with the *Rushmore* before we'd lifted off from Colby, and it was all playing out as discussed.

"I see the strobe," Captain Hogan reported.

He was obviously scanning the terrain through night vision goggles, focusing on a strip of smooth shore just south of town. Peering out a side window with the naked eye, I could not see what he was seeing—an infrared beacon flashing where our landing zone had been prepared. But I knew what it meant—we were almost home.

"We never discussed who's paying for gas?" Major James asked.

"You can bill the admiral," Schiavo said.

That was the plan. A quick stop on the beach to drop us off, and then the Marines would fly their Osprey to where the *Rushmore* had positioned itself offshore. They would land, be refueled, rest for a few hours, and then they would fly halfway across the country and return to their base.

Plans, though, were a luxury in the world as it was. We were all reminded of that just after the Osprey made a picture perfect landing and found Sgt. Lorenzen waiting for us, his expression on the grim side of serious.

"Captain," he said as we exited via the cargo ramp.

"It's Colonel Schiavo now," Genesee told him as he and Carter helped Martin onto the sandy beach.

"What is it, Sergeant?" Schiavo asked.

"We received a message from the *Rushmore* an hour ago," he said. "Admiral Adamson wants to see you immediately."

Lorenzen said no more, but it was clear he hadn't yet told all there was to tell.

"Go on," Schiavo prompted him.

"The *Rushmore* offloaded supplies yesterday, colonel," Lorenzen explained, adapting quickly to Schiavo's new rank. "Including a lot of weaponry."

Schiavo absorbed that as Major James came down the ramp, receiving a salute from the Army sergeant who'd greeted us with troubling news.

"Any idea when our gas station will be here?" the Marine officer asked.

"The *Rushmore* will be on station in an hour," Lorenzen answered.

Schiavo looked to Major James.

"We're going to have to hitch a ride out to the ship with you," she told him, her attention shifting quickly to me.

We...

I nodded at her. We'd made it home, yes, but we weren't done. Not yet. I was still attached to her at the hip. Mostly.

"Go see Elaine and Hope for a bit," Schiavo said.

"Gladly," I said.

* * *

I hitched a ride on the Humvee that had been tasked with taking Genesee and Martin to the hospital. Elaine was waiting just inside the door, alerted by the unmistakable sound of the Osprey a few minutes earlier that we'd arrived.

"That was the longest six hours of my life," she told me after I'd mounted the steps and looked at her through the screen door.

That's when word had reached Bandon that we were coming home, likely relayed by the *Rushmore* after Major

James had contacted the ship. Since then there had been radio silence, leaving everyone, including Elaine, to wonder if we would actually survive the trip across half the country, a thing that had once been so routine as to barely warrant any concern.

There was no more 'routine', though. Not in this new world.

"I took the first flight I could find," I told her, smiling.

She pushed the screen door open and I stepped past it, into our living room, like a neighbor might politely enter one's house. Elaine closed the screen door, then the front door, and came to me, putting her arms around me and laying her head against my chest. But there wasn't only relief in the embrace.

There was dread.

"Something's happening," she said.

The contents of the *Rushmore*'s delivery had sparked worry among those in town. And in my very own home. Elaine eased back from me and waited for some reply.

"I've heard intelligence that the Unified Government forces are on the move in California."

"Is that what this was all about?" Elaine asked. "The president passing on information to Angela?"

I didn't answer immediately, because I knew I couldn't answer truthfully. Or not with the whole truth. I was fully aware that Schiavo would bring Martin into her confidence at some point, but I could not do the same with Elaine. I was not the one who bore the burden that had been given to Schiavo in the guise of responsibility. What I'd been privy to I had to keep to myself.

Elaine, though, read into the silence precisely what I wanted to withhold—that there was more to what had happened. To what had been shared. Much more.

"Are we at war again?" she asked me.

"I honestly don't know," I said.

I also didn't know how long I had with my wife, and our daughter, before I would have to depart again, to do what was necessary to keep them safe. To keep everyone safe.

"Is Hope asleep?"

Elaine nodded.

"We can wake her," she told me. "You're reason enough to mess up her sleep schedule."

"We don't have to wake her," I said. "I just want to see her."

My wife took my hand and led me down the hall. We entered our daughter's room together and stood over her crib in the dark, watching our little girl sleep.

* * *

Thirty minutes later, as Elaine and I sat in the living room, holding each other on the couch, the time came.

There was no knock on the door. We both looked up and saw Schiavo, standing just past the threshold with the doorknob in one hand.

"Fletch," Schiavo said, a weary look of déjà vu about her. "It's time."

I'd spent ten minutes just staring at my daughter in the dark of her bedroom, and twice that much with my wife, hardly speaking a word. Neither of us knew with any specificity just what it was we might be facing as a town, but something was in the air. Something different. There was a sense of...finality. I didn't know how to describe it other than that.

"I'm ready," I said.

Elaine stood before I did and faced Schiavo, her posture almost challenging.

"Just don't leave me in the dark," Elaine said. "Please. Not knowing what was going on after he left with Clay was...hell. No matter what it is, I have to know what he's doing. All right?"

Schiavo didn't hesitate for a second, nodding to my wife's request that was verging on begging.

"I'll tell you myself," Schiavo promised. "You have my word."

I kissed Elaine on the cheek and grabbed my gear, leaving her once again. When Schiavo and I were in the Humvee, she glanced to me as she drove us back toward the beach where the Osprey would be waiting.

"I don't have a good feeling about this, Fletch."

"I don't, either."

She said no more, and neither did I, the short trip to the Osprey made in silence. Once aboard, we kept to ourselves, and as the awkward aircraft rose from the shore and sped low over the ocean, the quiet persisted, as if we were savoring some last bit of peace before a storm blew in.

Thirty Five

"They're moving," Admiral Lionel Adamson said once Schiavo and I were alone with him in his quarters. "Heading north."

There was no doubt as to whom he was referring—the Unified Government forces. We'd returned from Ohio by way of Kansas having been told of their position near the border with California. Now, apparently, the march they'd begun toward Bandon had resumed. They were coming to finish what they hadn't been able to during their previous siege of the town.

"Any estimation of their size?" Schiavo asked.

"Eight hundred to a thousand," the admiral answered.

The number, which would have hardly elicited worry in the military of the old world, was greeted with stunned silence. Their numbers had swelled since retreating from Bandon, taking on conscripts and volunteers after their conquest of Yuma, and then San Diego, and any other groups of survivors they'd steamrolled in between.

And now they were coming for us once again.

"I know," the admiral said.

"A thousand?" Schiavo pressed, seeking to truly confirm the size of the force moving north. "Actual fighting troops?"

"Yes," Adamson said. "Plus vehicles. Including a pair of Abrams tanks."

"Armor," I said, speaking the word as if marking the instruments of our defeat. "Even with what was offloaded, we can't stop that size of a force with armor support."

"Be thankful they have no air support," Adamson said. "It appears they shot their wad in that category with the drones they used on you before."

Schiavo considered the intelligence she'd been given, processing it as a military mind would. Weighing odds. Strategies. Tactics.

"Do you know where they are now?" she asked.

"The SEALs took their boat to observe from offshore," Adamson said. "They reported upon return that the entire force stopped just short of Pistol River for the night. But you can assume they will be moving again by dawn."

"Pistol River," I said, looking to Schiavo. "That's sixty miles."

She looked to me now, sensing where I was going with the fact of distance I'd just brought up.

"That has to be a safe distance," I said.

Adamson took in the exchange between us, clearly not from a place of ignorance.

"It will be zero three hundred in two hours," the Admiral said. "Your boomer will be listening."

As the president had told Schiavo, a ballistic missile submarine, or boomer, would monitor a specific frequency at the three o'clock hour each day, both a.m. and p.m. A radio message to it, with a clear target of Pistol River, would bring an end to the Unified Government forces on the west coast, just as it was hoped the president's forces had done to the enemy in Columbus. We were without confirmation that the latter had happened, but it was more than possible, and equally justified, that a nuclear hell could be unleashed in our part of the world.

"Sixty miles," Schiavo said, mostly to herself, it seemed. "What if that's not safe? What if there's fallout?"

"We don't have enough to fight them," I reminded Schiavo.

That wasn't a disputed fact, I knew. But she looked to the admiral for some chance that the odds might be turned.

"Do you have anyone you can let us have?" she asked. "SEALs, sailors, anyone who can shoot."

Adamson shook his head slowly, some true regret in the gesture.

"Colonel Schiavo, I have a skeleton crew," he said. "And with the damage we suffered during our encounter with the Unified Government flotilla on our way from Hawaii, I need every man and woman I've got just to keep the *Rushmore* seaworthy."

She had no choice but to accept what Adamson was telling her.

"There's no real option here," I told Schiavo. "And no time to waste. Every mile closer to Bandon they get, the more chance there is that we'll be affected by any blast or aftereffects."

"Aftereffects," she parroted. "That's a sanitized term that may not accurately reflect what happens if I do what you want me to do."

"I don't want you to do anything," I said. "But do you see any alternative?"

It seemed to me right then that she began to shake her head, but reconsidered. Her gaze almost snapped to Admiral Adamson.

"Do you have a map of the coast?"

"Yes, colonel, I do."

* * *

A few minutes later we were in the *Rushmore*'s combat control center. Where displays had once glowed with trained crewman monitoring each, only a few were lit up, displaying the most basic navigational information for the three sailors tasked with monitoring the stations. On a plotting table attached to one wall, Adamson spread a map, lines of terrain contours snaking across the colored landscape. Rivers coursed toward the Pacific, thin and blue. Towns were mixtures of criss-crossing avenues and bold names identifying each small burg.

Schiavo, though, was looking for something more specific.

"Bridges," she said, pointing to several that spanned the Rogue River. "They'll already be past the Pistol River by the time we could mount a defense, but if we move now we can blow these spans over the Rogue."

"They could still get troops across on boats," I told her. "They'd have to leave their armor and transport behind. That would slow them down."

"I'm not interested in slowing them down," she said. "I'm interested in destroying them. This has to be it. We can't look to a future where conflict is perpetual. This has to end. *They* have to be ended."

She had the power to wipe the Unified Government force off the face of the blighted earth in a small card tucked in her shirt pocket. Instead she was envisioning some other method of defense, or offense, which would crush the Unified Government forces. I wasn't seeing it.

Neither was Admiral Adamson.

"Colonel, they can just swing further east until they reach another crossing. Or another. You can't blow every bridge."

"We won't need to," she said, explaining her plan to the admiral and me over the next few minutes.

"There's a lot of bluff and choreography involved," Adamson said. "And timing."

"Timing is key," she agreed. "Which means I need the Osprey. We have to move assets to multiple locations miles from Bandon. And we have to start now."

Adamson thought for a moment. He had the authority to keep the Osprey and its crew here, and to engage them in the fight to come. Doing so, however, would put at risk an aircraft which had been assigned to block the Unified Government forces from moving east from the Rockies.

That fight, though, hadn't materialized, and was only a remote possibility going forward. This fight, here, was going to happen.

"You've got it, Colonel Schiavo."

* * *

Major James never had his few minutes with the admiral to discuss the situation in Kansas. Instead, Schiavo briefed him aboard the Osprey after we'd taken off from the *Rushmore* with the aircraft's cabin stripped of the auxiliary fuel cells which had made the cross-country trip possible. In Colby, when we'd first met the Marine officer, he'd looked the part of a worn-out fighter. A man longing for rest and respite from continually waiting for battle.

As it turned out, our estimation of the man had been wrong.

"A real fight," Major James said, quiet disbelief in his words.

"Yes," Schiavo confirmed.

The Marine thought for a moment, adjusting the microphone of his headset closer to his mouth, as if he wanted to make sure that what he was about to say was not misinterpreted.

"Colonel, I was trained to fight. It was drilled into me starting in boot camp that a Marine should be prepared to kill anything and anyone it sees. But since the world went to hell, I haven't seen an enemy worth killing. I've stared across prairies and mountains waiting for the war my men and I were told was coming. Waiting has been my assignment, Colonel Schiavo, and I'm tired of waiting. You just tell me where my crew and I can help, and we'll be there."

Schiavo smiled at the very lucid representation of what being *gung ho* truly meant.

"Thank you, major," Schiavo said.

Major James stood, heading forward, presumably to brief his pilots. Three Marines. That was the addition to our force. Them and their aircraft. Stowed just aft of us against the fuselage was one more thing they could bring to the coming fight—a minigun. The multi-barreled weapon could spit thousands of 7.62 millimeter rounds per minute from its mount on the cargo ramp. From his reaction, and the limited crew options, I had no doubt which Marine would be operating it, harnessed to a hardpoint on the floor, raining fire from the tail end of the aircraft.

"We're going to need help, Fletch."

"Camas Valley," I said, knowing that Schiavo had to be thinking the same thing. "Your push for an alliance looks like it's going to pay off."

She nodded, though there was uncertainty in the gesture.

"They're just part of the puzzle," Schiavo said. "Every piece has to fall into place at the right time for all this to work."

Timing...

Admiral Adamson had noted that critical component of Schiavo's plan to defeat the Unified Government forces. To wipe them out, once and for all, without using the terrible weapons at her disposal.

"As soon as we land, get someone out to Camas Valley to brief Dalton," Schiavo told me. "They'll have to move fast. Have them tell him that we'll pick them up. We'll need twelve shooters from him."

"I'll get Dave Arndt on it," I said. "He drives like a maniac."

The drive to Camas Valley, on good roads with no impediments, would normally take just over an hour. If the ash fall wasn't any more severe than what Genesee and I had experienced when passing through just days earlier, then the trip, with luck, might be made in two.

"I'm going to need you, Fletch," Schiavo said.

"I know."

"Martin will join us," she said. "Only because..."

"Because he'll refuse to stay in the hospital to recuperate," I said, completing the statement of fact for her. "Who else will you want?"

She scanned the Osprey's cabin. Empty as it was, it was not cavernous by any measure. The forces it could transport were limited.

"You and Martin, and my people," she said. "That's it."

I thought for a moment on what she had just said. It wasn't that I'd expected the numbers she'd indicated to be different, but the reality of what we were about to attempt based upon our limited resources was, in the most generous terms, daunting.

"That's twenty people," I said. "Plus three Marines and this aircraft."

"Against a thousand enemy with armor," she said. "I know."

Again, I thought of timing, and how that was, in many ways, the only part of her plan that really mattered. Without it, the Unified Government forces would eventually roll over us.

"Once I get Dave headed out to Camas Valley, what do you need me to do?"

"I need you to go to the library," she said.

At first I thought, for some reason, she'd decided to insert some joke into the very sobering moment. But she hadn't.

"The library?"

She nodded. Bandon's library was small in comparison to what had existed in most towns and cities before the blight, but it had one advantage over those repositories of literature and knowledge—it still existed. Because of the town's viability throughout the worldwide chaos, its library hadn't been looted and vandalized. The computers once connected to the internet sat unused, but the shelves brimmed with books and magazines of all kinds. The reason why Schiavo wanted me to venture there, though, eluded me.

"Yes," she confirmed. "I want you to find everything you can on the Johnstown Flood."

The event was only vaguely familiar, a historical morsel from some junior high class where I'd learned about the deadly disaster. Quickly, though, I understood why she was sending me on this errand. And what she hoped to learn from it.

"Speed," I said.

Schiavo nodded.

"Exactly."

Thirty Six

Sergeant Lorenzen supervised the loading of the Marine aircraft. An 81 millimeter mortar with four dozen rounds. Light machine guns with thousands of rounds.

And explosives. Demolition charges, to be exact. Enough to blow a bridge, and triple that amount for the big show far up river.

"I know you'd rather be with us," Schiavo told her husband. "But I need you with Dalton's people at the first bridge."

Martin might have resisted that order, but he didn't. A job needed to be done, and, in her mind, he was physically compromised. Operating the mortar from a stationary position was something he could reasonably be expected to do. Dalton's people would be tasked with blowing the bridge over the Rogue River at Gold Beach, all while presenting a defensive force meant to appear much larger than a baker's dozen. That would involve movement of small units, two people at times, from firing position to firing position.

"You've got to keep that mortar in action," she told him.

Martin had received a fifteen-minute crash course in use of the portable artillery piece from Corporal Enderson. Operation of the weapon was relatively simple, but targeting took both science and finesse.

"Manage your ammunition," she reminded him. "Walk the rounds east when they move inland."

"If they move inland," Martin said.

"They'll have no choice," Schiavo told him. "They see this as the decisive battle as much as we do. They're not pulling back. Just keep the pressure on them to move and kill as many as you can."

Kill...

The first action of this final battle might kill some enemy, but not enough. Degrading their numbers was only a secondary goal to blocking their advance along the coastal route. They had to move inland to the next bridge across the Rogue River. That was the only logical course they could take, and it was a lynchpin of Schiavo's plan.

"We'll send them on the run," Martin assured her.

He left Schiavo and me, joining Lorenzen and the rest of the garrison as they worked to finish loading the supplies as the clock ticked toward midnight.

"Dave will be there by now," I said.

Schiavo nodded, confident in that part of the plan. Dalton had proven himself to be a reliable, if wary, ally. He'd saved my life and ended Olin's. He would be among the dozen we'd requested to join us in battle, particularly if he grasped the finality of what we were about to attempt.

"Dalton will have his shooters ready," she said. "He'll—"

The Osprey' rotors spun up, whirling fast above the hard-packed sand, kicking up the last bit of ash which the tide hadn't yet washed out to sea. It was near impossible to hear anything now, but I didn't need to to notice the surprise washing over Schiavo's face. Surprise that had interrupted her.

"What's wrong?"

She didn't bother trying to answer my question, gesturing with a nod, instead. Motioning behind me. I turned and instantly understood what had given her pause.

Elaine was walking toward us, geared up, her MP5 strapped across the front of her vest and an M4 slung behind.

"What are you doing?" I challenged her.

She shook her head and pointed to her ear, half a smile added to the pantomime for effect. I put my hand on her back and guided her away from the waiting transport, far enough that some semblance of a conversation would be possible.

"What do you think you're doing?"

"I pumped enough milk for two days," my wife told me, sidestepping the direct question I'd posed. "There's always formula if that's not enough."

"Elaine, what are you—"

"Grace is going to watch Hope for us," she continued. "She has Krista to help, and every wannabe grandmother in town is itching to pitch in."

While I'd been at the library, Schiavo had very clearly followed through on her promise to Elaine, and I'd known innately upon first sight of her walking across the sand what her intent was. Hearing it, though, laid out through all the planning she'd instituted to make it happen, made it terrifyingly real.

"You're coming," I said.

"I am."

I took a breath. Behind us, Schiavo and every member of her garrison were readying themselves to board the Osprey. After a short hop to Camas Valley, Dalton and another eleven fighters would join us, if Dave Arndt's midnight race to inform them of the coming threat had been successful. With Martin and me, we'd planned this last chance defense to work with a force of twenty.

Now it would be twenty-one.

"Elaine, just for a minute, consider what you're doing."

"I have. Just like you have. If you fail, we're finished. Any chance for our daughter is finished. So my place is with you, trying to prevent that."

"And if something happens to both of us?" I challenged her.

"Then it will happen because we were doing what had to be done," she answered.

I could have fought her on her decision, but not on her reasoning, just as Schiavo might have tried to dissuade Martin, but had chosen not to.

"You're a hell of a woman, Elaine," I said.

"Good thing I married a hell of a man," she replied.

Behind us, Schiavo shouted that it was time to mount up.

"There may not be time for this later," I said, then pulled Elaine close, kissing her, too briefly for either of us.

She eased back from me, smiling.

"Let's go."

Elaine stepped past me and headed for the Osprey. I looked to the beach road, no throngs of residents there to send us off in the dead of night. Most were sleeping, or making preparations for another siege, one that would end far differently than the previous one when we'd driven off the Unified Government forces. I suspected that was why Schiavo hadn't called for a larger defensive force to be mustered from the civilian populace. She knew that if those of us about to set out on a mission to stop our enemy couldn't succeed, throwing a few hundred more armed civilians into the fray would not make a difference. Not against what they would face.

"Fifty to one," I said to myself.

Those were the rough odds. A handful more than twenty against a thousand troops and armor. I didn't know if there was any historical equivalence to match our situation, one where a force as outnumbered as we were had prevailed over their enemy.

Fifty to one...
I thought on that, without giving it voice again, as I followed my wife and boarded the Marine aircraft.

Thirty Seven

The flight to Camas Valley took fifteen minutes from takeoff to touchdown. Dave Arndt was waiting in a clearing just outside town, waving a road flare to guide us in. Loading Dalton, and Lo, and ten other fighters was accomplished in under two minutes before we lifted off once again and headed almost due south, the Osprey's rotors tilting forward once we were at altitude and speeding us toward our first destination.

Speed...

That was the key now. The speed with which we could reach our objectives and secure them. The speed with which the Unified Government forces would move. And, most importantly, the speed of raging waters.

"What's wrong?"

Elaine asked me directly, slipping out of the headset which tied us into the Osprey's intercom. She'd noticed the pad of paper on my lap. I'd removed it from my pocket, where I'd tucked it after poring over descriptions and numbers at the library, condensing the scant information there'd been about the Johnstown Flood to a scribble of calculations.

"Any one of these could be wrong," I said, removing my headset and pointing to the mix of equations I'd used to figure what Schiavo needed. "These aren't lengths of pipe or yards of concrete. I'm out of my element with this kind of math."

"You've done your best," she said.

I nodded, knowing that to be true. But there was no way to know the most important thing right now—whether my best was good enough.

* * *

"First drop off coming up," Captain Hogan reported from the cockpit.

The Osprey slowed, and the whine of its engine nacelles beginning to rotate rose, the large rotors at each end of the wings gently shifting from the mode that allowed swift forward flight to that which made a vertical landing and takeoff possible.

"Lieutenant, once we're down make your way aft to help me mount the minigun," Major James instructed through his headset.

"Yes sir," Lieutenant Grendel, the Osprey's copilot, acknowledged.

The oddly magnificent aircraft slowed further, settling toward the dark earth, just a hint of light from the half-moon filtering through scattered clouds and wisps of dark ash still dissipating in the atmosphere. But it was enough light to reveal what lay just aft of the Osprey as it touched down and its ramp lowered.

Water. A vast swath of it spreading out toward hills that contained it naturally, and what man had constructed to tame it on one side.

The William L. Jess Dam. A forty plus year old structure that formed Lost Creek Lake, capturing the waters of the Rogue River and releasing its bounty into the same, which flowed toward the coast and spilled into the Pacific at Gold Beach some ninety miles distant as the crow flies, and much more than that when accounting for the circuitous route followed by the river.

"It's topping the dam," Lorenzen said, scanning the lake as he slung demolition charges over his shoulder.

He was right. The lake was brimming, its excess spilling over the top of the structure which had created it. Excess snowmelt brought on by the ashfall to the north, or simple lack of maintenance, could account for it exceeding its designed capacity. What that meant to our plans, to my part of it in particular, I didn't know. Would more volume increase the speed of the outflow once the damn was breached? Would it have the opposite effect, creating some turbulence as the waters raced downstream, choking itself in narrow canyons?

"It might not be very stable, Paul," I told the sergeant.

He continued grabbing demo charges, as did Carter Laws. This would be their part of the plan, laying explosives which would destroy the dam, freeing the waters of Lost Creek Lake to race down the Rogue River and wipe out the Unified Government forces as they tried to cross upstream after having found the span at Gold Beach demolished.

"How long do we wait?" Lorenzen asked me.

That was my contribution to what Schiavo had conceived—timing the flow that would race down the river to intercept the Unified Government forces when they reached the secondary bridge in a narrow gorge. My uneducated calculations, based on historical flow rates of past disasters, said the torrent would reach that point in roughly fourteen hours.

Fourteen hours.

In that span of time, everything on our end had to go right. Everything.

"Do it as soon as you're set," I told Lorenzen.

He nodded and motioned for the young private he'd trained just weeks earlier.

"We'll see you in a while, sergeant," Schiavo said.

The demolition team exited down the ramp and jogged with their heavy load of explosives and personal gear onto the dam, their boots slapping through ankle high water pouring over. As soon as they were off, Major James and

Lieutenant Grendel mounted the minigun to a hardpoint on the aft ramp, connecting it to power and a large magazine box which would feed deadly rounds into the weapon.

"We're on the clock," James said as he clipped his tether to a point on the metal floor and sat behind the minigun, straddling it. "Let's move."

Grendel raced forward, the Osprey lifting off again just seconds after the co-pilot returned to the cockpit. If all went as planned, the aircraft would return after two more stops to retrieve Sergeant Lorenzen and Private Laws. By that time, the dam should be blown, and much of the contents of Lost Creek Lake should be racing toward the coast.

Should...

There was a lot of 'should' in our plan. And a lot of 'must' required to make it all work.

"Who dreamed this up?" Dalton asked from across the cabin, his fighters from Camas Valley seated to either side of him.

"I did," Schiavo told him.

Dalton thought on that for a moment.

"So far your ideas seem to work out," he said. "Otherwise my people wouldn't be here."

He smiled at her in the dim cabin as we turned west and headed for the coast.

Thirty Eight

Dawn was breaking as we reached the coast and turned south, the Osprey descending to land on a low hill overlooking Wedderburn Bridge.

"Second drop," the pilot announced as the Osprey settled to the earth atop the rise.

"Here we go," Martin said.

He stood and shouldered his gear, Schiavo reaching out to take hold of his hand before he was too far from her.

"I'll see you in a while," she said.

He nodded and ignored any sense of impropriety, leaning close to kiss his wife. She didn't resist, and, for the first time since I'd known her, willingly let her personal and professional selves come together in a public display. The embrace, though, did not last. It could not. Martin eased back and reached for a pair of packaged mortar rounds. Other hands seized the ammunition before he could.

"We've got it," Dalton said.

His people, in addition to their own weapons, hauled the 81 mm mortar and its 48 rounds of ammo down the ramp and off the Osprey, along with a trio of vintage M60 machine guns that had come ashore from the *Rushmore*. We were, in essence, unloading an augmented squad of fighters to stop the advance of a thousand enemy and force them to turn inland.

Inland was the key. With the Wedderburn Bridge blown, and with fire raining down upon them from the north side of the Rogue River, the Unified Government forces, if they wished to continue their advance, would have to move away from the coast to the next usable bridge upstream. That span across the Rogue at Lobster Creek would be where Elaine and I would be, with Schiavo, Westin, Hart, and Enderson. The six of us would have to keep our enemy at bay until the floodwaters reached that crossing point.

"Remember the procedures," Enderson told Martin. "Dalton has Lo calling out targets for you."

"You'll be behind the hill," Schiavo told her husband. "Stay there."

"You don't need to see what you're shooting at," Enderson reminded his pupil.

Martin, though, knew that more than instructions were being given to him, particularly from his wife. His place, in their mind, was out of the line of fire. Safe behind the hill while others exposed themselves along the shore of the Rogue River.

"When my rounds are complete, I'm not hiding," Martin said, fixing directly on his wife next. "You know that, right?"

She nodded. Martin Jay, savior of Bandon in many ways, was not going to let others bear all the risk to keep the town, his town, safe.

"Good luck," I said.

Martin gave me a quick tap on the shoulder and followed the last of Dalton's people off the Osprey. Within a minute we were airborne again, skimming the hilltops, heading northeast.

"We're going to get you as close as we can," Captain Hogan told us over the intercom. "If the mapping is still correct, that might be a beach on the south side of the river."

"Not a problem," Schiavo told him.

"You don't do anything heroic, okay?" I said, looking to my wife.

"Because you won't?"

It was a challenge neither of us could live down to. She would do whatever was necessary to see that our part of this mission was successful, just as I would. But we would be doing so apart.

"I don't want to see either of you within fifty yards of each other until the shooting stops," Schiavo admonished us. "Is that clear?"

We would be landing in just minutes. And once there, Elaine and I would be split up. That was by design, and insistence. Schiavo's insistence. That was the only way she'd allowed my wife to join the mission. Should something happen, the woman who'd conceived this operation didn't want it on her conscience that we'd be leaving an orphan behind.

"Opposite sides of valley," I promised her.

"Opposite sides," Elaine parroted, agreeing.

Schiavo gave us a nod. I looked past her, and past Major James and his minigun, catching a glimpse of the river just to the south. The waters, even without the catastrophic flow from Lost Creek Lake, were raging. Whatever beach the pilots hoped to put us in at was going to be inundated.

"You're gonna get wet," Captain Hogan warned us, as if on cue. "Beach is swamped."

"And the bridge?" Schiavo asked.

"Intact," he told her. "But it's taking a beating."

"Flashes to the west," Major James reported. "Big ones."

We all knew what that meant—the battle at Gold Beach was underway.

"It's too soon," Elaine said. "They couldn't have blown the bridge yet."

"Major," Schiavo said into her headset, and James turned from his position on the ramp to face her. "Once we're dropped off, get this bird back to the beach and assist there if necessary."

"Your men at the dam are going to get awful lonely," he said.

"They can wait," Schiavo said. "Destroying that bridge can't."

"Will do," James assured her.

Lorenzen and Carter, who by now had performed their task and, hopefully, destroyed the dam, would be in the dark as to why their ride would be absent. They might assume the worst, that it, and all of us, had gone down due to enemy fire, or that we'd simply crashed. A complete radio blackout was being enforced to prevent the Unified Government forces from gleaning any clue as to our actions, leaving them further in the dark.

"Twenty seconds," Captain Hogan said.

The six of us stood and took handholds as the Osprey slowed and settled into a hover just above the sloshing waters near the shore. We grabbed our gear, two squad automatic weapons and a pair of anti-tank rockets, then hustled down the ramp. It was a two-foot leap to the water from the hovering Osprey, and I was the first to make it, the water swallowing me to the waist by the time my boots hit the sandy bottom. Looking past the nose of the Osprey I could see the bridge and started to move ashore at an angle, closing the distance to the span with the current threatening to topple me. I heard multiple splashes behind, the rest of our team clearing the ramp, the rotors above and behind me now as the engines accelerated, lifting the grey aircraft higher between the hills. It banked left and soared over the rocky terrain to the north, disappearing behind it as it made its way back to the beach.

"Let's get across that thing before it collapses," Schiavo said.

The span, under assault by the unusually high flow, was holding, but there was no guarantee that it would. If it failed before the Unified Government forces reached it, they would likely move further upstream to the next bridge. Crossing that before the floodwaters came would render our entire operation pointless. Bandon would be lost.

But we had no control over this bridge at Lobster Creek. All we could do was execute the plan as it existed now. And hope.

We climbed the soggy bank of the river and found the road, its surface rutted by years of weathering and lack of maintenance. But it was easily passable. The enemy forces we expected would have no trouble traversing it to reach the bridge. Nor would their armor.

"Fletch," Schiavo said as we moved quickly along the road. "Look."

She pointed across the river, to the spot just east of the bridge where she, Private Westin, and I would take up positions.

"There's not as much cover as I expected," she said.

"We may need to shift more to the east," I said.

"I agree," Schiavo said, then looked to the garrison's medic. "Hart, Westin is going to take your assignment on the west side. You're going to be our scout."

"Scout, ma'am?"

The bridge was just ahead now, water thundering beneath it, kicking a spray up off the supports. Schiavo pointed past it, to a spot on the far side at the crest of the lowest hill downstream.

"You find cover there," she directed. "First sign of the enemy, you fire a warning. Two shots if infantry is in the lead, three if their armor is up front. You fall back then and join up with the western element."

I saw Hart react to that visibly, with uncertainty.

"Ma'am, that will leave just you and Fletch on the east," he reminded her.

"We'll be fine," she said. "I don't want you crossing the road if they're already at the bridge. I want you in action from cover. Understood?"

"Yes, ma'am," Hart said, then jogged up ahead of us, making it to the far side of the bridge just as we reached it.

"Fletch, we're taking both anti-tank weapons," Schiavo said.

She already had one of the AT-4 disposable launchers on her shoulder. I took the other from Elaine as we ran. The western element that she was assigned to would now be four strong, and would have both light machine guns, leaving Schiavo and me to deal with any armor that reached the bridge.

"If we—"

I never got the chance to offer my suggestion as to placement of the rockets we both carried. As we reached the mid-point of the bridge, a deep, concussive *THUD* rolled up the gorge, louder for a few seconds than the thundering torrents below us. We slowed, but didn't stop.

"That came from downstream," Enderson said.

"They blew the bridge," I said.

The sound could only have come from a massive detonation. Something large enough to echo this far up river.

"How long do we have?" I asked.

Schiavo had already considered most of the timing questions. But she took a moment now as we reached the northern end of the bridge and paused, stopping our progress.

"They won't all be together," she said. "The first units to reach the bridge at Gold Beach would be scouting elements."

The flashes Major James had seen from the back of the Osprey had been those reconnaissance troops probing ahead of the enemy's main force. This was Schiavo's working theory, and, even to a person lacking her tactical knowledge, it made perfect sense. Assuming that General Weatherly was still in command of the Unified Government forces, we could expect that he would carry out this operation as expertly as he had executed the siege of Bandon. An operation that had almost seen us defeated.

"It will take a while to maneuver everyone through town and to the river road," Schiavo continued.

"If Dalton is keeping the fire up, that will slow them down," Enderson said, shifting the weight of the SAW from one shoulder to the other.

"That mortar could really bottle them up if it hits them before they can regroup," Westin added.

Martin's part in the operation at Gold Beach was vital, but his ammunition was limited, as was his skill at operating the weapon and the indirect fire it delivered. If he could put even a half dozen rounds ahead of the main body as it turned to follow the river inland, that could slow them significantly, and reduce the time we would have to hold them off.

Schiavo, though, knew things were moving more quickly than she'd anticipated.

"We could have a four-hour fight on our hands," she said.

"Four hours?" Elaine asked, not sure how to imagine that.

Schiavo nodded and looked to the hills above the bridge, a road splitting off from it to follow the norther shore both west and east, and a smaller, narrower lane winding into what had once been lush forest directly north.

"We'll have decent cover against the infantry," Schiavo said. "Good fields of fire. But the armor..."

"If that even gets close to the bridge," Westin said.

"If the tanks get close," Schiavo said. "We stop them."

She looked to me. That was our task, each of us armed with an AT-4. One for each Abrams that might reach the bridge.

"We stop them," I agreed.

Schiavo nodded. Not at my words, nor at any confidence that she perceived, but at my commitment to the mission. In a very real sense, it was do or die.

"All right," she said. "Let's get in position."

Thirty Nine

The fate of the battle had yet to be determined. For the moment, we were just spectators waiting for it to unfold. To play our part and take up arms, which would be necessary. On our own we could not defeat the enemy surely to come our way, but we could, with some luck, hold them off until the weapon our absent friends had already unleashed at Lost Creek Lake roared down the gorge.

And if all went as planned, we would end the lives of a thousand people. A thousand human beings. A thousand of our enemies. That should have troubled me, if only a little.

But it didn't.

"People did hang on," I said, offering the observation without context.

Schiavo, crouched to the side of the boulder opposite me, shifted her attention my way.

"What do you mean, Fletch?"

"I know it worries you that so many of the survivors out there are military, but that doesn't negate the fact that they hung on. And they're from all over. Distant places."

She thought on that for a moment, maybe reaching back to the concern she'd expressed to me on the flight home to Bandon. Or, maybe not.

"Harker and Nguyen," she said. "Pell and Matheson."

"And Hammer," I said, joining in her recitation of those we'd crossed paths with on our travels over the past week.

"Borenstein," she continued.

"Robertson," I added.

"Who was the lieutenant in Colby?" she asked.

"Mason," I answered.

"Pedigrew, Handley," she said, recalling the two Air Force One pilots who'd saved us, but not themselves.

"Does MacDowell count?" I jokingly asked.

"Maybe," Schiavo said, allowing a smile. "Heckerford does."

She stopped the recollection there, as did I. We'd missed some, and were unable to give names to many who we had encountered. And that was a shame. In the old world, I would meet a half dozen new people a day, and they would flit in and out of my life anonymously, the 'who' that they were gone soon after the last time we met.

These people, these fellow human beings, they were not like those forgotten souls I'd had pass through my life. They could not be.

"They all have names," I told Schiavo. "And they lived. The same as you and me. Some are still fighting to stay alive, the same as you and me. The same as all of us, in uniform or out of it."

The words I offered, for reasons even I didn't fully understand, seemed to strike a chord with her. One not entirely happy.

"Do you think we'll remember those names, Fletch? In a month, or a year?"

"I will," I assured her. "I'll remember every last one of them, and what they did for us."

She quieted for a moment, then shook her head, almost to herself.

"How did we get here, Fletch? How did *I* get here? I was an Army musician, and now I'm a colonel with the codes to launch nuclear weapons. What makes me...special?"

"Everyone who's still alive is special, Angela. You, me, Martin. Everyone. As to why the president chose you...I'd say you know exactly why."

She challenged me with a look.

"He picked you because of this," I said, nodding my head to the rocky landscape surrounding us. "You didn't choose to use the power he gave you. You chose another way. You left that arrow in your quiver."

"This could still fail," she told me. "How pleased do you think the president will be with me then?"

"It could fail," I said. "You're right. But I don't think it will."

Schiavo accepted that with a slight nod and said no more, looking back to the bridge and the road beyond, both nearly a hundred feet below our location. I shifted my position slightly and looked across the shallow valley between our hill and the one just west of us, focusing in on the trio of figures hidden among the rocky outcroppings just below its crest. Two wore camouflage and manned the squad automatic weapons, each SAW propped on its bipod atop a low mound of earth, ready for action. The third figure wore grey, her form almost lost in the like-colored terrain.

Elaine lifted her hand and gave me a slight wave. She was watching me, too. Both our positions were above what the temporary water level should be as the billions of gallons surged down the gorge. Along the way to where we waited, the flood would slow as it passed through terrain that spread out, and speed up as the water was collected and funneled through valleys. These variables had made the calculations I'd performed approximate at best, but the time which the torrent arrived should be accurate within an hour, or two. And when that happened...

Elaine and I would be separated, the flood filling the depression between our two hills until it receded and continued toward the ocean. Dalton, his people, and Martin would have retreated to higher ground by then. They would be the only ones to witness the once dammed waters be swallowed by the Pacific.

I wished I could talk to my wife right then. Each element had a radio, but none were to be used until the battle was over. By that time we would be coordinating extractions by the Osprey to be transported back to Bandon and Camas Valley. Those of us who survived.

There would be casualties. I knew that. Even with a river separating us, the fire from our enemy would be withering in places. Already downstream at Gold Beach, it was possible that some had already fallen. People we knew.

Selfishly, I hoped it would not be the man I considered a friend. For a while after we'd taken our positions we'd heard distant thuds, each of the muffled explosions seeming a bit closer than the last. And then they'd stopped. It had seemed obvious to me, and to Schiavo, that what we'd heard was mortar fire, controlled by Martin, who was, as instructed, walking his rounds inland along the river road, harassing the enemy as it moved toward another crossing upstream. Our crossing.

The end of that fire, presumably his fire, could be attributed to completing the rounds available. It could also mean something worse.

"You comfortable with that?" Schiavo asked me, nodding toward the AT-4 leaning against the rocks next to me.

"I am."

Enderson had schooled me on use of the anti-tank weapon, the same as he'd drilled the basics of using the mortar in Martin. I knew I could fire it. Hitting what I was aiming at was another question.

Schiavo asked me no more. We waited in silence. For hours. And hours. Into the afternoon. Until the waiting itself spoke to something happening.

"We may have a problem," Schiavo said.

"What do you mean?"

"The scouting elements should have been here by now," she said. "If they're not, I can only think of one rational reason why."

"Which is?"

Before she could answer, three shots cracked to the west, Hart signaling confirmation of what she'd feared. She grabbed her AT-4 and positioned herself to see the road on the far side of the bridge.

"They moved their armor into the lead," she said.

Forty

The good news from the appearance of the Unified Government forces approaching our position was that the Wedderburn Bridge had been successfully demolished, redirecting their advance inland. That was the only good news.

"Here they come," Schiavo said.

I already had my AT-4 in hand as I stayed low and peered around my side of our rocky cover. What I saw matched with what I hadn't wanted to see—both Abrams tanks, painted all black in some macabrely pointless camouflage designed to intimidate, rolled along the road on the far side of the river, the bridge at Lobster Creek just a hundred yards ahead of them. Infantry followed close, with a few heavy trucks behind, and surely hundreds of additional troops beyond our view. The enemy had done just what Schiavo had suggested, slowed their move inland to reposition their most formidable weaponry at the front. The tanks were, effectively, the tip of their spear.

Even with that realignment which had delayed their arrival, they were early.

"How much longer, Fletch?"

Schiavo didn't have to specify what it was she was asking about. It was the timetable, *my* timetable, for the arrival of the floodwaters.

"Two hours," I said.

I looked to the advancing tanks and troops and knew that holding them off for that amount of time would take a miracle. And we had none to pull out of our bag of tricks.

"How do you want to do this?" I asked.

She thought for a moment as a few soldiers dashed ahead of the tanks, scanning the bridge before them with binoculars, searching for demolition charges. They'd been made wary by what they'd experienced at Gold Beach, and didn't want to do the same here. But the bridge was not wired for destruction. That had not been part of the plan. Getting them to this point where raging floodwaters would annihilate them was the goal, and that had happened. Just far too quickly.

"We could concentrate on one tank," Schiavo said, more possibility than suggestion in her words. "Try to disable the lead Abrams and block the other one."

Could the following tank maneuver around its disabled partner? Probably. Or could it simply push it out of the way? Maybe. In either case, as quickly as she'd voiced the scenario, Schiavo dismissed it.

"No," she said. "No."

We were going to have to make some decision quickly, as the advance that had paused resumed on the road across the river.

"Infantry is moving up," I said.

It wasn't just a few troops now. It was dozens. A full platoon, in old world military terms, raced toward the bridge, their boots just reaching the span when the fire began.

Both SAWs opened up at once, with rifle fire from Elaine and Hart, who'd reached their position, adding substantially to the attempt to repel the rush of troops. Two dropped, then four, others taking cover at the southern end of the bridge and returning fire toward our friends' position. Westin and Enderson managed their shooting, squeezing off long, aimed bursts. Quickly, though, they were faced with much more than bullets ricocheting off the rocks shielding them.

The flash and crack of the 120 millimeter cannon firing came at the same time, as did the terrible sound of the impact, rock and earth erupting into the air, arcing fully across the divide between our hill and the one my wife was stationed upon.

Elaine...

I chanced a quick look and saw her ducked fully behind a jagged mound of earth, the three soldiers with her rolling away from the explosion that had rocked their cover, already repositioning themselves.

Worse, though, was the continued rush of infantry onto the bridge as the fire against them stopped. I put the AT-4 down and took my AR in hand, about to squeeze off my first round when shooting erupted behind me and to the right, close to the edge of the hill that was our refuge. Had the enemy somehow crossed the raging river and flanked us?

No.

Schiavo looked at the same instant that I did, ready to react, but what we saw did not terrify us—it buoyed us. Sergeant Lorenzen and Private Laws were rushing forward, each firing their M4s at the advancing enemy on the bridge, momentarily stalling their progress.

"Sergeant!"

Lorenzen looked to his commander and saw her give him a solid thumbs up.

"The Osprey dropped us about a half mile north," he explained. "We heard the fire and double-timed it."

On the hill to the west, the SAWs were in action again, as were Elaine and Hart, an almost literal rain of lead stopping the flow of enemy onto the bridge. Another deafening blast from the lead Abrams' cannon shook our hill this time, spraying Lorenzen and Carter with shards of stone and metal.

"AHHHH!" Lorenzen screamed as he fell to the ground and slid toward the edge of the hill.

"Paul!" Schiavo called out, moving to leave her position to pull her second in command to safety.

Only a second cannon shot from the second Abrams stopped her, the round sailing overhead, missing us, a hot wash of air from its supersonic wake making both Schiavo and I dive for cover. I looked up and saw that one of our number was not planted face down, on the ground.

Carter laws ran out onto the exposed slope of the hill, firing as he crossed the open space, reaching his sergeant as the SAWs opened up again, providing covering fire. I didn't hear fire from either Elaine or Hart, but a glimpse across the way to their hill showed me that they were shifting positions, moving forward to have a better field of fire on the bridge.

"Covering fire!"

I followed Schiavo's direction and brought my AR up and around the boulder, squeezing off bursts not at the troops on the bridge, but at those beyond it. Tight knots of enemy soldiers had sought cover behind the armored vehicles, using them as moving screens as the force moved slowly, but steadily, toward the crossing.

"We can't hold this!" I shouted.

Schiavo didn't respond, looking behind to see that Carter had dragged Lorenzen into cover, the sergeant already shaking off the concussive effects of the near miss. He picked up his rifle and, with his helmet MIA, began firing again. Once more, the Abrams both fired, simultaneously this time, at the hill across the way, obscuring it in a blossom of dusty debris.

"More coming!" Lorenzen warned.

I looked and saw what he did, a scene not unlike what I'd experienced at the checkpoint by the bridge on the Coquille River where the Seattle Hordes had rushed toward our side. The drug-crazed attackers had been decimated then. Here, I could not see that happening.

"Angela, what do we do?" I asked.

"Keep firing!"

I did, but knew that what we were laying down was not going to stop what was pushing toward us. If even a half dozen troops reached our side, they could split our force, attacking our flanks and our rear. We'd worried about the tanks at the front of their column, but it was the foot soldiers making the attack, with direct support by the armor.

"We've gotta take those tanks out!" I told Schiavo.

"They're too far," she countered.

My estimate was four hundred yards. Within the range of the AT-4, but distance was one thing—actually hitting the beasts mattered more than anything. The unguided rockets would destroy or damage whatever they impacted, but—

"The bridge!" I shouted to Schiavo. "We hit the bridge!"

"What?" she asked between bursts from her M4.

Two more cannon shots blasted the slope just in front of our position, briefly shrouding the landscape ahead.

"If we fire at the bridge, it will at least be damaged," I said. "Maybe too much for the tanks to cross."

Schiavo took a quick look through the haze at the bridge below. It lay less than two hundred yards from our position. We could easily strike it with both rockets.

"That thing is beaten up by the current already," I told her. "All we need to do is weaken it more."

"And if it collapses?" Schiavo asked, challenging me. "Then they move upstream to the next bridge. Or they withdraw. And we have to fight again."

"We have to do something," I said.

"Another rush!" Lorenzen told us.

Yet another wave of Unified Government troops was pouring onto the bridge, just as cannon fire from the

Abrams forced the SAWs to stop shooting, Westin and Enderson taking cover.

"Angela..."

Schiavo looked to me, then to the two rockets leaning against the rocky mound that was our cover. After just a few seconds she dropped her M4 and took the AT-4 in hand. I followed suit, laying the short missile tube on my right shoulder and readying it as Enderson had shown me.

"Aim for the center of the bridge," Schiavo said. "On two."

I drew a breath.

"One," she said. "Covering fire!"

Behind and to the right of us, Lorenzen and Carter began shooting, drawing the enemy's attention toward them.

"Two!"

Schiavo and I both moved at the same instant, exposing ourselves just above the rocky ledge that shielded us. If I'd counted the time we were left without cover, I would have sworn it was minutes. But it was only a second or two, each of us taking aim at the agreed upon point, a part of the span that was not only steel and concrete at that moment, but flesh and bone as well. A dozen enemy troops had made it that far, passing the bodies of their fallen comrades. I fired my rocket just an instant before Schiavo, and before dropping back behind the boulders I saw both smoke trails sail true, the projectiles striking mid span. The blast that resulted tossed large chucks of the roadway into the air, along with limbs and torsos and a thick red spray that burst like some grotesque fireworks show.

We scrambled back to cover just as both tanks fired directly at our hill, one round detonating against the collection of massive stones in front of me, shifting its bulk a full two feet to the north, almost catching my left foot beneath as it lurched my direction.

"The tanks are holding!" Lorenzen reported.

I crawled toward Schiavo and, both of us on our stomachs, inched beyond the rocks to survey the scene with her.

"The bridge is a no go," she said, giving me an appreciative glance. "It worked."

Large sections of the span, roughly halfway between the north and south shores, had crumbled, blasted away by the AT-4 impacts. The way forward for the armor was impassable. But there was a downside to that.

"Infantry maneuvering!" Lorenzen said.

The enemy had lost upwards of thirty troops so far. Assuming the same number had fallen at Gold Beach, they still had over nine-hundred shooters to throw at us. And the bridge, though it had been rendered useless for vehicle traffic, was still viable for an assault on foot.

An assault with supporting fire.

Another tank round sailed high over our position, just missing the spot where Schiavo and I were hunkered down. The second tank, rolled up just behind its lead vehicle, loosed another shot, this one at the western hill. That round did not miss. Did not go high.

It impacted within ten feet of where I had last seen my wife firing from cover.

"Elaine!"

I knew she would never hear my voice yelling for her across the space between the hills, nor over the sounds of the continuing battle, but my reaction was instinctive. Schiavo began firing at the infantry which had resumed its push across the bridge, but I hesitated, straining to see through the dust and smoke to where Elaine had been. When enough had cleared, I was able to make out a form moving through the swirling haze.

But it was not her.

Specialist Trey Hart had sprinted across open terrain to where my wife lay, motionless.

"God, no..."

It was all I could think to say, almost under my breath, as I watched the garrison's medic huddle over her, pulling supplies from his bag, focusing fully on his patient as small arms fire chewed at the terrain around him.

"Fletch!"

I turned to Schiavo as she shouted my name. She saw the shattered panic on my face and looked across to the scene that held me rapt. For a brief instant she, too, was out of the fight, fixed on the sight of her friend, my wife, lying still on the dead earth. Then, she was back in it.

"She's alive, Fletch," Schiavo said. "Hart wouldn't be on her like that if she was gone. Now get back on the trigger."

She began firing again, adding to the rounds Lorenzen and Carter were sending toward our enemy. The SAWs, too, were in the fight, both Westin and Enderson covering their friend as he tended to my wife.

Elaine...

I pushed myself off the ground and found a firing position five yards from Schiavo and rejoined the fight, shooting between two slabs of angular rock. The first glimpse of the attack since my wife had gone down was almost as terrible as that event.

"They just keep coming!" Carter yelled.

He was right. Both tanks, prevented from moving across the bridge, were now, for better or worse, stationary gun platforms, each bombarding the hills where we'd positioned ourselves. The ground troops that we'd momentarily repelled with the AT-4 fire which had weakened the bridge were moving forward in force now, maneuvering around the holes in the span's center, bounding and firing, suppressing our ability to defend.

"We can't hold this!" Lorenzen shouted.

I looked back to the sergeant, who never stopped firing even as he pointed out the untenable situation. Blood streamed down his face, likely from rock fragments sprayed like shrapnel from the blast which had knocked him temporarily down. At his feet I could see a half dozen empty magazines for his M4. Before long his rifle would run dry, and any thought of further defense would be little more than folly.

"I'm low on ammo!" Carter reported, confirming what I'd noticed in relation to Lorenzen. "Three mags left!"

"Angela, I'm down to four," I said.

Schiavo didn't respond verbally, instead switching her M4 from burst to single shot. I followed suit.

"Make every round count!" I shouted toward Lorenzen and Carter.

Across the shallow valley, atop the other hill, only one SAW was firing. Westin had abandoned his light machine gun and was now helping Hart pull Elaine into a natural depression behind the crest of the hill. He popped up from that cover with only his M4 and began firing again. That could only mean one thing.

"Westin's SAW is out," I said.

"I know," Schiavo replied, still laser focused on the onslaught, firing calmly until the world before the both of us erupted in a flash and thunder.

"Colonel! Fletch!"

It was Lorenzen, I thought, calling out to us, not with warning, but with worry. I wondered briefly why he was doing that, but quickly some sense began to return. My nose burned with the stinging odor of an explosion. A close one.

We were hit...

I thought that, now, and opened my eyes, boiling dust and acrid grey smoke rolling over me. I reached to my body and felt around, probing for wounds or obvious injuries. There was no wetness, no blood, and all my extremities seemed to move as they should. Lying across my hips was my AR. My weapon. I had to get up. Had to get back into the fight. But...

Angela...

She would have gone down with me in the close hit. I scrambled to my feet, ready to look for her. As it turned out, that was unnecessary.

Colonel Angela Schiavo, former Army piano player, was already up, recovered from the blast, her helmet gone like her sergeant's, M4 spitting single shots at the enemy swarming our way.

"Fletch, you okay?" she asked.

"I am," I told her, and reclaimed my position between the rocky slabs.

I should have thought more about Elaine right then, but what she'd expressed before we'd boarded the Osprey was true. More true now than when she'd spoken the words to me. What we were doing mattered, and if we failed, we would fail giving our last full measure to protect our daughter, and those we loved.

"Too many," Schiavo said, pausing for just a second as she reloaded.

I looked over and could see that it was her last magazine.

"I'm out," Lorenzen reported to our right rear.

A quick glance his way and I saw him draw his M9, wielding the pistol, ready but holding fire for use when the enemy drew close enough for it to matter.

Carter continued firing. Schiavo, too. On the other hill, neither SAW was in action, both Enderson and Westin down to their M4s. I focused, and took aim at the lead element of troops, forty strong, no more than five yards from our side of the bridge. A hundred more were behind them, already on the span. And hundreds more were ready to cross.

We were about to be overrun.

I squeezed off one round, then another, but before I could fire a third I heard it. A most wonderful sound. Not the roar of water rushing down the gorge, but a deadly whine, like the scream of a saw blade spinning at full speed. Next I saw the ground around the troops on the bridge splinter and burst, bodies disintegrating before my eyes as the Osprey flew fast down the river, its aft-mounted minigun dragging a tail of fire left and right across the damaged crossing.

"Marines!" Carter screamed. "Yes!"

The tilt rotor aircraft swung low and fast to the south from its westerly course, a scene of utter destruction in its wake, bodies littering the bridge, and the road leading to it. Every survivor still able to fight turned their weapons skyward, unleashing a hellish fusillade against the unexpected.

"They're taking rounds," Schiavo said.

They were. Dozens, maybe hundreds of impacts. Small puffs bloomed from every part of the ungainly aircraft as the pilots, disregarding the safety or survivability of their bird, kept the nose pointed away from the battle, and their only weapon, manned by Major Stanley James, facing the storm of enemy fire without cover. He kept raining lead upon the Unified Government forces as the crew put the Osprey through shallow S turns and wobbles, maintaining contact with the enemy.

Until that heroic action ended in a ball of fire and flaming debris falling from the sky. A single tank round, not even a lucky shot, struck the Osprey just behind the right wing, cutting it in half, fuel tanks rupturing catastrophically. Pieces plummeted, dragging orange and black trails, leaving a swath of burning wreckage on the dead hills just south of the river.

An eerie quiet followed. One that seemed to be each side letting out a breath. One that was born of relief, and the other from grief.

"They're coming again," I said.

From the far side the enemy resumed its push. More than a hundred were dead already. Maybe a hundred and fifty. Two hundred. I wasn't sure. But they still had more than enough to hand us a defeat we could not afford.

"Get ready," Schiavo said.

She'd dropped her M4, no ammunition left to feed it, and now held her pistol. Carter was down to half of his last magazine. I had maybe ten rounds left for my AR. And on the other hill...

I took a moment to look that way. Enderson and Westin were still in position, M4s in hand. Their reserve of ammunition would be greater than ours, having used the SAWs for most of the battle. Hart was nowhere to be seen. Either he was obscured by cover tending to my wife, or...

Or he was gone, too.

"Single shots, private," Schiavo reminded her young recruit.

I looked back to the bridge. The wave of Unified Government forces was moving across it, lead elements firing, trying to keep our heads down. The turrets atop the Abrams were swinging in our direction, cannons taking aim.

That was when we heard the roar.

Forty One

From our left it came, thundering east to west. Once again, a pause stilled the battle, both sides shifting their attention to what was coming. To what was finally coming.

The waters announced themselves with sound first, then with a wash of spray pushed ahead of the flow by the pressure wave it generated. That misty cloud rolled fast over the bridge and the low terrain at either end, obscuring all until the torrent arrived a few seconds later.

It punched into the Unified Government forces with the force of a billion tons behind it, a tumbling mass of floodwaters that swallowed every living being, and those that had already fallen. The tanks, the trucks, the people, all simply were erased under seventy feet of water that filled the gorge, sloshing against the hill just fifteen feet below our position. The low valley between me and Elaine filled with churning whitecaps, the inundation reaching north and south, seeking low spots as it raced toward the ocean.

"It came early," Schiavo said. "Thank God it came early."

"The lake exploded past the dam when we blew it," Lorenzen said.

The excess volume in Lost Creek Lake had sped its flow, adding more mass to the relentless drive to the sea. It had moved quicker than I'd calculated, and I was ecstatic that I'd been wrong.

But I had little else to be happy about.

"I have to get to Elaine," I told Schiavo.

"You can't, Fletch. Not yet."

I walked toward the edge of the hill that tipped down into the valley. On the other side of the swirling water, Westin was covering the flood should any survivors appear, though that was almost impossible to imagine. Enderson had joined Hart where my wife had been taken to cover. From what I could see, it appeared that he was assisting the medic. Working frantically.

"The water will recede," Schiavo assured me. "We'll get there."

But how soon? That was my worry. If Elaine was hurt badly, she needed to get out of here and to the hospital without delay. Working against that was the fact that our planned ride out of the danger zone had been shot out of the sky. Men were dead, yes. They'd sacrificed themselves to best the enemy that threatened us and our way of life. But all I could think about was what I might lose. It was a selfish moment, and I didn't care.

"We need a helicopter," I told Schiavo.

She thought, then nodded toward Lorenzen.

"Sergeant, find some high ground and get on your radio. Contact the *Rushmore* and tell them we need a helicopter evac for wounded."

"On my way," Lorenzen said, taking his empty M4 with him as he fished the radio from his pack and sprinted toward a higher hill just to the north.

Carter approached, breathing fast, his heart racing.

"You did good," Schiavo said.

"Thank you, ma'am. But I'd rather not do that again."

"Me either, private."

* * *

The minutes ticked by, an interminably slow march of time. Five. Ten. Twenty minutes. Nearly a half hour after the flood had raged past, its remnants had receded enough that we were able to cross the valley and reach the others, sloshing through muddy tangles of stumps and whole trees uprooted by the destructive waters.

"Elaine," I said as I rushed into the low spot atop the hill.

"Babe?"

Her eyes were closed and splatters of blood covered one side of her face and the whole left side of her body where Hart had cut away her clothes.

"I'm here," I told her, shedding my gear to kneel next to her and take her hand. "Do you feel my hand?"

She squeezed my grip but said nothing. I looked to Hart.

"She took a lot of shrapnel," Hart explained. "Left side and back. The head wounds are superficial as far as I can see. But we need to get her to a doctor."

"Already working on it," Schiavo said.

Less than a minute later, Lorenzen ran up the hill, radio in hand.

"Adamson didn't want to send a chopper," Lorenzen said. "I told his comm officer that I would personally swim out to them and kick his ass if that bird wasn't here in twenty minutes."

Schiavo considered the insubordination her second in command had just admitted to. Maybe.

"Kick Adamson's ass, or his comm officer's?" she asked.

"I left that open to interpretation," Lorenzen answered. "But the helicopter is on the way. It should be here any minute."

Admiral Lionel Adamson had been beyond stingy when it came to using the two working Seahawk helicopters stationed aboard the *Rushmore*, allowing neither to be used for transport of supplies to shore, nor to move personnel. If he had not authorized their use now, in this medical evacuation of my wife, I would have joined Lorenzen in his swim out to the boat to make our displeasure known.

"I also was able to reach Dalton," Lorenzen said, looking to Schiavo. "They didn't lose anyone."

"No one?" Schiavo asked, incredulous and relieved all at once.

"He said once the mortars started and bridge blew, the enemy acted like they knew they were up against a large force."

Schiavo's plan had worked. With amazingly low casualties. That mattered little to me, though.

"Babe," Elaine said, her voice weak and thin. "Eric."

"I'm right here with you," I assured her.

"Is Hope all right?"

"Our baby is fine," I said.

"But we...Eric?"

"Elaine, I'm with you. Feel my hand."

"I can't," she said, her eyelids clamped shut.

In the distance the throbbing *wop wop wop* of helicopter blades could be heard.

"The helicopter is almost here," I told her.

"I can't feel anything," Elaine said, barely above a whisper. "I can't..."

She stilled.

"Elaine..."

I squeezed her hand. It was limp.

"Elaine!"

The helicopter appeared over the hilltop. Lorenzen waved it in with a flare as Hart pushed me aside and began administering CPR to my wife.

"Elaine!" I screamed as Schiavo held me back. "No!"

Part Five

The Unknown

Forty Two

I walked with my daughter through fir saplings as high as my shoulder.

"Daddy," Hope said, pointing, to a small bird flitting about the low branches, green needles quivering in the rush of air created by the bird's beating wings.

"That's a bird, sweetie," I said.

She ran toward the tiny finch, spooking it, and it maneuvered quickly away from her outstretched hand, swerving through the high branches of a dead, grey pine that had refused to succumb to time and weather.

A dead survivor, I thought.

We were not that. None of us. This I knew from experience, and through the pure joy of watching my two-year old daughter chase after the fleeing bird, giggling madly.

Two years...

She'd been born in the time between surviving and thriving. In the time when we fought our last true battle. Our final conflict of arms. She was a cooing baby that night and day, safe in the home of her Aunt Grace and her cousins Krista and Brandon. The titles of relation were not conferred because of blood lineage, but for more important reasons.

Love and loyalty.

"Bird!"

Hope's joyous screeching of the newly learned word buoyed me as I walked slowly behind, letting her stretch her metaphoric wings and explore the space before her. We were in the grove of new woods planted eighteen months ago on the border of the decaying forest. Soon, if plans moved forward, a swath of those grey and crumbling trees would be bulldozed, making way for still more replanting. The greenhouse operation at Remote was running at full capacity, and the hundred residents who now inhabited that settlement were already working on expanding their growing operation.

"Daddy!"

She looked back at me as she sprinted awkwardly, beaming.

"I'm coming," I assured her, adding playfully, "but you're so fast!"

She laughed and set her sights on some imagined point ahead, half-running, half-stumbling toward it. And if that didn't whimsically mirror how we'd all gotten to where we were now, through some focused bashing through the unknowns that defined the world after the blight, then nothing did. There were fewer of those surprises, now, but they hadn't disappeared entirely.

One had come not long after we'd eliminated the Unified Government forces in what became known as the Rogue River Battle. Just ten days past that event, Mayor Everett 'Doc' Allen did not show up for a Defense Council meeting. It was Dave Arndt who was dispatched to the man's house. He found him, in bed, gone. Sometime in the night he'd passed in his sleep.

The Defense Council, too, had changed, in name and in makeup. It became the Town Council, shedding the militaristic implications that its former name implied. Schiavo now sat as an advisor to the fully civilian leadership. Nelson Vickers had replaced me on the Council, voted into the seat I had willingly vacated. But he'd only accepted a one year term, requiring a new candidate to seek the office.

Or the office to seek the candidate.

It was Martin who'd approached the new mayor, expressing the Council's desire to have the full two-year term served. That would mean commitment. In the end, that was the only real question. Acceptability to the citizens was a given. Competence was without question. Integrity was beyond reproach.

And that was how I became the first husband of Bandon.

Elaine had been elected. Unanimously. And not in some Soviet-style election stinking of fraud and predestination. All those who'd lived in Bandon, and struggled, and survived, knew that Elaine Morales Fletcher was the exact person they wanted making decisions which would affect the future of every person who called our town home.

The wounds she'd suffered at Lobster Creek had almost taken her from me, and from our daughter. As I'd flown with her that day on the helicopter dispatched from the *Rushmore*, I'd thought we'd lost her. But she'd hung on as we were lifted from the wilderness and transported to Bandon. Genesee worked tirelessly, keeping her alive after Hart had revived her. Giving her a chance at the life we now had.

And it was a good life, despite the challenges.

She was well into her term, and was chairing a Town Council meeting as Hope and I wandered through the patch of growing woods. Two more survivor colonies had been located, one in Northern California, and another a hundred miles east of Bandon, the pair of enclaves requiring immediate support to move out of a purely survival mode. Our town, with regular resupply visits from the *Rushmore*, had become the hub of distribution to get foodstuffs, medical equipment, and, most importantly, seeds to these distant groups. Managing such a flow of material had put a strain on our town, and on those settlements, Remote and Camas Valley, through which supplies had to flow.

"The bird gone," Hope said, stopping just ahead and frowning at the empty sky.

"He'll come back," I assured my daughter.

She turned and glared at me.

"Not a boy bird," she scolded me. "A girl bird!"

I nodded and smiled. Our sweet, determined daughter was turning out to be just what the new world, our world, needed. One who would speak their mind, while at the same time appreciating the simple joy of wandering through greening woods. She was a handful, yes, and with Elaine devoting a great deal of time to her duties as mayor, she was usually *my* handful. And gladly so.

It did put a crimp in the contracting business I'd started, once again putting to use, on a smaller scale, those skills I'd honed in the old world. I was more hands on now, hanging doors and installing windows with hands that, in my old life, had become accustomed to shuffling contract paperwork and holding a cell phone to my ear. But it felt good to swing a hammer again, and to dig a trench. On occasion, when the job would allow it, I would bring Hope with me. Usually there was a willing resident who was more than happy to play with her as I completed whatever tasks were needed. That was the thing about Hope, and about any of the children born since the blight—they represented what we could get right.

And, mostly, they were as cute as hell.

"Go see mommy," Hope said, reaching up to me.

I scooped her up and was planting sloppy kisses on her neck that made her giggle when I heard it—my cell phone was ringing.

It wasn't the old days. I wasn't juggling paperwork with a customer in my ear. No, our world was different now, but a pair of enterprising engineers with expertise in communications had, almost six months ago, completed a year-long project to establish a rudimentary cellular network that covered Bandon, Remote, and Camas Valley. No caller ID existed, yet, but I was fairly certain who was on the other end of this call.

"Hi, babe," I said as I answered.

"You'd feel pretty foolish if this was Martin," Elaine said. "Or Clay."

"Maybe I call all my friends 'babe'."

"Mm-hm," she sighed and grunted at my weak humor. "Where are you two?"

"We are running through the woods chasing birds," I said.

"Mommy!" Hope shouted, grabbing at the phone.

"There's a request to have some mommy time," I said.

"It just so happens we're done with business for the day. You want to swing by and pick me up?"

"Mommy!" Hope shouted, laughing as I fended off her attempt to seize the phone in my hand.

"We're on our way," I said.

* * *

So much had changed, I thought, as I drove through town, Hope buckled in a booster seat next to me. I often had moments of nostalgia rear up, unannounced. More cars could be seen on the streets, products of mechanical ingenuity and an almost limitless supply of parts scavenged from abandoned vehicles scattered on roads up and down the coast. Stop signs had been repainted, and there was discussion of reenergizing a few traffic lights downtown to manage both traffic and pedestrians as they crossed the roads.

Bandon was different. It was growing. Becoming a town that, with every passing day, seemed more like what it had likely been before the blight. There was a time when I'd wanted to leave the very place I now called home, mostly because I felt it was too complacent. That those in charge had it on a steady course toward a slow decay. I'd been wrong, and I thought back now on those times with an unexpected fondness.

Now there were cars. And pedestrians who'd forgotten how to look both ways getting clipped by drivers who'd lived without speed limits for too long. There was a bar in town, serving a pretty good selection of, what else, local brews. And there were fights after too much imbibing mixed with too much talking.

The jail in Bandon found itself being used at least once a month, exclusively for one of these drunk and disorderly infractions, its inhabitants always the same combination of two or three people. A police force was in the works, which would relieve the town's garrison from having to deal with civilian infractions.

That military body now numbered eight, with the addition of two more recruits—Michael Poulson and Molly Anne Beck. The structure of the garrison had changed somewhat, with Schiavo giving battlefield promotions to those who'd served with her over the years. Lt. Lorenzen now had day to day responsibility for the troops, which included the newest recruits and Sergeants Enderson, Westin, and Hart. Corporal Carter Laws rounded out the tested and tried unit, and had proven himself to be a fine and reliable soldier.

A wedding, too, had changed the face of our town. And added to it. Grace had married Clay Genesee, and within a few months they were expecting, the baby born just two months ago, a little girl named Alice, who was doted on by her big sister Krista, and looked upon with some loving suspicion by her four-year-old brother, Brandon.

So much was different, yes, but so much was good, too. Every day I reminded myself how lucky I was to not only be alive, but to be alive here, with the people who'd become more than friends.

"Mommy!" Hope shouted, craning her neck to see above the dash of the old pickup as we pulled into the parking lot of the town hall. "Mommy there!"

Mommy was there. My love. Elaine. Beaming at the both of us from the wheelchair that no longer seemed like a reminder of loss. Shrapnel from the tank fire at the battle along the Rogue River had damaged her spinal cord and left her paralyzed from the waist down. Somehow, in the months after that terrible event, Elaine had not only been able to carry on with what she'd done to that point, she'd taken on more, adapting her physical limitations to any situation that presented itself. Including leading the town.

And exiting the town hall via the side stairs.

It was one of the things she loved to do to both terrify and inspire me, ignoring the ramp at the front of the building that she used upon entering, and instead pulling a wheelie and dropping expertly down the three steps to the sidewalk outside. As I stopped the truck near the exit she performed that very maneuver, wheels bouncing, chair tipped back, her balance never faltering.

"You love it when I do that, don't you?" she ribbed me.

"I always love watching my wife on the verge of splitting her skull open," I shot back.

"Hasn't happened yet," Elaine said, wheeling herself to the passenger door and pulling it open to see our beaming child clapping madly upon seeing her. "Hi, baby!"

I'd gotten used to not hopping from behind the wheel and helping her into the truck. That had lasted about a week until she'd perfected the choreography she executed now, hauling herself with her left hand up into the cab, and using her right to swing the compact wheelchair backward and over the side of the pickup, placing it perfectly in the bed where she could retrieve it just as easily. She grabbed her legs and swung them in, closing the door before leaning over our daughter to kiss me.

"Rough day running around the forest?"

"Brutal," I told her.

"Bootal!" Hope mimicked adorably.

Elaine turned her focus to our little girl, smothering her with sloppy mommy kisses. I pulled away from the town hall and out of the parking lot, driving my family home.

Forty Three

I was no longer among those who exercised authority in Bandon. That life, and those roles, I'd left behind. But I was not out of the loop as to decisions being made, and, on occasion, I was called upon to offer any expertise and advice that I could.

An instance such as that occurred on a glorious spring Tuesday.

"Have you thought about my offer?" Dave Arndt asked me as he slipped into the headset and plugged it into the Cessna's intercom and radio system.

"I have," I told the man, adjusting the mic so that it was closer to my mouth. "And I decline."

We sat in the aircraft that had been restored from the useless state it had been found in on a stretch of road outside Coos Bay. Our expanding scouting patrols had discovered it, and another almost identical aircraft in an old farm field, more than a year ago. A Bandon transplant, Chris Beekman, who'd been a bush pilot in Alaska in the old world, had taken it upon himself to not only haul the Cessnas south to town, but also to restore them to working order. Once he'd completed that, he'd offered lessons to any who were interested, most paying through some sort of barter. Dave had helped Chris renovate a small hangar at the airport to secure his lessons.

"You would love it," Dave told me.

"I love being a passenger," I said.

He smiled and started the engine, the 172's propeller jerking, then settling into a steady, blurring rotation as the engine revved up. The high-winged aircraft was one of the most familiar in the old world, and its usefulness had transferred to our time. It, and its near twin, had been used to establish initial face to face contact with the recently discovered survivor colonies, Dave landing on stretches of road to deposit Schiavo or Martin to meet those who'd come through the blight and all that had followed.

This day, though, Dave Arndt was flying me not to some group who'd beaten the odds and survived, but to a place north of Bandon, along the coast, where the Siuslaw River spilled into the Pacific at Florence. A scouting mission had reported that the bridge spanning that river might not be structurally sound, and I was tasked with making the call to either certify the crossing as usable, or suggest it for demolition to prevent collapse when some unaware traveler was unlucky enough to be upon it.

"Wheels up," Dave reported as we lifted off, keying the radio mic on his yoke next. "BC, this is SF One, departing north out of the field."

There was no control tower at the actual airport. Any pilot taking off was responsible for making sure the runway and the airspace was clear, the latter being a virtual certainty. Still, Chris Beekman had drilled it into his students that they could not be complacent simply because they might be the only thing in the air within a thousand miles, or more.

"Scouting Flight One, this is Bandon Center, copy."

The voice that acknowledged us over the radio was more than familiar. Krista, who'd years ago taken a shine to all aspects of the communication system left behind by Micah, had further educated herself on the use of the town's radio system, to the point that even Westin, the garrison's com specialist, turned to her on occasion for assistance when troubleshooting links between his equipment and distant receivers in Remote and Camas Valley.

"Did you hear her talk show last week?" Dave asked me.

Krista had begun broadcasting a radio show one night a month, with guests who would answer questions related to town issues, or livestock, or cooking.

"Was that her sixth episode?" I asked.

"It was. And it was good. She had Hap Killion on talking about smoking meat. I am seriously thinking about building a smokehouse after listening to him."

"Have you tasted his spareribs?" I asked, and Dave shook his head, instantly envious. "They are unbelievable."

Talk shows. Recipes. Pork ribs. We'd gotten to this place in our recovery so easily that all the struggles we'd faced, all the dangers we'd survived, seemed distant. Not out of memory, but somehow those difficulties now existed in some minimized form. That we'd all nearly died on multiple occasions did not seem strange as we looked back upon those times. That was the curse, and the blessing, of the blight.

It had harmed us, and it had toughened us.

Some obstacles, though, we could not simply force our way through. Fog was one of them.

"Great," Dave said, taking note of the thick layer of mist creeping inland from the ocean, sliding over the landscape precisely where we were heading. "Can't fly through that."

"Another day," I said, taking in the sight of the wide blue sky above, unsullied by the marine layer that would soon shroud it from any earthbound view.

"BC, this is SF One, returning to field due to weather."

Dave began a gentle left turn, skirting the coast, lines of whitecaps curling toward the shore. A minute later he frowned at the controls and glanced to me.

"She must be grabbing a snack or something."

Krista was diligent. But she was still young. A full-fledged teenager now. A quick run to the refrigerator, or to the bathroom, or to say high to a visiting friend, could all be explanations for her not acknowledging the call. But her dedication always, at least in my experience, led her to notify all stations that she would be away from the radio for a brief period, or signed off entirely for the night, or while she was in school or tending to things at home with her family. She hadn't done that this time. We would have heard her.

"Call again," I suggested.

"BC, this is SF One, returning to field due to fog over our destination. Do you copy?"

Once again, there was silence.

"Maybe it's the radio," Dave said, checking the unit.

"Well?"

He adjusted controls, flipped the power on and off, then keyed the mic several times.

"Something's wrong," Dave said.

"It's not working?"

He shook his head, but not to confirm what I was suggesting.

"It's working fine," he said. "But the receiver is pegged. It's overwhelmed by a signal."

"You mean jammed?"

"I don't know," he said, pointing to the signal strength readout. "That's holding at the top of the limit."

"What are you saying?"

"I'm not an expert," Dave said. "But we don't have a transmitter strong enough to do that."

He looked out the windshield, scanning in all directions before his gaze settled on me.

"The signal is coming from somewhere else," he said.

Forty Four

It wasn't just the radio in the Cessna.

"Every communications device that isn't hard wired is completely jammed," Westin said.

Dave and I had hurried from the airport to Micah's old radio room. Krista was there, along with Westin, Martin, and Schiavo.

"So we are being jammed," I said.

"Not exactly," Krista said. "Just swamped. The receivers can't handle the signal load. No broadcast we make can get through."

"Some receivers have actually failed," Westin reported. "Mostly cell phones. Their circuitry is more susceptible to frying."

"Is this some sort of EMP event?" Schiavo asked.

An electromagnetic pulse, product of nuclear explosions at altitude, could render sensitive electronics useless, destroying the intricate collection microchips and relays within. But there'd been no indication of any such event.

"No," Westin told his commander. "Imagine you have someone screaming into your ear with a bullhorn. You won't hear anything but that, even if a dozen other people are talking to you a few feet away."

"So someone somewhere is transmitting...silence?" Schiavo asked, puzzled.

"That's right," Westin confirmed.

"On every frequency?"

Westin looked from his commander to Krista.

"Every frequency I've scanned," the teenager said.

"Which means every frequency," Martin said, gesturing to the equipment that his late son had used to serve and, ultimately save, Bandon. "Micah built this to listen across the radio spectrum. If Krista used this, we know it's everything."

"I ran his scanning program," Krista said.

"Why is this happening?" Westin asked, voicing the question that vexed him, and others. "Why now?"

It wasn't the most salient inquiry, though. Not to Schiavo's way of thinking.

"I'd rather know who," she said. "And where."

"Something with the power to do this, it can't be too distant," Westin said.

"What about satellite?" Martin asked.

Krista shook her head and pointed to a signal analyzer running on one of Micah's computers that was still functioning, though another had recently failed and was awaiting scavenged parts for repair.

"The signature points to a terrestrial signal," Krista explained, tracing her extended finger over a wave form on screen that, other than Westin, we lacked the expertise to fully understand.

"Terrestrial?" I parroted. "You mean, right here. On land."

Krista half nodded, half shrugged.

"Or sea," she said.

"So how do we find out where it's coming from?" Schiavo asked.

"Can we triangulate?" Martin asked.

Using multiple receivers to pinpoint the direction of a signal was a known technique. But both Krista's and Westin's reaction indicated that we would have to find an alternative.

"The signal is so strong, we would have trouble determining any variance that would indicate a direction," Westin said.

"Even with a directional collector, there's back scatter from a broadcast this powerful," Krista said. "That can affect any reading."

Something that had been repeated several times suddenly struck me as a salient point of interest.

"How much power are we talking about here?" I asked.

"There's no way to know with the equipment we have," Westin said. "Millions of watts."

"Millions?" I asked.

"I'm guessing here, Fletch," Westin said. "But I've never seen anything like this. It's off every scale I've ever been taught."

Schiavo thought for a moment, then looked to Krista, smiling.

"Sweetie, thank you for working on this. When do you have to be home?"

"In about an hour," Krista answered.

"Can you keep monitoring until then?" Schiavo asked. "And use the landline to let the garrison office know if anything changes?"

"Absolutely."

Schiavo looked to us, and then the door, the signal plain enough—she wanted to talk without Krista listening.

* * *

"Sergeant Westin," Schiavo began when we were outside, standing near the former meeting hall across the street from Micah and Martin's old house, "I need you to step up."

"Ma'am?"

"That's a child in there," Schiavo said. "But this is your area of expertise. I need you to figure this out. Finding where that signal is coming from is not an option, so I'm not interested in why *you* can't locate it—I'm interested in what *you* have to do to change that. Is that clear?"

Westin absorbed the mild dressing down, which Schiavo had, surprisingly, offered in the presence of relative outsiders.

"Very clear, ma'am," Westin said.

"Get to it," Schiavo said.

He backed away, then headed off toward the garrison headquarters next to the town hall up the street. Neither Martin or I said anything about what we'd just witnessed, but Schiavo looked to us both when her com specialist was gone.

"We've had two years of peace," Schiavo said. "Two years of normalcy. We've all grown a little soft."

"Angela," Martin said.

She responded with a knowing look.

"You disagree? And what about you, Fletch? Are you still the hardened, finely tuned civilian warrior that you were back at the Rogue River?"

"Angela," Martin said again, admonishing his wife mildly for the tone she was taking.

"How about it, Fletch?" she pressed the matter. "Where is your Springfield?"

She nodded toward my hip, nothing there but the pocket of my jeans.

"When was the last time you wore a sidearm? When?"

She was right. It had been a while. Like others, I'd embraced the calm after the storm, though it had taken some time to come down from that place of perpetual readiness.

"We don't know what this is, Angela," Martin said.

She laid a hard look on her husband.

"Exactly," she said. "And when was the last unknown we faced that turned out to be a good thing?"

Martin didn't have an answer. Neither did I. Schiavo, though, did.

"Never," she told us, then turned and followed the same path that Westin had taken toward the garrison headquarters.

Forty Five

Corporal Enderson had summoned me, stopping by our house on an eerily silent motorcycle, one of three recently delivered from the shop set up in Camas Valley. It was an example of commerce. People building things. Making things. Doing things. All for compensation, which had been made possible in the last seven months by the introduction of a currency. Pieces of paper created in a print facility operating in Remote. For now the exchange of money for goods and services was limited to non-necessary items. Food, medicine, shelter were all still provided, but already some residents who'd become adept at growing particular fruits or vegetables were requesting the ability to charge for what they were producing in light of rising customer requests. Supply and demand was coming, once again, to our world.

The bike that Enderson had ridden to our house was his personal vehicle. He'd made money during his off duty time working for me. The truth was, there was enough repairing and outright building going on between Bandon, Remote, and Camas Valley that I, and the other fellow who'd set up a contracting business in town, could use a half dozen workers on a half time basis. But Mo, as I'd taught myself to call him during his off duty hours, did not come to talk work or business as I ate with Elaine and Hope. He came to tell me that Schiavo wanted to see me down at the beach.

I drove toward the spot he'd directed me, headlights of my pickup sweeping across the road and the sandy shore beyond. It was not in those bright beams that I found the colonel, though. Instead it was in the glow of a small fire burning on the beach that she was revealed to me.

"Fletch," Schiavo greeted me as I approached from where I'd parked on the nearby road.

"Angela."

She stood close to the fire in civilian clothes, a light jacket to keep the night's mild chill at bay. Sparks from an array of old wood she'd ignited drifted past us and burnt out against the dark sky. Shards of planks and jagged ends of snapped rafters were her fuel of choice, obviously hauled to the spot from the old shack which had finally collapsed. It was the place where I'd chased Olin, or thought I had. I never was able to convince myself that he had actually been there, that close, taunting me.

This, though, was real. Schiavo was here, as was I. For what purpose, though, I had no idea. Not yet.

"Thanks for coming," Schiavo said.

"I could have brought some marshmallows and a stick," I joked.

She smiled. It was good to see that expression on her. After defeating the Unified Government forces two years earlier, it had taken her time to adjust to an existence not rife with conflict, or the threat of it. It was only a few months ago that I'd noticed her actually relaxed at times. Enjoying life, especially with Martin. Losing their child before birth still hurt, I knew. Time wouldn't heal that wound, but it mellowed the grief, letting it exist as a memory in competition with all that was still very good with their world, and with the world as a whole.

Still, I knew that this was not a moment where humor would exist for long.

"I'm sorry, Fletch."

I knew what she was referencing. But there was no need for an apology. Her motives in how she'd taken me to task for my waning readiness were pure, if harsh.

"You don't have to—"

"No, I do," she said. "I have to because...because..."

"Because why?"

"Because I'm afraid, Fletch. Of something starting again."

"The signal."

She nodded.

"I hate feeling this way," she said. "But it's what I'm supposed to do—be ready. Something like this, out of the blue, it turns that switch back on and suddenly I'm back on Mary Island, or in the pit in Skagway, or—"

"On a hill looking down at the Rogue River," I said.

Again, she nodded, frustration plain in her gaze.

"I hate that it's so automatic," she said. "I'm either at five miles an hour or a hundred and five. There's no in between."

I understood what she was saying, even if I couldn't relate fully. The world after the blight had become a place where one often slept with the proverbial one eye open. Or with a sidearm at the ready.

We'd moved beyond that state of simmering fear, mostly. As prodded by Schiavo the night before, I didn't always wear my Springfield now. But what she didn't know, and couldn't see, last night or now, was the Glock 30 holstered inside my waistband, covered by my shirt. Contrary to what she'd thought, I hadn't entirely dropped my guard. And I never would.

"Angela..."

"Yes, Fletch?"

"You didn't build a fire and ask to meet me way out here to apologize."

"Not entirely," she said.

She looked at me for a moment, as if finalizing some decision she'd thought was already made. Then she reached into the front pocket of her jeans and retrieved a familiar object—the sleeve containing the code card that would authorize the use of nuclear weapons.

"I can't fathom any circumstance where I would use what's on this card," she said. "Even if I could, and needed to, there's every reason to believe that the sub that's supposed to be listening for my call is out of commission. Two years is a long time to be on station."

I knew that Schiavo had considered seeking information on the continued presence of the missile submarine from the *Rushmore*'s commander, but with Admiral Adamson having shifted his command to dry land on Hawaii, doing so would bring another person into the realm of needing to know. And I was certain that Schiavo had no desire to allow a new individual, however trustworthy, into the secret signified by what she carried in the small plastic sleeve.

"The president was right, Fletch. He couldn't keep the power exclusively to himself. Not in this world. And I can't either."

There was every likelihood that the president we hadn't heard from since fleeing Columbus two years ago was dead. Killed by the Unified Government attack on the city outright, or by the nuclear blast he'd envisioned as the last chance to stop the enemy from completely absorbing the eastern half of the country. That he'd shared part of his duties, the ability to launch a strategic strike, with Schiavo had been a prescient move, it seemed. Now, she was taking steps to do the same.

And I knew who she had in mind to bear the same awful burden she'd known for the last twenty-four months.

"How's your memory, Fletch? A contractor seems like the kind of person who'd have to keep a laundry list of measurements and parts numbers in their head."

She held the code card out to me over the fire.

"Take it," she said. "Memorize it. I already have."

I didn't reach for what she was offering me. In many ways it was an invitation to a club that would exclude any too eager to join. A club whose members had the power to set in motion actions which could kill millions.

Only there were no more millions to kill. Some calculations performed by a former professor of statistics who resided in Bandon pointed to there being fewer than three million survivors scattered about the entire planet.

Three million.

Down from more than seven billion and change when the blight struck. A nuke might now only kill thousands as it devastated a city, or an area. Oddly, that made using it almost more potent, with a near guarantee that a foe would be obliterated.

"If something happens to me, Fletch, there needs to be another who can do what needs to be done."

"Did you discuss this with the council?"

She shook her head.

"Only Martin knows," she said.

There'd been no discussion with anyone as to the specifics of what the president had said, and had given her, during our meeting with him in Columbus. By necessity she'd let her husband in on the secret, if for no other reason than to inoculate him against any surprise should he find the code card amongst her belongings. Beyond him, though, no one else knew what power Schiavo had been charged with, and the colonel hadn't taken any steps to expand that small circle of knowledge.

"Would the president approve of this?"

"If he takes issue with it, he can let me know when and if he makes contact again," Schiavo said.

I could continue to resist, but in the end I would take her at her word. And I would do what she thought was best.

"Take it," she prompted me.

I did, sliding the card out and looking over the mix of letters and numbers, reading them again, and again, and again. Then I closed my eyes and imagined what I'd just seen. Schiavo was right, I had once been adept at quickly seizing measurements and parts numbers and contract dates, and holding each in memory. A length of schedule 40 PVC from my favored supplier was still item 86-8A in my mind.

"Do you have it?" Schiavo asked me.

I opened my eyes and looked to the card again, confirming that what I'd committed to memory was an exact representation of what was printed on the card.

"I have it," I said.

She reached out and took the card back, slipping it into its sleeve. But she didn't return it to her pocket. Instead she held it over the fire and let it fall.

"Angela..."

Flames seized the small rectangle of plastic and paper, twisting it. Melting it. Consuming it. In a few seconds it was blackened and unrecognizable. Reduced to ashy embers glowing at the base of the blaze.

"I don't want what you and I know to exist in any form that can be found, or taken, or given."

"Given?" I asked, surprised that she'd allowed that as some option.

"We don't need another BA Four Twelve out there, somewhere."

She was rightly worried about the unconfirmed existence of the human virus equivalent of the blight. But her suggestion as to its disposition was off base.

"Neil never gave that to anyone," I told her.

"You don't know that, Fletch. All he told us in that note he hid was that the sample of Four Twelve was somewhere safe. That could be with some*one*."

"I don't think so, Angela."

"That really doesn't matter," she said. "The code you and I know has to stay that way—with you and I knowing. Understood?"

"Of course," I answered.

She glanced down to the fire, no remnants of the card and its sleeve remaining. It was gone. For good.

"Do you remember the call sign?" Schiavo asked me.

"Viper Diamond Nine," I answered.

She nodded, satisfied.

"Let's hope we die of old age never needing to use what we know," she said.

"Yes," I agreed. "Let's hope."

Forty Six

I heard the thud in the hallway and cringed. A moment later, Elaine wheeled herself into our bedroom and stopped just inside.

"The bathroom door?"

"I know," I said. "I know."

She rolled closer to our bed and slid herself in and under the covers.

"I'm married to a contractor," she reminded me. "You'd think I could get some work done."

"By next weekend," I said. "I promise."

I'd widened all the doorways in our house, and replaced all the doors. Except one.

"I can live with banging my knuckles occasionally when I come in and out of the bathroom, but every time that happens we have a fifty percent chance of waking you know who if she's sleeping."

Hope had entered the 'terrible twos' a full half year early, particularly when it came to falling asleep, either for naps or when going down for the night, and staying asleep. One of us coughing in the living room was often enough to wake her. A banging from the bathroom just across the hall from her bedroom was just asking for trouble.

"We can write up a contract if you want," I offered. "I'll sign my name and everything. Bathroom door will be widened and replaced by insert date."

"Funny," Elaine said, then rolled toward me and snuggled close, nuzzling her head against my shoulder. "What did Angela want?"

She hadn't asked when I'd returned home from our discussion on the beach. And I hadn't offered any explanation outright. But I knew, somehow, the question would arise.

"If you wanted to tell me, you would have told me," Elaine said. "Unless you were waiting for me to ask. So I'm asking."

I thought for a moment, weighing what I knew against what I needed to keep to myself. Schiavo had told Martin, her husband, though there was some consideration there that had to be given to the existence of a physical item which, if discovered, could elicit more than a little curiosity. Here, though, with Elaine, there would be nothing such as that. All that existed relating to what Schiavo had shared was in my head.

"Was it about the signal?" Elaine pressed.

"No," I told her.

I knew I could trust her. But could I burden her?

"It wasn't about the signal," I said.

"Then what was it?"

I shifted position and rolled toward her so that we were facing each other. Light from the half moon drizzled through the curtains, just enough that we could see each other.

"Eric..."

For the next few minutes I explained it all to her. Not once did I impress upon her the need to maintain complete secrecy. This, I knew, she would do on her own. When I was done, she looked slightly away from me and shook her head.

"That's what this was about," Elaine said. "Blowing up the world."

"In a sense," I mostly agreed with her shocked realization.

She'd had questions when we returned two years ago from Schiavo's meeting with the president. Everyone had. But all that had been given in explanation was that the contents of their discussion were classified. That hadn't sat well with many, who saw a secretive streak suddenly introduced into our community. To some, that smacked of the old world, and of the deceitful traits exhibited by the government which had abandoned its citizens as the blight exploded across the globe.

To Elaine, though, there was a deeper meaning to knowing what she now knew. One closer to the person she'd become, and the broken body she now inhabited.

"She could have used that against the Unified Government," Elaine said. "Before they ever reached the Rogue River."

I hadn't considered the possibility that bringing my wife into my confidence about the matter would lead to where she'd taken it. But I should have.

"She was worried about effects on the town if a nuclear blast went off down the coast," I explained. "The town was her concern."

I wondered if Elaine was feeling a sense of anger. Some burning animus toward Schiavo, who hadn't employed the weapon which would have prevented her from becoming paralyzed.

As it turned out, I was a hundred and eighty degrees incorrect in my supposition.

"That had to be the toughest decision," Elaine said. "And she made the right one."

For a moment I puzzled at my wife's response, but that reaction was quickly replaced by familiar admiration. She wasn't weighing what she'd just learned against what she'd lost—she was weighing it against the toll it must have taken on Schiavo to make the choice she had.

"You're pretty amazing," I said.

Elaine eyed me, almost amused at what I'd said. She grinned and put a hand gently upon my cheek.

"You're right," she said, smiling outright now. "But so are you."

Forty Seven

Two days after the appearance of the signal, we had an answer as to its origin. A partial answer.

"It's where?" I asked.

It was Elaine who'd shared the news with me, using the landline to reach me at home during a break in the Town Council meeting called to discuss efforts to investigate the transmission. Westin had, it appeared, found some way to filter out any scatter from the powerful signal, allowing a directional antenna to take readings from multiple points, triangulating the source to a place that we'd known was possible, but unlikely.

Not anymore.

"One hundred and thirty miles west south west," Elaine explained. "Out in the Pacific."

"So there's a ship out there," I said.

"It looks that way."

"The *Rushmore* can have a look then."

"The *Rushmore* isn't due back for another five weeks," Elaine reminded me.

Every six to eight weeks we would have a visit from the Navy ship, which would offload supplies, food, livestock. All things deemed necessary to supporting the recovery of our town and the settlements nearby. What we needed, though, sooner rather than later, was information.

"What does the council want to do?" I asked.

"We want to send a plane out there to have a look."

There were two viable aircraft in Bandon, and several pilots. But flying that far over open water would be a challenge for those who'd only recently learned to pilot the aircraft. Not, though, for the man who'd taught them.

"You need Chris Beekman," I said. "What you're asking is beyond what Dave, or Jeffrey, or Nicole are capable of right now."

"We know that," Elaine said. "That's why I called you."

"I'm not following you."

"Angela wants to be flown out for a look," Elaine said, and I understood instantly why this wasn't going to be as straightforward as I'd expected. "We need you to arrange it."

Years earlier, more than forty residents of Bandon had left the town to found the settlement at Remote. Chris Beekman had almost been among them.

"He will not go for that," I told Elaine.

If hate was too strong a word for what the fifty-year-old plane mechanic and flight instructor felt toward the town's senior military officer, it was not by much. Schiavo's actions during the siege of Bandon orchestrated by the Unified Government, particularly her near confiscation of ammunition held by private individuals, had been seen as a dangerous overstepping of authority by those who'd ending up leaving. And even more so by one who'd stayed—Chris Beekman.

"The only reason he's even still here is because the people who settled Remote can't stand him," I said. "Few can."

"You're one of the few," Elaine said.

I was. And it wasn't even a mystery to me. The man, minus the caustic persona he wore openly, reminded me of a friend. A friend who was gone. The first friend I'd made after the blight.

Del Drake.

Hellfire *303*

In Chris Beekman I saw an individualist. A man committed to survival who possessed the wherewithal, and the fortitude, to see himself through to an end he might not be able to yet imagine. Del was like that. He'd been prepared to live out his days alone in the woods north of Whitefish. Only my arrival had upended that scenario. We'd ended up fast friends, and remained close until the day he sacrificed himself to weaken our enemy at the time.

I was in no way a close friend of Chris Beekman, but I hadn't held him at arm's length, either, as many had. And, most importantly to Elaine, I knew, was the simple fact that I wasn't Angela Schiavo.

"Will you talk to him?"

She already knew the answer I would give, and as soon as she returned home and took over 'Hope duties', as we called it, I headed out.

* * *

Chris Beekman lived in a large house just south of the airport. He'd taken up residence in the abandoned home a few months before my arrival in Bandon. Like many of us he'd followed the beacon Micah had sent out, reaching what we'd come to know as Eagle One with only the clothes he wore and a deer rifle on his back. That same rifle was slung over one shoulder when I found him moving cans of gas just outside the hangar Dave Arndt had helped him refurbish.

"Chris."

"Fletch," he greeted me, never stopping the chores he'd set out to complete.

"You have a minute?"

"I have lots of minutes," he answered.

"Your teachers must have loved your smartass answers in school," I said.

"Probably why they celebrated when I graduated," Chris shot back.

He didn't take crap from anyone, and he appreciated those who acted similarly, I thought, which explained some of the acceptance he'd always shown me.

"You need a hand with those?" I asked.

He set a pair of red cans next to the open hangar door, one of the Cessna 172s within, and slapped the dirt from his hands as he faced me.

"All done. The next minute is all yours."

I didn't beat around the bush, and dove right into the request the Town Council was making. He listened, almost smiling when I came to the part about Schiavo accompanying him on the reconnaissance flight.

"What do you say, Chris?"

"You already know what I'm going to say. That's why they sent you, because I won't haul off and punch you for wasting my time with such a suggestion."

"You know we need to figure this out, right? Aircraft in the air without any communication is asking for trouble. This affects you as much as people who can't use their cell phones."

"I'm well aware of that, Fletch. I'm also aware that Colonel Schiavo is willing to dictate actions to people who really have no inclination to be dictated to. That's how juntas in banana republics begin, my friend."

"Chris, that's not even close to being fair," I told him.

"Look, I know you're close to her, and to Martin. I have no beef with how you live your life, and who you choose to associate with. You're one of the good ones, Fletch. She, my good fellow, is not."

I hadn't any real idea how the exchange with Chris Beekman would go, but I'd hoped it would progress better than this.

"You want me to tell the council that you're refusing the request?" I pressed him. "That's what you want?"

"Hell no," he said. "I've got no problem with flying out there to see what the story is. I just won't do it with her."

I had half failed, half succeeded, it appeared, and was prepared to report that to Elaine when Chris added something I hadn't expected.

"I'll take you out there, Fletch."

"Me?"

"You know damn well that they'll go for that just fine," Chris said. "And you can see whatever's out there as well as she could. Hell, you've practically been her right hand for how many years?"

He was stating an outdated truth, to be sure. But it was still a truth. There would be annoyance at his refusal to take Schiavo, but acceptance that I would fill in for her.

Another truth, though, was that I wasn't entirely overjoyed at the thought of such a journey.

"That's a long way out to sea," I said.

"That's why you need the best pilot you can find," Chris countered.

I wasn't exactly being drafted into service. It was more of a forced substitution.

"I've got a suggestion on when we should takeoff," Chris said. "You probably won't like it."

He was right.

Forty Eight

We sped down the airport's single runway and lifted off heading north, lights of the town ahead until we made a gentle, sweeping turn to the west. Only black water and the night sky lay before us.

"I'm going to level off at three-thousand and cruise to our target," Chris told me over the intercom. "Then we can head down to the deck if you need a closer look."

"That'll work," I said.

An hour flight lay ahead of us, assuming that the location Westin had calculated was correct.

See you in a couple hours...

That was what Elaine had said to me just before I'd boarded the Cessna, its prop already spinning at idle. I'd leaned down and kissed her, then I'd given both Martin and Schiavo a nod. Despite Chris's refusal to have her as a passenger, she'd insisted on being present for the flight's departure. It might have been a way to show the man that she was not cowed by his intransigence, though the official reasoning was that we were departing on a flight sanctioned by both the civilian and military entities that served Bandon. I suspected there was a bit of both in the very overt helping of face time she was serving on the man's home turf.

"She agreed with you," I told Chris as we climbed through low, broken clouds. "You know that?"

"I don't know why she would have disagreed."

Night. That had been Chris's suggestion, that we carry out our reconnaissance flight under the cover of darkness, with just under half a moon shining in the eastern sky behind us. Doing so made complete tactical sense, particularly since we had no idea what we were going to find out there. It could be a buoy with a transmitter strapped to it. Or a barge, manned by hostiles, though that made less sense the more anyone entertained the notion. The bottom line was that we had no idea, and ignorance demanded prudence.

"How far can you see with those things?" Chris asked, nodding toward the case on my lap.

"Miles," I said, referencing the night vision binoculars within. "It really depends on how small our target is."

"If it's too small we may never find it," Chris said.

That was a possibility. There were no guarantees that this would be a successful mission. It could turn out to be just a waste of gas and time.

* * *

The hour passed slowly, with our attention focused on the dark waters ahead of us, both of us scanning the distance with the naked eye. Searching for lights. A shape. Something. The clouds had cleared, the glow from the moon highlighting lines of waves stretched across the ocean surface more than half a mile below.

Except in one spot just ahead. One very large spot.

"You see that?" I asked.

He nodded, checking his instruments and the folded map strapped to his thigh.

"We're just about on target," he reported.

This had to be it, what we were seeing. Or not seeing, to be more precise. Something big down there was blocking the constant movement of waves, in one spot, as if erasing them from the surface of the Pacific.

"We're going down for a look," Chris said.

I took the night vision binoculars from their case and brought them up as we descended. Before I even had the chance to look through them, the necessity of doing so became moot.

"Do you see that, Fletch?" Chris asked as he leveled out just a few hundred feet above the ocean. "Tell me you see that."

"I see it, Chris."

The light of the half moon washed over the massive ship, painting it with ashen hues, giving it definition as Chris put us into a low orbit around it.

"That's an aircraft carrier, Fletch."

He was right. It was. Huge and modern. Dark and lifeless. A ghost ship at anchor more than a hundred miles off shore.

"What's that?" Chris asked, pointing through the windshield as he passed low over the ship. "On the flight deck."

Now I brought the night vision binoculars up and activated them, the world beyond the lenses brightened with a grey-green luminescence. Through the optics I could make out the superstructure, antennas and radar dishes still upon it. And the wide, long flight deck, devoid of any aircraft. But not empty, as Chris had noticed.

A large square object sat on it, a perfect cube placed equidistant from each edge of the ship, and each end. Thick cables ran from it, four in total, and disappeared below decks after snaking down through the opening created by a lowered aircraft elevator.

"This is crazy, Fletch," Chris said.

It was. And more. The unknown we'd hoped to explain had just become another unknown, and even more inexplicable.

"What do we do?" Chris asked me.

I lowered the binoculars and thought for a moment.

"I think we should get the hell out of here," I told him.

He nodded and did one more low orbit around the aircraft carrier, then turned northeast, putting us on a course for home.

"That box, Fletch..."

"I know."

"It's as big as a house."

"Yeah."

Chris, the fine pilot that he was, kept his attention forward, focused on flying the plane. But at least a portion of his thoughts, like mine, were fixed on the aircraft carrier we'd just discovered.

"Chris..."

"What, Fletch?"

"Could you land on that?"

For an instant, the man turned to me and considered what I'd asked as if the question had been posed by a madman.

"Could you?" I repeated.

"That box is blocking a lot of the flight deck, but...it's possible."

"Good," I said. "Let's go home."

The time would come, I knew, sooner rather than later, that there would be a return visit to the carrier. There had to be.

This was one unknown, one mystery, that we would have to confront.

Thank You

I hope you enjoyed *Hellfire*. Please look for other books in *The Bugging Out Series*.

About The Author

Noah Mann lives in the West and has been involved in personal survival and disaster preparedness for more than two decades. He has extensive training in firearms, as well as urban and wilderness Search & Rescue operations, including tracking and the application of technology in victim searches.

Made in the USA
San Bernardino, CA
21 June 2017